My Aim Is True

LEE PATTON

REAMSPINNER
PRESS

Published by
DREAMSPINNER PRESS

5032 Capital Circle SW, Suite 2, PMB# 279, Tallahassee, FL 32305-7886 USA
www.dreamspinnerpress.com/

My Aim Is True
© 2015 Lee Patton.

Cover Art
© 2015 Valerie Tibbs | Tibbs Design.
Cover content is for illustrative purposes only and any person depicted on the cover is a model.

ISBN: 978-1-63476-534-3
Digital ISBN: 978-1-63476-535-0
Library of Congress Control Number: 2015943924
First Edition October 2015

Printed in the United States of America
∞
This paper meets the requirements of
ANSI/NISO Z39.48-1992 (Permanence of Paper).

For George

Acknowledgments

Special thanks to theater director and playwright Jeremy Cole for his intrepid dedication and guidance on ongoing drafts of this novel; to novelist Chris Kenry for his encouragement and suggestions; to George Ware, Kristen Hannum, John Serini, and the late, great Jack Long for invaluable feedback; to Peter Knapp and Bruce Morgan for specific revision advice.

Chapter 1

February, 1978

WHILE WE posed for our first team photo, the Pest told me a complicated joke involving a triple-A-cup bra, the miracle of Lourdes, and a gay donkey.

"Sorry, Rob," I said, "I don't quite get it."

"You're getting to be a real drag these days, Guy," declared Rob Pescatore, my tennis teammate and best friend since our first days in Catholic school. "You would've gotten that joke back in sixth grade."

"You lost me with the gay donkey."

"That was the punch line!" Rob spat in disgust.

I probably could have figured it out, but I wasn't really paying attention to the Pest just then. Our coach's son and new assistant, a blond hunk, was rearranging us on the court bleachers. I freaked out when the hunk slapped my butt and ordered me to the top row. "Get up there, big guy."

Then the hunky blond ordered the Pest to climb up the bleachers beside me, but without the butt slap. The tallest guys on the team now, Rob and I both shot up past six feet by the middle of junior year. On that warm, sunny February afternoon, rare for the ocean side of San Francisco, the group photo marked the start of Walt Whitman High School's 1978 varsity tennis season. Since I was the most mediocre player on our mediocre team, I felt like a hypocrite standing in the highest spot.

"Come on, you've gotta laugh a little now and then, Guy," Rob said, elbowing my ribs while we took our places. "Like you used to. At least we're not stuck next to Darren Kennedy."

"Keep your voice down, Rob, okay? You don't have to hurt the poor guy's feelings. We've all been kind of lousy at tryouts."

"Well, at least Darren makes the rest of us look good," he stage-whispered. "He spends more time chasing the balls than hitting them. When he's not chasing after every guy that has balls."

"That would be just about every guy on the planet. Anyway," I said, trying to steer Rob away from the topic of Darren's queerhood and into queerdom as a general idea. "I hate to ruin your punch line, but we just studied research about animals having homosexual tendencies. Even donkeys, probably."

"No way," Rob the Pest said. "That's just AP Biology bullshit. Nature wouldn't stand for it. If the donkeys go queer, where will all the mules come from?"

"Aren't they born sterile anyway?"

"So what, Guy? If boy donkeys mess around only with other boy donkeys, there's still gonna be a mule shortage."

Our conversation, as usual, wasn't making much sense. I was feeling as sterile and misbegotten as a mule myself. I was sick of going along when Rob and everybody else took it for granted I was straight. The hunky blond was still arranging the guys in the first row, that sizzle still fresh from when he slapped my behind. Now the hunk was glancing at me with this sly half smile, like he was in on the truth, like he knew I was as gay as poor skinny Darren Kennedy. Nobody took for granted that Darren was straight, not even in grade school. Hands flailing, hips sashaying, acting like central casting sent him to play the Class Queer, Darren even lisped.

Darren, Rob, and I were the only three from our original Precious Suffering kindergarten opting to attend public high school. So I figured all three of us were kind of connected, though nobody was supposed to associate with Darren. As we grew up, though, I kind of appreciated ol' Darren for his bitter sense of humor and his never-ending quest to get good at tennis. I could sure relate to that.

I still felt crappy about the way I used to help torment the poor guy, joining the packs of bigger Catholic boys during recess at Most Precious Suffering. Smearing the queer, I'd called Darren the same mean names as everybody else and shouted the same raunchy taunts, not knowing I was just insulting my future self. Or maybe I did know, on some kid level, and went along with torturing Darren to cover up the truth about myself.

After Most Precious Suffering, when I started eyeing every good-looking guy I saw at Walt Whitman High School, I decided to stop being such a two-faced jackass. On that thought, just as we all finally smiled for the camera, Darren turned around from the lowest bleacher, looked up, and caught my eye. Saying something to Coach, Darren smiled toward me, his hand flailing in that girly wave. I waved back, a quick palm up, *muy macho* style.

"Ah, there's your old gay buddy," the Pest said, nudging me. When I didn't react, Rob told me I was being a drag again. "Not to mention morose and morbid, Guy. I know what's bugging you too. Now you're all hung up that you're another pathetic kid from a broken home. Smile for the camera, you poor semi-orphan."

I was nowhere near an orphan of any kind, with both my youngish parents still alive and well. Okay, I had been brooding about my parents' separation back in the fall, when their marriage hit the rocks over my mom's decision to go to art school in Oakland. Our house up in Ashbury Heights was still *un*broken, though, and I expected my mother to move back after she got watercolors out of her system.

What the Pest didn't know was that I was being a drag mostly over this Gay Honesty Crisis. I wasn't really hung up on *coming out* since I accepted that I liked guys in ninth grade. I didn't really think that was as taboo as my classmates, even in San Francisco, seemed to think it was. Coach's son's flirting prodded me to tell Rob the truth, and soon.

When the team picture finally got snapped, I realized what Darren and Coach had been yakking about, why Darren had been pointing at me, and why Coach wrinkled his brow and then smiled up at me in wonder. "I don't know why I never put two and two together, Dimchek," Coach said to me, slapping my arm as Rob and I clambered off the bleachers. "I just never linked you to your dad. Wow!"

I tried to smile, to show a little pride for my dad's celebrity. Paul Dimchek became a household name around the Bay when he won the 1960 silver medal, then made gold in 1964 for the vaulted high jump. His fame was more than Wheaties boxes too, when he became one of pro volleyball's national champions for the San Francisco Claimjumpers. Two years back, in 1976, he became their manager.

The Pest had watched Coach's wonderment, barely able to contain his contempt until Coach was out of earshot. "Guy, I told you Coach Blanding was mentally deficient. How could he be so clueless about your dad? How many *Dimcheks* run around this neck of the city? Or the Bay Area? Or California? Or the world?"

"Must be tons of 'em in Yugoslavia, where my dad's ancestors live." I figured Coach, though he was new to us this season, really had put two and two together, and it just couldn't add up. He couldn't believe a gold medal athlete and Claimjumper star could have produced a klutz like me.

As the team disbanded, Darren Kennedy patted my shoulder. "I thought Coach should know. Something to be proud of, big guy."

"Thanks a lot. You know I can't stand everybody going ape over my dad's heroics."

"Not to mention, now he's the Finish Line man. Staring down from billboards like an Olympic god all over again. Get over it, Guy." Darren wandered away, winking at me. "You ought to bask in the reflected glory!"

"Yeah, kid." It was the blond hunk, Randy Blanding, who'd been hovering around the bleachers. His big hazel eyes and thick lashes blew me away. Up close, he looked younger and less intimidating.

I could tell the Pest was a little freaked-out, looking from Randy's face to mine as the blond hunk and I locked eyes in a prolonged silence. Rob broke it by asking Randy, "So where the heck have you been? We could've used an assistant coach last season too."

"I live out in the Delta. Joaquin Island." Randy told Rob he was attending junior college for freshman year, out where his mother lived, but that his girlfriend was a senior here at Walt Whitman. *Girl*friend? Randy kept his eyes on mine. "But I'll help out some Fridays, most weekends, whenever I can. Plus, I'll be teaching a tennis clinic on Saturdays. But after I transfer to State in the fall," he added, "I'll be your full-time assistant coach." He pointed over his shoulder to the San Francisco State University campus, just down the avenue from Walt Whitman's playing fields.

Manly, Randy shook both our hands. But he turned away quick, tagging after his disappearing father like a little kid. "I better hitch a ride with Dad," he shouted to us.

"Yeah! Hope to see you at practice sometime soon," I said, embarrassed by my own eagerness.

"Hope to see you at the clinic," Randy yelled.

"The proof's in our next practice," Rob said in Randy's wake. "We don't even know if he plays any better than we do."

"Well, he's gotta be better than me," I said. "I'm looking forward to whatever he can do for my stroke."

THE NEXT Sunday morning, I took the chance to try out my Gay Honesty Project on the Pest. Rob and I were practicing on the courts under Lone Mountain, next to the Catholic Kremlin, under the watchful windows of St. Ignatius Church and Bleeding Sacred Heart High School. Bleeding Heart's plaster arteries pumped right into our old primary school, Most Precious Suffering, just across the street. I always hoped this holy precinct would inspire divine intervention to save my half-assed serves—talk about chasing balls—but Rob kept acing me out, as usual. When we were sick of playing, we took a breather on the benches facing Ashbury Street and watched a nun escorting a bawling little kid out of the school doors, probably from a First Communion prep class between Masses. "Hey," the Pest cried out, "isn't that Sister Fred?"

"Yep. She probably still wields that ruler like a light saber." My sweat chilled in the breeze, remembering our Great Confirmation Heresy back when the Pest and I were ninth graders. It still freaked me out to consider what Sister Fredericka would have thought, after all those years drilling God and sin into us during religion class, if she knew that Rob and I took a vow to leave the Church the minute we were confirmed. We swore our confirmation would be our last church service besides funerals, preferably our own. Since our parents paid for and put up with eight years of our whining about Catholic school, Rob and I just went along with the program until Confirmation Day, making them proud that we became adults in the eyes of the church, then faking everybody out by never dipping our paws into the holy water after the ceremony.

That's what I always liked best about the Pest. He understood our schemes with no need for explanations or persuasion. That's why I hoped he'd take my pronouncement in his usual cool way. If he didn't care that I was a godless heathen, why should he care that I was gay?

We watched Sister Fred deliver the bawling boy to a young mother we recognized from sightings on the Masonic bus route. Wearing tiny miniskirts and go-go boots, and with her huge breasts bulging out of tight blouses, she looked like she was still stuck in the Swingin' Sixties as she took her kid to school. Miniskirt Mom looked hilarious towering over Sister Fred. Even in February, the mom just wore a flimsy wrap over her shoulders, showing more skin on the street than the little nun probably showed in the shower. She acted all nicey-nice for Sister Fred, hugging her kid close and smoothing his hair. She even popped a crucifix from between her boobs, then twirled the gold chain while Sister Fred talked.

"Man, that crucifix is probably getting cold," Rob said, shivering in his T-shirt and shorts. "That little Jesus probably misses his warm nest down there between her tits."

Talk about AAA cups. Talk about heresy. "You want to join him down there?"

"God no," the Pest said, sticking out his tongue for a loud *phfft*. "That chick is gross. And old. Probably thirty or something."

As soon as Sister Fred waved farewell and returned inside the school doors, Miniskirt Mom swatted the poor kid on the head, right where she'd just been caressing him. "You wanna boohoo during sister school," she said, almost shouting, "I'll give you something to cry about, buster!"

The little boy tried to stanch his tears right then, blubbering as his mom yanked him toward the church.

"Not exactly the saint we took her for," Rob said. "What about you, Guy? Think she's hot?"

"Definitely not my type. She'd probably make me cry too."

The Pest laughed, and I figured it was now or never, if I ever wanted to end the next *think she's hot?* bullshit session—coming up on No. 4,489 since puberty knocked us more senseless than Sister Fred's ruler ever did. Since he had the Beast, his mother's rusty old Ford Galaxie, for the day, Rob asked if I still wanted to go jogging at Ocean Beach.

"Yeah, I've to get in better shape for the season," I said, thinking it might be easier to ease into the Topic while we jogged side by side at the surf line.

But the Topic popped up in the Beast, thanks to an old hit song from 1974. "Don't Lose that Number" came on the radio the minute Rob turned the Beast onto Fulton Avenue toward the beach. Along with every other kid in America, we kept up the four-year-old debate about the story behind the song's lyrics. Rob turned it up, leaning in. "Yeah, I'm still sure the whole song's about a drug deal. This chick, Rikki, can't find the guy's stash of pot, and he's reminding her, one more time, not to lose that *number*. A joint."

"But like I told you before, the kid's name is *Ricky*. And the guy singing the song is telling Ricky not to lose his *phone* number. He even says not to call anybody else."

"That is a very queer interpretation, Mr. Dimchek."

"Nothing wrong with that, Mr. Pescatore. It's about time we had gay love songs too."

"Why?"

"It's 1978, for the love of Jesus."

"What does 1978 have to do with anything, Guy? You always read too much into things, even songs. Like in school, always pontificating about your own private interpretation of everything and making our teachers slobber over your brilliance." Rob glanced at me, smiling. "Okay, so you're smart. I admit it. But you're wrong about this damn song."

"You're smarter than I am about a lot of things, and a way better tennis player, but you'll never know more than I do about this song. Listen. The guy singing it even wants Ricky to go out to Slow Hand Road with him—"

"Stop! You're ruining the song for all time, now. Who wants it to be about some fags with their hands in each other's pants?"

The Steely Dan song segued into a commercial about skin lotion, and I held my breath, glad it wasn't my dad's voice this time, hawking some of the Finish Line male wrinkle cream he'd been endorsing in radio ads for the past few months. We'd reached the parking lot across Great Highway, not very full on this blustery Sunday noon, and Rob eased the car close to the sea wall. He turned off the engine. He looked at his hair in the rearview mirror and tried to tamp down his mass of black curls. His question still hung in the stale Ford air between us.

"Well? Am I right, then, Guy? Once and for all, who wants the song to be about two fags?"

I looked at the ocean, all wild with whitecaps. I cleared my throat. "I do."

"Why? Just for the sake of winning another damn argument?"

"No, Rob. Because I like having at least one song I can relate to."

"So what are you saying? Not that you're, like, gay?"

I couldn't look at him, so I aimed my gaze at a seagull. "Yep."

"Since when?"

"Since you started noticing girls and I started noticing boys."

Rob tapped the steering wheel. He also stared ahead, becoming fascinated with the same seagull. After a while, he said, "So now you tell me?"

"I was too chicken. You're my oldest friend."

"But you still thought I was some dickhead? That you couldn't tell me?"

"You're the first person I've ever told."

Rob was silent for way too long. I was reduced to counting the Cheetos (eight and a half) littering the floor mat just to keep my nerve. Finally he said, "Man, when I think of the times we've showered together after a practice. Or in gym class. Were you perving over my ass? And during all those sleepovers? And campouts, when we shared that backpacker tent? Jesus, Guy."

"It's not like that, Rob. It's never been like that." I grabbed my hooded sweatshirt from the backseat and got out of the car. I hated the way the whole Topic was going, surging as out of control and stinking as a red tide. But what did I expect? Rob was just one of millions of funny, smart, red-blooded straight guys who hated fags. I knew that and didn't have any reason to be surprised or act all disappointed. I pulled the hood over my head and sat on the sea wall, staring at nothing, just feeling my heart thumping.

I heard the Beast's door slam behind me. Rob wrestled into his own hooded sweatshirt against the wind. Talk about faggy. There we were, identical in our team logo, Walt Whitman Tennis, our gray shorts, and mud-splattered running shoes. Rob leaned against the sea wall, his back to it and to me. "Were you embarrassed, then, lusting after me when we passed into puberty?"

"Do you lust after your sister?"

"That's psycho!"

"You're like a brother to me, okay, Rob? I've never even *wanted* to see you naked. You're all dark-haired and greasy but pasty. And you smell funky. In other words, you're Italian."

I couldn't see if our old ethnic put-down routine forced a smile out of him and hoped he would have a comeback about even smellier Yugoslavian subhumans.

"So," he asked instead, tonelessly, "I'm not your type?"

I shook my head. "You're not *any* type. You're just Rob the Pest, my best friend since first grade. Nothing's different, okay?"

I turned to watch Rob shove himself away from the sea wall. I practically held out my damn hand, imagining we'd shake or some other manly gesture, making everything okay again like old friends usually do. Instead Rob tossed his keys from hand to hand. "No, Guy. Everything's different." He stood beside the Beast's driver's door. "Want to know the truth? I think fags are disgusting."

"Get real, Rob. We see five million gay guys at Seventeenth and Castro every time we transfer to the M Car."

"And they're disgusting. Just more Castro clones, man. But my best friend messing with other guys?"

"I never have. But maybe someday I'll get a chance."

"Are you kidding me? Gay sex makes me sick."

"Come on, Rob." I finally turned around to face him, surprised he wasn't flashing a snide smile. "That's not funny."

"You're damn right it isn't. Man, I've got to think about this, okay? All the things you said and did that I probably took a different way. The normal way."

I moved forward, trying to think of the right words to straighten him out and make him understand that I never perved over him or any of our friends, but he held up his palm in a keep-the-hell-back-you-pervert gesture and opened the car door. "You're okay to take the Fulton bus home? I want to think."

That blew my mind. So I was too disgusting now to ride in his mother's fucking Cheetos-fouled rust bucket? "It's okay, buddy," I told him. "I can jog home through the park."

"Come on. You need some change for the bus, don't you?" Rob tossed some quarters my way. "As usual."

I let the coins clatter at my feet as I watched him drive away.

THE AMUSEMENT park, once right across Great Highway, had been torn down years before. Now a Safeway buried good ol' Playland at the Beach. Thirsty and in need of a pay phone, I stepped through the whooshing doors, imagining they replaced the exact spot of the fun house gates, opening to the mirrors, the slide, the spinning disk. I conjured all the foul, loud old rides, no matter how contradicted now by aisles of junk food or the tinkly supermarket music. I remembered when my parents used to treat Rob and me to rides out here, Sundays after Mass when we were still semiholy Precious Suffering tykes. Rob's folks didn't have much extra money back then, not even quarters for the Barrel of Laughs.

Now he had plenty of quarters to toss at my feet, Judas's blood money to bar me from the Beast. So Rob Pescatore did turn out to be too much of a dickhead for the truth.

There was a time when he hung around our house so much, always welcome for dinner or a sleepover, that my mother would call me "Rob" and Rob "Guy" by mistake. At six or seven, brotherless, I sometimes confused the words "friend" and "brother."

Lately, I didn't even like to go home to our lonesome, motherless house, with my dad almost always out at some investor or Claimjumper or political meeting. When I was little, though, life was so easy in our skinny three-story in Ashbury Heights, I also confused "home" with "family" during noun lessons in grade school. Rob was there in the next desk, laughing his head off when Sister Fred tried to set me straight, so to speak, by whacking me with a flash card.

I never did pick up the quarters the Pest tossed. As usual, I didn't have any, so I connected to my dad's answering service by reversing the charges. That annoyed the voice at the other end, but since I was the Great Man's son, the service always put up with me. I just asked them to let my dad know I'd be late. Who knew how long it would take me to jog the five miles through Golden Gate Park?

I stepped away from the pay phone, numb-headed, staring at a scary-smelling soup bar. It made me think of how my mom used soup crackers in that watery old Playland chili soup to pretend to Rob and me that she could read them like tea leaves for our fortunes. "I wish the future spelled itself out like this," she'd said. "It'd be so much easier." (Dad had said, "Try alphabet soup.")

A manager appeared, asking me what I was buying and who I was with. I said nothing and no one.

"Please leave, then, son. We don't allow loitering."

I left without arguing. *Loitering.* I never got accused of that when I was still a shrimp, but now my height seemed to make adults think I was some kind of delinquent or brain-damaged outcast. I felt pathetic, an ex-Catholic wandering alone, godless, queer, and newly friendless through an oversanitized fluorescent purgatory, shooed away like a little kid. But I was too old to pretend the past could be fixed. Tired of being morose and morbid, I crossed the Great Highway and drifted down to the beach.

Under slapping wind, hardly anyone strolled the strand. I jogged to the surf, meaning to scream something outrageous. But the ocean growled, whitecapped and roiling. When I yelled, "At least I'm being honest!" every word was lost against the uproar, blown away like flash cards of familiar nouns.

YOU KNOW the expression "you look like you just lost your best friend"? Well, I don't know what I looked like, but I sure felt like hell. I had plenty of time to think on that five-mile run. Leaving Ocean Beach, I took the section south of the polo field, where Golden Gate Park stopped being tended and reverted to being a chunk of wild woods, dark and winter-like that afternoon, the tall grass blades still wet from the last rains. Piles of fresh-cut pines along muddy paths made me miss the real woods and wonder if my dad and I would ever take another backpack up in the Lost Coast or High Sierra, like in the good old days when Rob would sometimes come along—except now the Pest was too scared to share a tent with the Queer. Jogging out of the park near Kezar Stadium, I was hoping Rob would get over the shock and remember that I was still the same old Guy I always was.

Cooling down on the last block, turning from Ashbury Street into Montes Terrace, I was shocked myself. My dad was actually home and outside on a Sunday afternoon. Hunched on his haunches, he was weeding the ice plant border by our front steps, my mom's old chore. He turned to look at me. "How'd the sets go with you and Rob? You guys planning on a championship season?"

"Didn't you once say," I said, still catching my breath, "a fairy sport like tennis didn't really matter?"

"I would never say such a narrow-minded thing. Especially when I make my living on a fairy sport like volleyball." He yanked a weed. "And, after all, everything matters."

"I'm going to take a tennis clinic from Coach's son on weekends. My serve and backstroke are severely disabled."

"Could be a damn good thing if you're in the hands of a capable clinician."

I sat on the brick rim nearby, trying to catch a stray sunbeam before the clouds over Twin Peaks blotted it out. I didn't want to ruin the moment by pointing out that he was actually doing something healthy. During the past months of licking his wounds over the separation, if Dad was ever home, he headed into the TV den for *Charlie's Angels* 'n' scotch. After my mom split to her Oakland apartment, Dad retreated from everything that mattered, even kissing off practice with the Claimjumpers, benching himself from jogging and pickup basketball games at the Catholic Kremlin's courts. He sometimes even skipped cocktail hour with Adrian, his best friend, business partner—and my godfather. In boxers and sweatshirt, his wavy hair matted under his faded "McGovern in '72" baseball cap, Dad preferred to drink alone as he retired to the guns, laugh tracks, and mammary glands of all six TV channels.

He smelled most of the time, a mixture of stale booze and nervous sweat. Every morning while I made coffee and toast, he'd lurch into the kitchen like a low-budget zombie, groaning, arms dangling. Our most absorbing conversation involved which Charlie's Angel was endowed by her creator with the perkiest breasts. Of course, Dad's imaginary measuring tape lassoing Farrah, Jaclyn, and Kate didn't rope my fascination a hell of a lot. Almost as stimulating were his most frequent questions, to which I never knew the answer: "Guy, when is one of us gonna clean up the damn kitchen?" and "Guy, where did I put the damn *TV Guide*?"

As for my mom, I didn't see much of her. I stayed with Dad by choice, clinging to the old-timey security of our narrow old house on Lola Montes Terrace and wanting to stay at Walt Whitman with my friends (you know, like Rob).

At least my parents weren't making a show of fighting over who got stuck with me. I'd come home after school to make countless dinners of canned stew drizzled with stale Fritos—my mom's own invention and her only gift to the cuisine of California. Now and then she offered me enticing weekends across the Bay in Oakland, but I made excuses. I didn't want to wear my poker face when she tried to pretend she wasn't sleeping with Lester, the Marxist watercolor art professor who lured her across the Bay to Oakland in the first place.

Sitting on the front planter box, I kind of liked hanging out with Dad for a while, so I started digging up the weeds around me until we both turned our heads toward these soft, powdery explosions a few doors down. On the corner with Ashbury, from the half arch that half guarded the entry to Lola Montes Terrace, another piece of plaster rained down. Fat crows were prancing across the arch's outer edge, cawing in triumph and kicking more loose plaster. A bad omen, I thought.

"You know the arch story, the real story, don't you, Guy? Why it stayed only half-finished?"

I did, having already heard it 4,489 times. But I let Dad tell it anyway, just to hear his voice again. He pointed at the arch, reminding me it was built after the 1906 earthquake to signal the rebirth of Ashbury Heights, then jumped to the punch line: "The city aborted the project when the contractor claimed a prostitute's services as a *public erection outlay*."

I laughed for his benefit. Maybe, now that he had actually crawled out of the TV den and spoken actual words to me, Dad and I could take up that theme, erections, and discuss why Farrah, Jaclyn, and Kate's bouncing boobs didn't give me any.

But he stood up and pulled on my arm. "Okay, kid, we've got our work cut out for us. Come on," he said, leading me into our cramped back yard. "I got started earlier." In bunches around him, dead plants were plopped along the brick walkway. The patch of lawn had gone wild, its green spears a foot tall, with much taller weeds poking up everywhere. The last surviving rose petal sighed on a slight breeze, then got stuck on thorns. "How'd we let this happen, Guy?"

I knew we'd let it happen for the obvious reason that my mom had always tended our garden and kindly reminded me to mow our dinky lawn. Whatever gifts she lacked in the kitchen were compensated with her natural genius in the garden. I'd taken our small, sunken paradise for granted my whole life. Now it dawned on me that the jungles of bougainvillea might need some hacking back during the city's winter rains.

I pulled a plastic trash can from behind the hydrangea and started cleaning up after Dad.

"Yeah, good," he said, "let's get this looking decent again."

I was just about to bring up a spring backpacking trip to the redwoods when Dad looked at his watch and sprang to his feet. "Hey, Guy, hack back that monster shrub and stack up these cuttings, would ya? I gotta get out of here for a while. Take you out for Chinese later?"

Before I could respond, he'd bounded through the dwarf-sized garden door and was pounding up the back steps to the kitchen. I started battling with this Godzilla-sized rhododendron when I heard footsteps *down* the stairs. I turned to see my mother squeeze through the door. Her smile of greeting quickly withered.

"Guy! My God! What's happened to the garden?"

I kept snipping. "Our gardener abandoned us."

Her face tightened even more, eyes wide, cords in her neck pulsating. Frozen on the doorway steps, she stared at me. For a crazy second, I thought she'd march across the ankle-high sod and slap me right across my smart mouth.

Instead she sighed, dropped her gaze to the weeds between the walkway bricks, then sank to her knees. She began yanking them, making a neat pile. "I've missed you so much, Guy. I came down here to give you a hug. But I can see you're in no mood for that."

"I'm not in any mood at all, Mom. Dad and I just realized how bad we've been at taking care of your garden. I guess he knew you were coming over." I crouched down nearby, attacking another patch of weeds. "I didn't."

"I'm surprised he didn't tell you."

"You haven't been over here for a while."

"Not because I haven't wanted to. Guy, you know I have that extra room at my place in Oakland. It's all set up for you, any time you want it."

"Don't you need it for your art stuff?"

"It doesn't take up that much room. Nothing I can't move. I just don't want the whole season to pass before we—"

"But I'm doin' okay, Mom. I made varsity tennis. And for pocket change, Dad's hired me to haul junk out of one of the slums he's investing in."

She made a face, identical to the one she made just before she took off, when she decided Dad was becoming a capitalist pig for investing in rental properties.

"Why don't you come over here more often, like you used to?" I asked her. "When you come into the city to stop by Aspirations Unlimited, can't you just swing by here?"

"I'd love to. But I'm not really needed that much these days. My new manager's so good at running the school she's just made me... superfluous. Happily superfluous."

I knew it was true. Her new manager was a woman I knew only on the phone, a sharp, all-business voice with a slight European accent.

As my mother spent less time at Aspirations Limited, her modeling school for teenaged girls, it started to make a profit. So Mom came to think of herself as an "executive" in her school's administration, which meant she worked less and paid herself a higher salary.

"And you know," she went on, pointing back to the house, "it's still awkward between your father and me. But it is getting better. We just had a nice, civil conversation on the stairs. But, Guy, it's still hard."

Oh, sweet baby Jesus, now she was crying. I tried to keep weeding for a while, hoping she'd get a grip. I'd tried so hard to pretend I didn't miss her flaky presence around our house.

I kind of wanted to get weepy too, thinking of what all three of us had lost. We could thrive just fine as individuals, but my parents had cast something better into perdition. I wanted to stop and just grieve for what had died between them, not just for Mom or Dad but for Mom-*and*-Dad, the gravitational pull that used to hold my universe together.

But I didn't join in her boohooing. I hardened my heart to any tears. I tossed my pile of weeds atop hers, then reached across the space between us and clasped her hand, urging her up to her feet.

My gesture seemed to calm her. She sniffled, swiped her nose with the back of her hand, ceased her weeping, and leaned against my shoulder, her arm around my waist. I liked Penelope O'Malley Dimchek more than I had for months. I liked her straightforward emotions now. I liked how she was dressed in jeans, sneakers, and a T-shirt, and how her hair was growing out, longer and kind of wild. Penni steadied herself against me, bussed my cheek, and pronounced: "You're getting so grown-up, Guy. My God. I'm so proud of you. But aren't you getting cold in those running shorts?"

So she was going to make aren't-you-getting-cold suggestions like I was still a kid? I ignored her question. Anyway, I had a crazy idea. Penni was coming back to us with her tail between her legs, as if she was a little kid who'd run away from home. She'd outgrown her artsy Oakland adventure, and now she wanted back inside. That's probably what her "nice, civil conversation" with my dad on the stairs had been about. I decided I'd invite her to have Chinese with me and Dad. You never knew what magic a little moo shu might work. Just as I started the invitation, "Mom, why don't you—" there were more footsteps on the basement stairs.

The rest of that moment played out of focus and fast-forward. A middle-aged man appeared in the garden doorway, hunching his lanky frame, grinning, inquisitive, excusing himself for interrupting our intimate mother-son moment. This had to be Lester, her watercolor professor. ("This guy professes watercolors?" my dad asked my mom just before they separated, when he first heard Penni obsessing about her teacher. "He's done actual research on, say, red and yellow?") The guy was a long-faced blur of thinning, graying hair; skinny chest, and tie-dye T-shirt. Its random designs swirled around a clear, inked image of Chairman Mao.

Great, a Maoist loser. "Nice to meet you, Professor," I lied after our handshake. "My mom's told me all about you too." I knew I'd never look at watercolors the same way since he touched Mom's life with the finest horsehair brushes.

"What do you want me to do with the sheets?" the watercolor professor asked my mom. "There's room in the big box with the photo albums, baby."

Baby? Okay, for all my supposed brains, I was so damn dense. Penni hadn't stopped by to see me or to reconcile with Dad but to collect the rest of her possessions before the divorce proceedings made this salvage mission more complicated. I didn't know why Dad didn't have the guts to tell me, let alone fess up to why he was trying to make the garden presentable to Lester and Penni as they sacked and pillaged our household. Blindsided, I blurted, "'Scuse me, I've gotta go. Homework. Tons, due tomorrow. First thing."

"What's going on, Guy?" Penni asked. "We were hoping to take you out to dinner after we've packed a few things."

"Got a date later with Dad at the Lotus Moon, Mom. You know how great the Happy Family is there?"

Yeah, it was great, great, Lester and Penni agreed, and after a magnanimous kiss good-bye on Penni's cheek, I was gone, gone.

It was weird, weird now going up all the stairway flights, half basement, kitchen and living room, master bedroom and den each taking up their small floor as the house darkened and the short afternoon drooped to evening. As I passed by my parents'—my dad's—room, now that I knew the truth about Penni's plans, the whole place felt hollowed out. My footsteps echoed louder than I'd ever noticed before. So much for the six-year-old who once confused "home" and "family." Now that I was sixteen, I wasn't sure if either word really meant anything.

I could tell Dad was hiding in his den, probably nursing a beer and cursing Lester and Penni as he watched some financial program with my godfather, Adrian. Dad's early fame earned our house, this old Ashbury Heights fixer-upper, mortgaged for an off-tune whistle to San Francisco's 1964 Gold Medal Boy. His sunken career arc also explained why our house still looked like a bombed-out set in a war movie. Pro volleyball was not exactly catching fire with many fans, which was why Dad had to dream up slum investment schemes with Adrian and pose for Finish Line's billboards of male powder puffs. Anyway, I grew up thinking everybody's stairwell led to a wooden gangplank over a gutted hallway. The narrow house narrowed even more to my attic room, over the plank and another flight of stripped-bare, groaning stairs.

My dad's inner drive to improve the world always led him far from any actual home improvement. He was gung ho for liberal politics. With his gold medal fame still fresh, he angled for an appointment to a civil rights board. Disgusted that blacks still got banned from voting, he volunteered in Mississippi for fair elections in 1966. Back home, he volunteered for Robert Kennedy's 1968 presidential bid and marched with Kennedy, Cesar Chavez, and Dolores Huerta during the United Farm Workers' strike. Later, though his face had disappeared from Wheaties boxes, Dad lent his dimming star quality—for free—to antipollution commercials for Save the Bay. Then he served on Save the Bay's board of directors, along with being our precinct captain. That's how he got involved in Castro Camera store owner Harvey Milk's successful election campaign for supervisor from our district, helping Harvey Milk just get elected as the first openly gay city official.

After I tackled trig and my AP Biology assignments, I decided to end with the fun stuff, Geography on a Threatened Planet. I had to predict trouble spots on a mimeographed map based on my teacher's theory that global cooling meant a new ice age was coming, but before I switched on the lamp, I just sat there for a while. I needed to have food and a shower at some point, but that's how Dad and I lived these days, hungry and stinking. My desk was shoved up against an alcove cut in for an attic window, with an unreal view that I was so used to I hardly ever noticed.

Between Ashbury Heights and the Catholic Kremlin were some skanky neighborhoods, including Rob's, some run-down blocks across from Haight-Ashbury, but the evening light mellowed everything. And now, with the house getting dark, the Catholic Kremlin across from the Panhandle of Golden Gate Park lit up. Lone Mountain looked just like the shining castle I thought it was when I was little. The spires of St. Ignatius Church and the Catholic schools floated on their hilltop beside it.

So instead of identifying the possible new glaciers of the new ice age, I drifted into a memory of that fateful Confirmation Day two years ago up at St. Ignatius, my pact with Rob to abandon the faith after the ceremony. I'd taken a quick glance back inside, giving a final nod to the statues, the crucifix, the stiff, oily pews. I inhaled that Sunday smell, cleaning chemicals mixed with old wood and the vanishing sweetness of all the moms' perfumes. How sterile the church had felt when nobody else was around. If there really was a God, I was sure he wasn't hanging around this lifeless, brainless joint. Penni had been clueless about our pact and often hinted "how natural" it would be that I went across the street to Most Sacred Bleeding Heart High School, and then, of course, just across the next street to the Catholic university. She probably thought I would be elected Pope after that. Confirmation morning, she'd come into my room, and looking straight at my completely dressed self as I buttoned my cuffs, she asked, "Are you dressed yet, Guy?"

"No, Mom. Remember that birth defect? How my skin is a polycotton blend?"

"This is a big day for you. I'm so proud."

"Proud of what, Mom? I turn fourteen, they burn a bunch of incense and shake some shiny dealybobs." That morning, I thought about breaking my godless news while I had my mom in my grip, but she looked too happy. So I just joked around, stuck in the old family replay. "I haven't accomplished one thing. Well, I did grow a little hair under my arms. Wanna see?"

She'd laughed and retreated to the doorway. "Now hurry up and finish dressing. Comb your hair. The ones on top of your head." Her voice trailed off, bouncing off the bare stairwell. "I'm fixing you a special brunch."

I could've pretended I didn't hear, but I figured what the hell, she'd been slaving over something smelly on the old stove.

Even when I was little, I came to think of my mother as "Penni," in honor of her own moment of youthful fame. The summer she met my father, a visiting Catholic jock from Sacramento, at a Bleeding Heart High School dance, teenaged Penelope O'Malley was the official hostess for Penny Wise Family Discount Stores. After she graduated from Bleeding Heart High, the boss hired her back to work full-time, a girl model in hokey local TV commercials. Meanwhile Penni entered and dropped out of art school at nineteen, then married my dad when he got back from the 1960 Summer Olympics in Rome. As a bride she was only a little pregnant with me. After the cord was cut, she picked up her career again and just to be extra cute, rechristened herself as "Penni Wise," a mascot for new products. She posed in a space suit to fake excitement over Supersonic Orbital Bottle Washers. On the back of a terrified burro, Penni Wise introduced the World's First Fully Automatic Tortilla Warmer.

When I was in the early grades, my mom was promoted to a "mother" Penni Wise who led classes in etiquette, modeling techniques, and good posture to twelve-year-olds lured in by big ads in the Sunday *Chronicle*. These featured a head shot of Penni, looking too sensitive ever to belch. And beautiful, with a sly lipstick smile. In a few years, though, when the style got reshaped into being "natural," scowling, and slumping, the daughters stopped signing up, the bosses dropped the classes, and Penni had to scuffle for freelance modeling jobs. But just like Dad, she got the message she was getting irrelevant and decided to go into business for herself, starting her own modeling school, Aspirations Unlimited, one of those pose-and-posture deals that run ads in back of magazines like *Zits*.

When I walked into the kitchen that Confirmation morning, I was still crazy about my mom. She smiled, standing at our vintage 1945 gas stove, warming leftover tripe stew. "My favorite south-of-the-border recipe." *Huevos rancheros de menudo.* Which translated into my mother gooping tripe over eggs and automatically warmed tortillas.

Time traveling back to the present, February 1978, I flicked on my desk lamp and tried not to think about people like Penni and Rob. They both had unexcused absences from my life.

Just as I turned back to the global cooling map, Adrian stopped by my room for one of his godfather ambushes. "Your dad's on the phone with the LA people. They're going to take Finish Line to a whole new level. Not just billboards and radio around the city. Professional, filmed commercials, all over California and the West, then maybe nationwide."

"Does that mean shooting ads in LA?"

"Most likely. We're talking slick productions. Nothing like the little ol' black-and-white local things like your mom—and all of us—had to endure back in the days of Penni Wise."

"Yeah, but she had fun. And she was home in time to make dinner for us. Wholesome home cooking, like octopus eyeballs in a seaweed curry."

Adrian smiled, peering over my shoulder at my geography homework. "I know you must feel kind of marooned these days. But you know how much your old dad cares about you. It's just that he doesn't have time right now to…."

"Time to express it?" I surveyed pestilential lowlands and frozen, nonarable highlands. "Wow, that's a busy old dad."

He shrugged, changing the subject. "I hope you've been surviving this AP track you're on. Are you capable of making friends among those brainy kids at Walt Whitman?"

I made apelike snarls and animal snorts. "Me try. Me screw up. Me cry."

"More to the point. Have you discovered girls yet?"

I still wanted to blurt out the Truth. Long before today's disaster with the Pest, I figured I could practice Coming Out to Other People on Adrian. But being direct wasn't as easy as I hoped, so I started slow. "So, what is there to discover about girls, exactly?"

Adrian laughed. "That's a good one. Just be careful out there, little Guy. You're not too hideous, and who knows how many young temptresses are going to throw themselves at you before they discover your… defect."

"That I'm kind of… different?"

"That you're kind of… mentally impaired."

I laughed at the old joke. Ever since I started bringing home my goody-good kiddie report cards from Most Precious Suffering, Adrian thought it was his duty to keep me from thinking too highly of myself. *Not to worry*, I thought to this Jewish atheist my parents chose as my godfather in Catholic morality. Today I felt plenty lowly. Like, say, a pile of steaming hyena crap. "Just think of how the temptresses are going to go nuts for me when they see Dad on TV, selling his soul for Finish Line male wrinkle cream."

Adrian tugged at his black mustache. He looked even thinner than usual and jumpier, his dark eyes darting around my room until they finally settled on mine. "Think how much good Paul's endorsements are going to do for you guys. His political volunteering sure doesn't put food on the table. You don't want your father to be a wadded-up old jock all his life, do you? Isn't that where he was headed, an old has-been down at the Claimjumpers business office, promoting volleyball for geriatric clinics?"

"Come on, Adrian. There's got to be a raised bar for somebody who can jump that high!"

"Well, then, genius… what?"

"Whaddaya mean?"

"What would you like your dad to do?"

"Who am I to say?"

"Well, then…."

Adrian and I had this conversation, or a close replica, 4,489 times without my ever getting up the guts to let him know that his godson was a homo.

After Adrian left, I noticed the boxes and contents of Penni's bedroom drawers and closets were no longer exploded throughout the stairwell. Penni had carried it all away except for a left-behind item, blown up against the floorboards. It was a black-and-white snapshot I'd never seen, "March '61" scrawled in blue ink. I turned it over to see a teenager facing an errand into the unknown, a solitary Penni, stomach swollen with me. The photographer's shadow—most likely my dad's—fell across her feet on Granny's Sacramento porch.

In the stairway, where the ancient paint droppings and carpet glue still splotched the exposed boards, my hollow footfalls were answered by the steady pounding, across the gangplank, in Dad's room, along with banging and scooting.

He sighed, groaning to his knees and facing me amid the chaos of the bed frame, the emptied, still-opened drawers and closet. The room looked barren, deprived of the king-sized bed Penni and Lester must have claimed. All that was left was a cleaner, darker-green spot in the carpet squared by a fringe of dust bunnies.

"Your mother found a box full of stuff from your baby days, Guy. Snapshots, bronzed shoes, shower invitations. Penni thought she should take it, being as she was the one who kept track of all that crap."

"So now you're going to move back in here? No more falling asleep on the sofa in the den to Veg-O-Matic commercials?"

"Yep, I finally have my chance to try out the waterbed again." Penni had hated the contraption, claiming seasickness and Aleutian chill and probably even barnacles, and banished it to the basement.

As I looked around, a polar current swept through me as it all sank in. My *baby box* was going to Oakland with Penni, along with the freakin' king-sized matrimonial bed. Why was she making off with our ancient family mementos? I'd never imagined any of that stuff ever leaving Montes Terrace. In lame hope of some misunderstanding, I asked Dad, "Didn't Mom say she was just, kind of, *staying* in Oakland while she finished art school?"

"Come on, Guy." He exhaled, then bounced his fist against the bed frame. "Our divorce is going to be final. She wants a life of her own in a place of her own." He looked out the bay windows, which had a dead-on, street-lamp-lit view of the half arch's plaster cherubs taking wing into nothingness. "Hell, I'm sure going to miss her."

Dad's voice cracked, which he tried to disguise by knocking a metal beam. Still sprawled on the floor, he started fighting with the frame. "You're not a kid anymore, and judging by the pain in my back, I'm sure as hell not one either. So get over here and help me. Then we'll get some takeout from the Lotus Moon."

Little did I know, I was now an accomplice, helping him set up that waterbed. Each of us would eventually float toward whole new seas of pain and danger. But first we'd drift into our separate whirlpools of sex. Then, cast apart, Dad and I each would get caught in a more treacherous current.

You know. Love.

Chapter 2

EARLY ONE morning that week, as I crossed the gangplank, past the exposed joists in the stairwell, I heard high-pitched giggles that sure as hell weren't my dad's. When I tiptoed past his room off the second floor landing, the gasps grew distinct. Then heavy breathing turned to squeals.

I made coffee, expecting to share it once again with one of Dad's "companions," like I had to during the past Thanksgiving weekend. I'd been stumbling across the gangplank, then almost got smacked by the door opening to my dad's bedroom, to be shell-shocked by the sight of an older woman tangled in her red party dress. Through his still-open bedroom door, I glimpsed Dad, still asleep, muttering, his bare back only half covered by the sheets. I looked away and into an awkward pause with the woman in the red dress.

As she struggled to close her back zipper, she'd grinned at me, her red-orange hair coiled like a wig of wires. Deep eye makeup caught in cobwebs of wrinkles. "Honey," she asked, cloying, "would you zip the back for me?"

I did, silently, lapsed into a stupor. She flinched when I managed to squeeze her flab in a final upward tug.

"Oh, sweetie, that tickles! Oh my, if I weren't too much of a lady, I might rob the cradle...." She slipped around, ambushing me with a sloppy kiss on the lips. "Thanks, doll. Tell your dad I had to leave early. Family business." She cackled. "He'll know."

Later, Dad explained he'd met the old gal at an evening reception for Finish Line investors. ("She was very interested in our men's product line.") She was hardly the only female to take the product for a long test drive after Penni moved out in the fall. After that our house became a one-night hostel for women seeking the Paul Dimchek Experience. Secretaries came and went in three varieties: clerical, legal, and part-time. (Adrian said it was the same pattern with his Jewish girlfriends: "Orthodox, Reform, and retail.") My favorite of Dad's overnight guests, though, was a belly dancer from South Dakota.

Strangely, I never saw her again that fall. Before Christmas, Dad had just stopped bringing women home. But then he didn't sleep at home that much either.

Noises like this morning's hadn't shivered the house's timbers for months. For a crazy second, heating the coffee water, I fantasized that Penni and Dad had reconciled secretly in the night. Crossing the Bay like an epic Greek, Dad had recaptured his exiled bride.

The coffee filter remained in the sink exactly where I'd set it on Friday morning before school, the cone brittle, the grounds caked dry. I was sure if I placed a skinned goat on the kitchen table, it would rot there until Zeus himself demanded we set the horned beast ablaze. The only sign that Dad had passed through the kitchen in the past week were two cocktail glasses beside the sink, half-bitten cherries floating in the melted ice.

When I was pouring the last drip of almost-sour milk into my coffee, a slightly accented voice wafted toward me from the doorway.

"Normally, I would just slip outside without any fuss, but your father is still sleeping, and I must get to work."

Well, it sure wasn't Penni or the Dakota belly dancer, the tone way too formal and precise.

I dimly recognized that voice but couldn't place it as it neared the kitchen.

"So, are you as sweet as your father? You are almost as tall."

I turned to see a gorgeous blonde stranger smiling as she clutched the lapels of my dad's white terry cloth robe.

"Oh, you are his mirror image!"

"Maybe. But I'm not nearly as sweet," I said, fighting through the cup collection for one that wasn't a wobbly remnant of Penni's failed pottery phase. The only decent mug was left over from a political fundraiser, captioned "JERRY FOR ZEN MASTER," with a cartoon of Jerry Brown cross-legged, meditating, his thought in a cloud: "And Governor Too!"

Pouring, I said, "I hope you're a Democrat."

The woman just smiled before she accepted the coffee. I offered to trade if she took it with milk.

"Thank you, but I take it black and strong. You have wonderful manners, just like your father. No wonder politicians like to have their pictures taken with him. Are you going to follow in his footsteps?"

The ones leading where, I wondered. To the gates of the next Olympiad? Probably not—our tennis team just got creamed at our first tourney.

The beauty was studying me with a quizzical smile. The floppy terry cloth lapels had fallen open, revealing a mighty vista of her cleavage. Now her gaze caught mine, and she smiled even broader, then gently covered herself and tightened the sash.

"So you *are* going to follow in his footsteps."

"I'll say this much. Dad taught me to appreciate women."

"It certainly shows."

She tapped the Jerry Brown cup while she glanced around, her face neutral, as if she were trying to hide her disapproval. Cracks welted the ugly yellow paint. Penni had once painted projects in here for her first art class, Color Technique, splashing pale acrylic squiggles on the kitchen table. Since they dried, it always looked like colorful drunks had just partied overnight. Otherwise the place hadn't changed a bit, probably, since the Great Depression.

"Such an old-fashioned... well, homey kitchen. Think of all the wonderful meals that must've been prepared here."

I suppressed a laugh. "Meals without number," I said in tribute to the culinary battles Penni waged against that helpless, well-meaning old gas stove.

"Thank you so much for the coffee."

The beauty poured more into her own cup to take up to my dad. So she knew he liked it black and strong too. I figured at least some of his mysterious late-night "meetings," when Dad showed up at home the next morning only to make sure I hadn't burned the house down or died of starvation, were probably conducted at the blonde's place. The woman drifted upstairs, bearing the steaming coffee like a goddess.

I DIDN'T see much of my dad for the rest of February, but I'm sure the blonde did. I'd come home after tennis practice to find the same tattered note from Dad reclipped to the fridge:

Eating out again. Some bucks attached for you. P.S. Not for candy, beer, or premarital sex.

I had dinner at this Mexican joint on Haight Street so often my order became known as "Guy's Big Burrito." Some evenings I sipped cappuccino and played checkers at Café Amalfi with the old Italians who'd survived all of Haight-Ashbury's incarnations. Other nights I joined the eternal pickup basketball games at the Catholic Kremlin. Nobody seemed to care how lousy I was. Then, sweaty, I'd suffer over my homework at the branch library, only half conscious that I was avoiding our empty house.

Haight Street, where the flower children of the late sixties got plucked by the junkies of the early seventies, mutated into a big singles scene. Gay and straight bars sprouted in abandoned head shops and methadone clinics. Meanwhile the clones started to spill over the hill from the Castro district. In tight jeans, flannel shirts, trimmed mustaches, and short haircuts, aggressive young guys strode down Haight Street hand in hand. Some evenings as I slunk away from the Mexican joint, a lone clone would shoot me an eyeful so hungry he must've thought Guy's Big Burrito was ready for takeout.

Not quite. It probably sounds weird. There I was, a tall, healthy gay teenager wandering San Francisco streets alone as 1978 started spurting to its climax. In my very own neighborhood, a great homosexual migration was morphing into history's greatest gay sexcapade. Those new arrivals tempted but scared the hell out of me. The clones were ten or fifteen years older, their biceps straining their T-shirt sleeves, their lust throbbing in their jeans. It wasn't just Jimmy Carter who sinned in his heart. How could I avoid a thousand wicked fantasies while Castro and Haight each hosted a street carnival of mind-blowing bulges and sculpted butts under skintight denim?

The problem was, like President Jimmy, I still thought in terms of "sin." Deep in my nonbelieving soul, that Catholic schoolboy still choked my own liberation. My dad was way more liberated from Catholic sex phobias than I was. Years before Harvey Milk finally won office, with each of us still dressed for Mass, Dad took Penni and me marching with Harvey's faction in Sunday gay rights parades. And when his best college buddy came out to his unforgiving family, Dad was the only friend he turned to. The guy spent weeks crashing in our den on the Hide-A-Bed.

So I fantasized about the guys on the street but held back from doing anything about it. In the cold fog of reality, I rode the 33 Muni bus every school morning down to my transfer point, Seventeenth and Castro, the global epicenter of the gay street revolution. Turned-off and turned-on in equal parts, I dodged my mixed feelings while the M streetcar tunneled me under Twin Peaks.

Every afternoon at the Castro transfer point, I endured more of the same in reverse direction. It was especially weird without Rob, who used to join me for the return trip. Now, if we happened to take the same streetcar home, he'd sit wherever the farthest point was from me, acting all engrossed in a textbook for the whole ride. Caught out alone at the transfer spot, I must've looked like a lost preppie. That's when I wished I'd come out to Dad a lot sooner. I invented hokey pep talks in his absence. "Guy," he'd say, "you're smart to wait until the right guy comes along." But outside of my imagination, he was never around for the Big Conversation. The few times I saw him at all, he'd mutter about the floundering attendance for the Claimjumpers, the better prospects of the Finish Line male cosmetics project, and his plan, with Adrian and other investors, to buy more half-decomposed slums in West Oakland. (I wondered if this was his sneaky excuse to visit Penni's side of the Bay Bridge.)

So I stuck it out there at Seventeenth and Castro by myself—not that I had any choice. Individual wolves among the roving clones smiled at me, baring their teeth in sinister snarls, rubbing their crotches and licking their lips. There I stood, tennis racket poking from my book bag, a native gay guy scorned by some Midwestern twinkie. I hunched my shoulders, hummed old Stevie Wonder tunes, and prayed that the 33 Muni bus would snatch me up to Ashbury Heights before I involuntarily lost my virginity to some clone from Kansas.

So ONE Saturday morning in early March, when I left the city for a Saturday sleepover in the Sacramento River Delta, I still took along my virginity. I didn't realize how close I would come to losing it.

My first field trip into gay sex came about, so to speak, when Randy Blanding, Coach's hunky blond son, overheard at the Saturday morning tennis clinic that I needed to collect pond scum for my marine biology class project.

Randy had a natural way of giving pointers and spreading around positive reinforcement, of which I needed plenty. It threw me off, though, when he kept me after, stretching his arms beside mine to demonstrate a better backstroke, yakking with me about his favorite subject—girls—then inviting me for a sleepover at his mother's place on Joaquin Island. "It's nothing but scum out there, Guy. You'll have the best collection in class."

He had a point. Thinking about where the fresh water of the Sacramento and San Joaquin Rivers met the tidewaters of the Bay, I could make a hypothesis about habitat destruction in the Sacramento River Delta.

Randy's thick arm pressing against my skinny one, his bare thigh pressed against mine, I scanned my addled brain to answer, "Like, sure. Sounds great. I'd love to collect your scum," which earned me another swat on the butt.

That Saturday afternoon, Randy's father was driving Randy and me across the Bay. Coach Blanding dropped Randy off at his ex-wife's place on Joaquin Island while he picked up Randy's little sister for her city weekend with Dad. "A great transportation epic, most weekends," Coach explained to me, his eyes catching mine in the rearview mirror as he yelled over the open windows' roar. "But if you can survive my ex-wife's so-called hospitality, you might have a great time on the island. If you want ugly microbes in murky water, Guy, Joaquin Island's crawling with 'em."

"True, Dad," Randy said, scrunched beside Coach in the beat-up old Beetle's passenger seat. "But Guy needs to prove that they're endangered due to pollution and urban sprawl."

"Randy, you're sure this has been okayed by your mother and we're not going to have any scenes?"

"What does she care, Dad? Like, about anything? She's fine with Guy spending the night, if that's what you're asking."

"Okay. But is she entertaining any of her gentleman callers this weekend?"

"I think Mom's still seeing that part-time preacher guy. The bald one who took over the propane service."

"Yeah, Harold Pruedhoe," Coach said, sighing. "Old Gas 'n' Jesus. Makes me nervous she's got such bad taste in men. Makes me wonder where I once marched in her parade of losers."

"Don't worry, Dad. She still hates your guts."

"That's a relief. Thanks, Son."

"No big compliment, though. She hates everyone."

"Even Gas 'n' Jesus?"

"She gets that nice discount on her propane bill. Mellows her out."

"And the Bible verses are free of charge."

So it went, past Concord and Antioch, out where the subdivisions subsided and the rain-greened hills clumped along the Bayshore. As the traffic dwindled, the country opened and flattened. The sky seemed broader here, and I daydreamed about jogging past the live oaks in the warm spring sun. But I was trapped, with legs cramped sidesaddle in the rear seat of a Volkswagen Bug, stuck in some other family's postdivorce psychodrama.

Beyond Brentwood, the highway narrowed and skirted a high river levee. As lonely mailboxes sprouted among hedges and along orchard groves, we crossed a one-lane bridge onto Joaquin Island. Coach Blanding waved to a bald, overweight man climbing into a truck with Island Propane spelled across its cab. Gas 'n' Jesus didn't wave back.

To my surprise, no herons flew from the palm-frond swamps that arose in my imagination when I heard the phrase, "out in the Delta." Joaquin Island was a flat landscape of farmhouses and just-planted fields. But it was warm and calm, far inland from the breezy Pacific chill at Walt Whitman High School.

Finally, after zigzagging on farm lanes, we arrived at Randy's mom's place, snug against the levee and shaded under eucalyptus trees. With Mrs. Blanding watching, arms folded, from the front porch, a little girl walked alone down the path to the gate, clutching her overnight bag and a plush toy alligator. After Randy hugged her, Coach snapped her up with a kiss. It seemed so weird, this custody exchange, Coach trading big, hulking Randy for this tiny little girl.

Randy and I hardly had time to yank our own overnight bags from the Bug's front trunk before Coach shook our hands, wished us a good scum search, buckled little sister into the front seat, and jammed into first gear as if some curse forbade one word with the watchful woman on the porch.

Mrs. Blanding seemed mild and frumpy. She got right to the point. "So, Randy, is your dad still seeing that shopgirl?"

"You mean Andrea? Or Michelle?"

"Andrea, I think. Who's Michelle?"

"Nobody, Mom. I'm sorry I mentioned it."

Before long, we organized a plan of attack for my research project. Driving around the island in his mom's pickup and armed with her Mason jars, we gathered river water from various sites along the levee. We rowed out to the middle of the river for an open-water sample, yelping as we fought the current's urge to sweep us into Suisun Bay. Finally we stripped off our T-shirts, jeans, and shoes and waded in our boxer shorts through muddy, reedy shallows to get a sample from the island's westernmost edge.

An hour later, on the dock just over the levee from his family's spread, Randy and I soaked in the sun's last rays. We'd dunked our ankles into the river to wash off the mud, then folded our jeans and T-shirts as pillows and lay back, side by side, in the warm breeze. I ignored the golden sheen on Randy's face and chest from the late afternoon sun. I ignored the smooth contours of his chest as his ribs rose and sank with soft breaths. I ignored the neat striations his abdominals formed. Above all, I ignored the darker hairs gathered in a line leading from his navel down to the elastic of his boxer shorts.

I sat up, arms squeezing knees. I forced my mind to focus on something other than Randy's flesh as he dozed inches from my side.

I tried to concentrate on other aspects of nature, that entire universe that didn't involve Randy's naked skin. The sun sank as battalions of birds sang and swooped under soft pink-orange clouds. The smooth, broad river swooshed under the dock. Oaks darkened, spiny and solitary, across the surging river, absorbing the sky's last colors.

Randy sat up beside me, hugging his own legs and resting his chin on his knees as he admired the dusk. "It's weird we didn't see any crawdads in the swamp. Geez, I figured we'd find at least a few."

"Think it's a massive die-off?" I told Randy about my hypothesis, which was based on things I'd heard about when my dad was fighting for Save the Bay. There was so much pollution that entire species of fish were disappearing. "I'm going to try to show how the polluted runoff is affecting the microbes here, where freshwater meets tidal bay."

Randy nodded, pointing upriver. "See the skeletons of that subdivision going up? A couple hundred new 'patio homes.' A yacht club, new power lines, a huge sewage lagoon. Might as well drop a neutron bomb on the old Delta life."

I detected an undertow in his sorrow for the Delta. A loss closer to home, kids traded off, zigzagged between two houses, two lives, city and country. And now his old countryside was vanishing along every shore.

I wanted more than anything to run my fingers along Randy's arm in consolation. But straight guys didn't go in for that stuff, did they? For all I knew, gay guys didn't either. But now, to my everlasting wonder, Randy was running his fingers along *my* arm. I swore I could feel every electron explode in every atom of my skin under his touch.

Still, I didn't know if this was any kind of gay green light. After all, Randy had a girlfriend and blabbered about girls in general all the time. Maybe older straight guys were more relaxed in their affection. Maybe he thought of me as a kid-brother type. For some reason, I was terrified of glancing over to see the expression on his face. With my arm practically radioactive with exposed nerve endings, fake casual, I muttered my thanks for his help with the biology project.

"Do you really think that's why I took you out here?" Randy's caress became a clench, his big grip clutching my skinny forearm. "I mean, I like mucking around in the mud as much as the next guy, but afterwards I like to… mess around."

"Out here?"

"It's getting dark now. Anyway, nobody ever comes around here."

"So… what do you wanna…?"

"Let's start with this." Randy's next move felt like an ambush, the harsh way he leaned in, moving his grip from my arm to the back of my neck, while he steadied himself over me and guided me down so that I lay on my side against the dock's rough wood. I thrilled to this, no matter how scared I was. My first kiss.

With his lips mashed against mine, I marveled at the perfect fit. All my energy felt sucked up against those warm, wet fleshly curvatures. I figured it would go on like this for a while, so I braced myself against his bulk with my hand on his back while I dared to open my eyes.

His were closed tight, which was the last observation I made before his lips opened and his mouth began to pry at mine with the full force of his jaw. His tongue began to lap against my teeth, then thrust inward to tangle with my tongue, into heat and saliva and delicious, wet hidden spaces. It was a lot more of a kiss, and more from a kiss, than I'd ever imagined.

The trouble was, I hadn't done much imagining beyond that. When Randy's hand slipped down my spine while his tongue continued slithering around mine, I somehow didn't quite expect his reach to extend under the waistband of my boxers. I didn't expect his fingers to fan out across my butt, to squeeze each cheek and seek their way between them. I flinched, my rear involuntarily arching away from his grasp, which only made his hand more determined and his grip on my ass stronger. I could smell his ardor now, sweat mixed with our river mud and microbes, while I felt him pressing hard through our shorts' fabric.

Fabric he'd had enough of. He yanked my shorts down my thighs, exposing my bare butt to the entire Sacramento River. "I love this," he whispered, breaking our kiss for the first time. "I've been after this since our first practice. Can't you tell?" His fingers explored, probing what he was after. "I want your butt so bad."

Despite how the lead-up switched on my circuitry, those words blew my fuses. In all my fantasies of Randy, I'd never quite pictured actual male-to-male… penetration. As exciting as Randy's searching, prodding fingers might be, they also hurt like hell. I couldn't imagine taking any more mass or bulk up my backside. So my body responded with human history's entire survival instinct. I yelped, wrenching myself from Randy's fingers' pumping and thrusting, and skittered away with such force I almost launched myself over the dock into the river.

Randy, startled, pulled me by my arms back to dry safety. Shorts shoved to our ankles, we kneeled, face to face.

"What's the matter, Guy?"

"Sorry. I got scared."

"Scared? Haven't you ever done this before?"

I looked at his beautiful torso outlined in the twilight, his perfect, flat stomach, the twin rounded halves of his chest, his still-hardened nipples. The thick biceps, their strong vein lines distinct even in the wavering, distant marina lights. The thick, sleepy lashes over his sharp, eyes regarding me quizzically, kindly. But exasperated all the same.

Why couldn't I go through this like a real man? "No," I finally answered, looking away, looking beyond. "That was my first kiss."

"With a guy, you mean?"

"With anybody."

"Sorry, Guy. I got carried away. Way far. I thought you were experienced, okay?" He yanked up his shorts. "You're so damn tall for a junior, and you act like Mr. Cool."

"Me?" I pulled up mine, light-headed. And ashamed, as if I'd actually given up my virginity. All that for a kiss and a little below-the-elastic second-base action. "No, I'm not cool. I'm sorry," I finally said. "I really like you, Randy. I've had this crush on you, okay? And I'm sure I'm gay. I mean, no girlfriends. No copies of *Hustler* in my sock drawer. Okay?"

"Okay. That's cool with me. You're a damn good kisser for a beginner. Better than my girlfriend." Reaching for his jeans and T-shirt, he got up. "You're a hell of a better kisser than you are a tennis player."

In a flurry of denim and zippers and laces, he was off. From the rickety steps that led to the levee, he called back, "Get dressed, Guy."

"Yeah. I'll just collect my stuff here." Along with what was left of my good judgment.

"Okay, kid. See you back at the house. My mom will have some grub for us."

As I listened to Randy's footfalls, I pulled on my clothes but was still barefoot, moored to the dock. With my head propped on my sneakers, even though it was getting cool now, I watched the stars come out and pondered what on earth could be wrong with me. Everyone else on the planet was sexing into a frenzy without scaredy-cat second thoughts about their own virgin asses, so what was my deal? Copulating clones in the Castro and fornicating Cosmo Girls in the Marina had conquered my native city. Even my dad had gotten in on the action.

Now that all our practice had finally led to a real game, I'd refused to play. Was I some kind of sex-averse freak? I was coming of age as a teenaged monk in the very decade that was making a religion of easy sex. Worst of all, I was sure I'd blown any chance that Randy and I would ever become friends, let alone boyfriends. As if to underline my disgrace in dripping ink, I was bawling now. Whimpering there on the dock like a brain-damaged maiden who'd swallowed the key to her own chastity belt.

But if I didn't follow Randy to the house, where else could I go? Not real bright to find myself in this fix, free to be alone fifty miles from home but stranded at the same time, no bus service, nothing to drive. Jesus, did I ever want a car of my own. What could I do, call Penni in Oakland, for God's sake? Wait for my mother and her boyfriend to pick me up from an aborted sleepover? Right. It would be even more humiliating to call my dad, and it being Saturday night, he wouldn't be home anyway. I could shoot a message into his answering service, but what the hell would I say? "Daddy, I'm a'scared. Too scared to let my coach's son screw me, and now I want to come home with you and your date for the night. Can you give me a ride?"

Above the tulle haze on the horizon, the first stars blazed. Below, the dock rocked, and I realized that I lay there beside a kind of water highway, barges and pleasure craft slipping by, their lights doubled in the placid, lapping river. Could I untie this dock and light out for the territories like Huck Finn? Better yet, hitch a ride on an upriver yacht all the way to Sacramento, where my granny was probably making minestra and pasta.

In the end, hunger won out over the urge for escape. I sighed, rubbed away the tracks of my tears with spit, and laughed at myself. Then I hustled into my shoes and over the levee in search of kitchen lights.

I passed by the pickup's bed, where my Mason jar samples were stored in a fruit crate. My only Delta spoils, contaminated swamp scum. Framed in the kitchen panes, I could see Randy at the table, his back to the window, and his mother hovering by the oven. Just in time! I salivated, smelling fried chicken as I bounded up the porch steps. Then, breathless and embarrassed, I lurked in the doorway.

"Oh, good, Guy… I was worried about you," Randy's mom said. "Why don't you wash up and have some supper?"

Yes, ma'am! I scrubbed up in the laundry room sink and ducked back through the doorway. My appetite overcame my uneasiness about faking small talk with Randy for his mom's sake.

But the talk didn't sound small at all.

"But who could they possibly be, Harold," Randy's mom was asking, "these enemies of the family?"

"Haven't you heard of gay liberation, Caroline?"

My neck snapped toward the table. That wasn't Randy. I vaguely remembered that face from my glimpse that morning when we'd arrived on the island. Gas 'n' Jesus was one of those bald guys who comb a few long, dark strands over their shiny skin dome. He wore a yellow golf shirt, burgundy slacks, yellow socks, and Hush Puppies. In front of him, sucked clean of all meat, bones were piled on a plastic plate. In one hand he clutched a coffee mug, in the other a Bible, which rested on his knee. God knows what verses, marked by a little red ribbon, had ignited this conversation.

"Well, come on in, Guy, don't be shy," Randy's mom said. "You're welcome to join us."

"Pull up a chair, son. Caroline has some chicken heated up just for you."

It soon became clear that I'd missed the meal. Randy had hustled to the bunkhouse to watch TV with a plastic plate full of chicken and mashed potatoes. After Mrs. Blanding served me at the table and sat with her coffee, I had no choice but to sit before the reheated drumstick, the lumpy, watery mashed potatoes, and a can of Coke. She and Harold were so pleased to have a captive teenager in their company that they both sat in silence for a moment, smiling at me, awaiting the miracle of The Adolescent Who Actually Ate at the Table. I could only oblige, not only because of their kindness but because by now I was ready to swoon from food lust. Smiling, I wielded a drumstick.

Gas 'n' Jesus prompted me, lowering his head, "Bless us, oh Lord…"

"…for these thy gifts, which we are about to receive…." I finished the blessing, waving the drumstick like a bishop's crosier, and cracked open the Coke. I'd been drinking wine with dinner, first diluted with water, now full strength, since I was seven or so, along with competing lectures from Dad and Penni about the proper variety to complement that meal's sautéed squirming mollusk. Coke with dinner seemed interestingly mid-American, as if to prove the Midwest started at the Sacramento River Delta. I was also mighty thankful for the whole concept of chicken and mashed potatoes. I'd fantasized forever that in the great nation that undulated eastward from San Francisco, real people were sitting down to meals like this, meals composed of familiar barnyard animals and garden vegetables.

Satisfied that the dining miracle had been consummated, Gas 'n' Jesus returned to his earlier point. "Caroline, haven't you heard about this homosexual who's infiltrated the Board of Supervisors over in the city?"

"Harold, now, please. I don't think we should discuss this in front of the boy."

"All right. But I am working up a sermon about it, and I want you to hear it before I go before the congregation."

"I'd be proud to."

"I'm telling you, there are enemies untold out there." He pointed his Bible out the window, toward the surrounding dark. "Immoral men and women who mean to undermine the American family."

"Well," Caroline said, surprising me by getting up and reaching for my empty plate, "I still can't fathom who these enemies are and why they'd have anything against the American family. Everyone's part of *some* family!"

God bless you, Caroline, I thought. Even if I only had one single solitary drumstick, I liked the way she put that. She refused my offer to bus my own dishes and directed me toward my sleeping quarters in the bunkhouse.

"Randy has a king-sized waterbed, Guy, with more than enough room for two big strapping boys. Why, he's had plenty of his friends sleep over."

Gas 'n' Jesus put his Bible on the table and pulled Randy's mother onto his lap. They both merrily wished me good night, making no secret of why they were terminating our little family meal and hurrying me out of the main house. On my way out to the bunkhouse, I noticed Gas 'n' Jesus had parked his propane truck in the eucalyptus grove, well hidden from prying island eyes.

Everywhere around me, straight couples were uncoupling from their sacred vows and forming new sex alliances. Everywhere, their kids were having lonesome burritos or hauling plastic plates out to bedrooms to snarf down meals alone with the TV. Yeah, Gas 'n' Jesus, it was me, the immoral Enemy of Families, who caused the downfall of society.

I stood on the kitchen porch, taking a deep breath to fortify my courage for the journey across the gravel driveway to Randy's bunkhouse. Its windows shifted cold with blue TV light. From the kitchen, Caroline giggled like a schoolgirl. Beyond the levee, a barge snorted at some tooting, smaller craft. The eucalyptus trees caught the faint lights in their fingery leaves, wavering on the slight river breeze and smelling sweet and medicinal, a salve to my nerves. Wafting to Ashbury Heights the few blocks from Golden Gate Park, eucalyptus scent made me homesick even when I was home.

Okay, enough self-distraction. I had to face that king-sized waterbed. Would I even be welcome there, now that Randy knew me for the sex coward I was? Would he even let me sleep on his floor?

After a quiet rap on the door, I eased into Randy's room. Beside a plateful of chicken bones, still fully clothed, he lay on his stomach, watching a relic from the sixties, *Bob and Carol and Ted and Alice*, with the sound off. I thought Randy was asleep until he stirred, turning to face me. "I'm sorry about what I said, Guy. You're not such a bad player." He patted the space right beside him. "There's lots of hope for you yet, with the proper coaching."

So I joined him on the waterbed as we watched the rest of the movie, a comedy about straight people swapping spouses. Then we fell asleep wrapped in our clothes and each other's arms.

Chapter 3

SUNDAY EVENING, Randy helped me carry my river samples into the foyer. He asked, "Think your dad's home?"

"Probably not. I think he's staying with some new girlfriend most nights now."

"Good. Then I can kiss you." He did, quick but deep, then slapped my butt. "Gotta go, babe. Dad's double-parked. See you at our next practice."

Simple as that. I stared out the open door, weak-kneed, clutching my box full of swamp scum while Randy hopped into the Beetle.

I ducked into the kitchen in search of domestic vital signs. None, just a corpse-like silence broken by my own Randy-rattled heart pumping in rhythm with the refrigerator. My mug and the "JERRY BROWN FOR ZEN MASTER" cup were exactly where I'd put them on the drain. I thought of the blonde beauty again and figured they were out for dinner. Dad had turned over the note I'd left about Joaquin Island and written his own.

> Welcome back, Guy. Here's dinner in case (!)
> you're hungry.
> Love ya, Dad

He'd stuck some bucks to the magnetic clip. I knew I couldn't eat—my stomach was still churning from Randy's kiss—so I saved the bills for my Datsun 240Z fund. I set the sample box beside my tennis racket and other school stuff, then imagined myself standing at Castro and Seventeenth early the next morning. Yep, the dutiful schoolboy with his Mason jars, waiting to transfer to the M Car while the clones crept homeward from their bathhouse all-nighters, as brimming with exotic microbes as my swamp water.

I hadn't slept so well on the island, mangled all night by Randy's fully clothed bear hugs, so I headed straight to my room. Before I'd reached the second floor, I could already detect giggles and snorfling and moaning coming from Dad's closed bedroom door. So they'd skipped dinner and gone straight upstairs for bump and grind.

I lay on my bed, trying to ignore the Catholic Kremlin's hilltop glow taunting me. A female voice rose, faint. Then Dad's shouted response. Then the toilet flushing. Soon the giggling, snorfling, and moaning started up again. At least, thanks to Dad's waterbed, I was spared squeaky springs.

When I could actually detect my father's rhythmic grunts, I put my head between both pillows, embarrassed that my father was a sex fiend, just like me and everybody else in the whole screwing world.

THE REST of the semester challenged my wit—and my wits—even more than my father's going AWOL with the mystery Finish Line meetings—sometimes in LA—and his mystery blonde. How could I know spring was going to snare me into my own entanglements with no finish line in sight?

It started when I decided to make new friends to make up for the fact that Rob continued to treat me like a nonperson. He wasn't a complete jerk about it. Maybe true jerkhood never was in the Pest's character. If we had to talk about team stuff or even share a ride somewhere, he talked with me like any teammate would. Rob even hand delivered a homemade invitation from his sister to attend her birthday party like I usually did, so I guess he hadn't badmouthed me to his family. But we'd become just teammates, not friends.

Rob acted like my being gay was a bad choice I'd made, like stealing lunch money from little kids to shoot up heroin. When would it occur to him being gay was an orientation starting at birth, like left-handedness? He looked at me, shrugging, acting like he was so evenhanded but pure, sidelined from my great sin. *Well, if that's what you've got to do, child-robber-addict, who am I to judge you?* I got that shrug, plus the old Pescatore evil eye, especially at Saturday clinics with Randy. Rob seemed to pick up on whatever electric current passed between Randy and me and shook his head in mild wonder and disgust.

That prompted the most uncool thing I overheard him say all season, when Randy took me on in a practice volley: "So who's serving and who's taking it in the sweet spot?"

Anyway, I decided to start finding new friends away from the playing fields of Walt Whitman. As the last quarter got started, just when

I figured my college prep teachers would start easing up a little, my classes got more and more demanding. Worst of all, I was the only junior and one of the few guys in our tiny AP Biology class, which focused on marine ecologies. It was completely dominated by brash senior girls I called the Science Amazons. They attacked any topic, brilliant and fearless, and luckily my swamp-sample project had impressed them.

"Young Mr. Dimchek may have actually found some evidence of new and destructive change where the salt water ecologies meet the freshwater in the Delta," one of the Amazons wrote in her critique after my presentation, "though it appears he isn't quite aware of how significant his samples are." Which was typical, even though I'd already decided aquatic ecology was my favorite subject and studied like a demon to keep up. These senior science Amazons treated me like I was a dunce who got the right answer now and then, by accident.

I volunteered to be the science department's lab rat during my free period. I was trusted with lab setups and cleanups for the biology teachers and earned the grudging appreciation of the Amazons.

After my presentation, my favorite senior Amazon, Janine, was effusive. "Guy, even though you're one of the least developed biotic forms on Earth—a junior and a male—your project is probably the most important experiment in the whole science department this year. I can see how much heart and passion you put into your research."

I blushed like a baboon's bottom. Soon I was hanging out with Janine, sharing a seat if we caught the same M Car at Seventeenth and Castro, sitting with her at lunch, and even walking her to her next class.

The other science Amazons mocked me as Janine's new dumb-shit sidekick.

"She's always taken on some awkward dolt as a project, Dimchek," one of them told me, "just for laughs, ever since elementary school."

Maybe I was a dolt, but I really did adore Janine. Not only was she beautiful and nice, an unusual combination, but she helped me with difficult concepts and coached me before big tests. Naturally, the other senior Amazons assumed I was in love with her. How tragic for the mere junior, helplessly infatuated with pretty, busty, brainy Janine.

"Guy's predicament is practically Shakespearean," one of the Amazons commented, "impossible, star-crossed, unattainable love."

Oh yeah, it was one helluva sixteenth-century sitcom. During their lab-rat chores like injecting infection samples into petri dishes, then studying the oval portraits of venereal disease, I was sorely tempted to come out as a homo to the whole bunch.

But I decided to try coming out to Janine first, one fine March day when we were brown-bagging lunch on the so-called lawn of the campus quad. She asked me if I had a serious girlfriend "I was hiding somewhere."

"No," I told her, "I'm not really drawn that way." If this went the way of my attempt with the Pest, at least I would be losing my newest friend, not my oldest.

"What do you mean, Guy? At six foot one, you've got to have shot past puberty a while ago. Girls still aren't a draw for you?"

"I do feel drawn, just not to girls."

Janine absorbed it all calmly, nodding and smiling in the right places, encouraging me to go on. Then she told me her gay aunt was her favorite human on the planet.

"I knew you'd be cool about it," I told her, summarizing how Rob reacted. "It still kills me, Janine."

She grew thoughtful, picking at some weeds in the patchy lawn. "My guess is that Rob has great qualities if you two have been friends so long. I'm sure he still loves you, but he isn't sure how your sexuality might threaten your friendship. He's probably not sure how to relate, but he's got to be worried about you. For sure, the poor guy just doesn't know what to say or do now."

Janine's whole response kind of bowled me over. I never thought of looking at it from Rob's point of view, really, that he might be as freaked about our lost friendship as I was.

But more than anything, it felt so good to be accepted without question by someone I admired so much. I hardly had time to digest my baloney sandwich before two of the Amazons from biology approached, pretending they were standing over us without noticing us. "My goodness gracious," one said, feigning shock, "Janine's really robbing the cradle with the Dimchek boy."

"Yep. I caught them on the quad, sharing baloney sandwiches," said the other. "And here she is, practically engaged—to a college man!"

Janine laughed, tossing a handful of fresh-cut weeds at their ankles. "I like to cover all my bases, ladies. My college man is getting up there, pushing twenty. I like keeping young Guy around as a kind of fall back. You know how junior boys perform!"

I could've joked about my own college man love troubles but decided to keep that drama to myself for a while. I thought I understood gay and straight attractions, at least in the abstract, but I guessed Randy was that one rare and frustrating creature in the ecology, a bisexual. Randy had mentioned his awe for the senior women he'd met through his Walt Whitman girlfriend, the one he never introduced me to.

Janine and I officially became lab partners for the unit on California Tidal Ecosystems. After that school week, while I headed off to tennis practice, she headed home to start studying all weekend on her piles of AP coursework.

Meanwhile, Randy kept inviting me "out for a flick" on those weekends when he stayed in the city for our tennis clinic and his girlfriend had other plans. He and I would sit in the dark together in the back row at the Surf or Clay, our knees pressed together, our hands locked. After, he'd invite me to his room at his dad's place to "talk about the movie." Even though I always begged off, Randy would kiss me good night, leaning across his dad's VW Bug, and I would kiss him back. Caught in a swampy surge of confusion about his promises to his girlfriend—I didn't ask—I didn't know what to feel, beyond the mandatory ex-Catholic Twinges of Guilt. I hoped Randy's girlfriend would just disappear in some painless, mutually agreed way. Then Randy would be free to fall in love with me.

Meanwhile, I was determined to upgrade my driver's permit to a full-fledged license on my seventeenth birthday in early April. Pretty soon, I figured, I'd be driving to school, senior year, in my red Datsun 240Z. Penniless and godless, I still believed in miracles.

Janine helped me out with the driver's exam booklet, giving me tips during one Friday lunch on the quad. She was serene, having just passed a passel of tough exams in several classes.

"I'm caught up! It's such a relief to study the California Vehicle Code instead of tidal mollusk reproduction. I think I'll even visit your tennis practice today."

I thought that was a weird way to pass her rare free time, but if she wanted to witness a klutz in action, I was glad for her company. After school, just as Janine and I reached the bleachers and I turned to head into the locker room, Janine hooted at a blond figure in the courts.

Adjusting the nets, the blond turned, hooting back. "Hey, baby!"

"I'm glad you're here today, Randy." Janine waved and smiled, then went running down to meet him. They kissed, a long smooch, over the drooping net.

"This is a surprise, Janine! You always study after school."

"Not today. So I invited myself to come with Guy to today's practice."

"Guy? You know Guy?"

I waved from the locker room doorway, trying to keep my cool. "Yeah. Janine and I go way back, Randy," I called out. "We've been hanging out for like, at least a week."

"Huh," Randy said, keeping his own cool just fine, as usual. "Well, I'm glad you two are becoming friends." He turned back to Janine, holding both her hands. "Anyway, after my last class this morning, I realized I'm free for a long weekend in the city. Say, aren't your parents out of town?"

Janine laughed. "Like you don't remember. Come over, like I said. I'll cook you my specialty."

Randy kissed her again. "Which is?"

"My mother's leftover spaghetti."

I was about to turn into the locker room when I realized Darren Kennedy was standing a few feet away, absorbing the scene.

He looked at me, nodding toward the court, and smirked. "Aw. That's the cutest thing. The big dumb jock and his brainy girlfriend playing house this weekend."

"I don't know anything about that," I told Darren, actually telling the whole truth for once.

"And here I thought public displays of affection were forbidden on campus," Darren hissed, his voice whispery but high-pitched. "But I guess that doesn't apply to the special ones."

"Yeah," Rob said, coming out of the locker room, ready in his tennis gear. "That rule doesn't apply to special cases, Darren." Bouncing a ball on his racket like a yo-yo, he glanced at me and added, "Like a nice, normal kiss between straight people."

I glanced back, shaking my head and keeping my mouth shut, and ducked into the dark doorway.

FOR THE rest of the month, I literally tried to outrun my Randy-Janine predicament. After practice, hoping I could dash away from any more accidental encounters with either one, I took long runs down the wide, untrafficked expanses of the Great Highway. I loved jogging with the ocean fog in my lungs and moisture dripping down my face, trying to escape the Puzzle of Other People:

One, my dad's spending almost zero time at the house while practicing intimacy with a mystery woman somewhere and getting more and more unavailable to me.

Two, Randy's casual weekend overtures to me, his good-night kisses prowling deeper each time.

Three, Janine's sudden silences and sullenness during our lab work.

Did she suspect I was making out with Randy? If that were the case, I'd force myself to take a sharp turn west into the frigid Pacific current until I died of hypothermia.

"Are you mad at me, Janine?" I asked after school still early in April, the day of the most important exam of my life. Free after practice, Randy had offered to drive me to Motor Vehicles for my full-license driver's test. "I'm really sorry," I told her, "if I did or said something stupid."

Janine stared at me with her big brown doe's eyes, mixed with pain, sympathy, and natural warmth. "Oh, Guy!" She clasped my head with both hands and tiptoed to kiss me on the forehead. "You haven't done a thing except be a great new friend. I couldn't have made it through Tidal Ecosystems without having you for my lab partner."

"I think it was the other way around." Now we were standing face to face, our hands clasped. "You've just seemed so upset lately."

"It's just a mess of my own making. Nothing I can even think about until after the big push into final exams, so—"

"Ah-hah!" Randy said, treading into the lab, beaming as usual. He watched us, his head cocked, jiggling the keys in his pocket. "Geez, I can't leave you two alone for a second."

Since she'd figured out our mutual connection, Janine thought it was so "cute" that Randy and I had become such "good friends" and confided to me that Randy considered me his special project during weekend clinics. I was gooned by the unholy fact that my heart's real project was her boyfriend and surprised at myself for lusting after Randy through it all.

But Janine immediately wrested her hands from mine and propelled herself at warp speed into Randy's arms. I hustled from the lab while they smooched, pacing alone in the hallway. I could hear their voices after that but not their words, their serious, muttered tones. I distracted myself with mental reviews from the test booklet: Four. *At an uncontrolled intersection, which driver has the right of way?*

LATER THAT afternoon, I stepped from the driver's bureau with a full-blooded, no-restrictions California motor vehicle license. All I needed now was a vehicle. When I waved my temporary copy gaily and thanked Randy for waiting, he shrugged, hunched on the fender of his Dad's old VW Beetle, staring at the gutter. "Hey," I said, chucking his chin. "What's the matter?"

He grabbed my hand right there, squeezing it, then kissed me on the cheek. At rush hour three lanes of traffic clogged Oak Street, a captive audience for this homosexual act. Randy's closeted openness still blew my mind.

"Guy, when we were kids, remember how hippies talked about free love? I didn't even know what it meant, but I thought it was a great idea. I still do. But I know it's not the way the world works. Come on, let's get out of the traffic noise."

He led me to a bench, deeper into the Panhandle, where a eucalyptus grove muted the rush-hour roar between Oak and Fell Streets.

"I wanted to spend some time with you this weekend, celebrate your birthday, Guy, but that's not going to work. I've got to be with Janine." He explained that Janine had just learned it was definite. "I'm going to be a father. Which is okay with me. Really. But what the hell are we going to do about the next several years of college?"

Whatever powers of empathy I ever had suddenly stopped transmitting, a total blackout. Rather than imagine the responsibility my friends faced while still in their teens—crummy apartment, scramble to juggle job shifts and night school, then home to colicky, sleepless, spit-up squalor—I went blank and waited for the gray-green expanse of Panhandle lawn to come back into focus. I wanted the gauzy April sun to stop swirling so I could concentrate. As far as I was concerned, my best hopes about ever connecting with Randy were finished. A deeper isolation was going to stalk me like an armed mugger in broad daylight. I felt the pressure of Randy's hand on mine, but for once I pulled it away and clutched the bench's wooden slats. Sweet baby Jesus, enough was enough.

But Randy persisted and pressed his fingers over mine.

"Guy, I've got to tell you the truth. It hasn't been a big secret, has it? And I know it's been tough for you, but it hasn't been easy for me either. During this whole thing, I've wished you were older. I didn't want to fall in love with a schoolboy. But I did. Okay? I fell hard, babe."

"God, Randy! I wish you wouldn't even tell me this. What about Janine?"

"Maybe I could be accused of using Janine. Doing with her what I wanted to do with you."

"How would you answer that accusation?"

"I'd say it was half true. Because I really do love Janine. But I love you more. I'm just sorry you're a boy."

On those words, I got to my feet and told Randy I wanted to walk home. No more smooching with the Beetle's gearshift digging into my leg, no more "See ya next time." I muttered some white lie about my dad planning something for my birthday and bolted alone under an evening sky that suddenly had the texture and density of overcooked oatmeal.

I was enraged. Everything Randy had said on the bench felt condescending. He'd been ladling too much sugar to make it tasty for "the boy," oversimplifying everything. If Randy knew he'd abandon me for Janine, why torture me with that confession of love?

I'm just sorry you're a boy. Well, I wasn't. I loved being a boy, and I had news for Randy. I planned to be a man worth waiting for.

Okay, okay. I would just have to keep putting one foot in front of the other, into a future without the expectation of Randy's love or Janine's friendship. I'd had practice when I managed to lose my mom's presence in our lives and even my dad's companionship, though we supposedly lived under the same roof. I was even getting used to being rejected by my best friend. I glanced north toward the Pescatores' house on Hayes Street, recalling all the birthdays Rob and I had celebrated there, always doubled up so that Rob's mom made a scrumptious cake for me and Penni tried her best to create an edible one for Rob. It felt so hollow to head south now, as if I wasn't invited to my own birthday party. I was a freaking genius at the art of losing.

One foot in front of the other. I realized I was retracing the route Penni once used to take me home, hand in hand from Most Precious Suffering School, south one block on Masonic, east on Page, south again on Ashbury, crossing Haight. The intersection bustled with pedestrians. Did they all hurry to wives, husbands, lovers, kids? Was I the only one heading to dinner by myself?

One foot in front of the other. I felt a little better now, treading uphill, the half arch in sight where Lola Montes Terrace began to jag into Ashbury. Maybe by some miracle Dad would be home and I could make my white lie come true, inviting him to join me for my seventeenth birthday Big Burrito down at the Mexican joint.

Double-parked cars clogged dead-end Montes Terrace. TinkerToy Hondas and tanker Mercedes expelled well-dressed strangers at our front steps while the drivers angled back to Ashbury in search of parking spaces. At the door, I found myself stepping aside to allow a lone middle-aged woman to enter.

"Baby doll!" she cried, a total unknown to me. "Nice to see you again," she gushed, so I kissed her hand and helped her out of her evening wrap.

Now I got it. Since I'd been intimate with its back zipper, I recognized the red party dress immediately. With her makeup and hair all perfect, Dad's oldest (known) gal pal didn't look like a floozy anymore. In the open doorway, her gold and diamond jewelry bounced light around the foyer. A gray-haired man bounded in behind her to shake my hand. The red-dress woman introduced him proudly as her husband before they vanished into the noisy hallway.

Around the bend, the entire ground floor roared with twenty clustered conversations. Among a gaggle of people sitting on the steps, sipping from plastic tumblers, I spotted Leon, handsome ex-Claimjumper, star of my nocturnal blue movies before Randy replaced him in the lead role. With his arm around a woman in a shapely Afro and skimpy dress, Leon held up his drink to me, calling out, "Guy! Where you been, man? The show's about ready to start."

I just smiled and shrugged. What the hell was all this? I could hear Penni's laughter pitched high above the living room's din and caught a glimpse of Lester as he navigated his way back to her from the kitchen, bearing two tall tumblers full of ice and brown booze. Adrian waved to me as he schmoozed with the investment company's accountant. Nodding toward a silky couple, Adrian muttered, "Yeah, LA people," out of the side of his mouth.

The unexpected party's only expected thing was my dad's usual hosting style. Open bottles of top-shelf liquor spread around the kitchen table amid paper plates full of potato chips, Beer Nuts, and my personal favorite, gooey Vienna sausages. A woman in pearls and a slinky black dress rooted through our plastic cooler for a beer. Various Claimjumpers lined the countertops, looking uncomfortable with so much skin covered up in flared slacks and button-downs. Several of my dad's friends, coinvestors, and even a few familiar faces from Aspirations Limited bumped into me with, "Where have you been, Guy? We were afraid you were going to miss the first one!"

Just as I invented an hors d'oeuvre for myself, Celery Stick in Congealing Velveeta, a scream shrilled from the living room, followed by squeals and lots of oohs and ahs. Caught in the general crush through the open archway, I was propelled with the human tide to watch the television. Apparently this amazing show's first station break had come, inspiring the uproar. But it looked to be an old movie on Channel 2, *How to Marry a Millionaire*. What was the big deal?

Dad had raised the TV by stacking a coffee table atop an old console record player and stood beside it now. He turned up the sound so we could all hear, "Tonight's featured movie is sponsored by Finish Line," to hoots and applause. I realized I hardly recognized my dad in a wild magenta rayon shirt, puffy at the sleeves, floppy at the collar. When had his hair gotten so long?

Then the crowd hushed. Horns and percussion thumped over a high-angle shot, Olympic-victory music. Young women lined up along a track, cheering for Paul Dimchek, who loped toward the high jump, fully dressed in sports coat, tie, slacks, and street shoes. After close-ups of worshipful girls' faces, he vaulted into the air, just as the younger Paul Dimchek suddenly leaped in the older Paul's place, in ancient color shots from the 1964 games. Then, just as the young Olympian stood on the topmost raised platform to be anointed with gold, the older Paul Dimchek, in a business suit, took his place among the thronging, surging mass of adoring females, the gold medal replaced by a little vat of Finish Line cologne, which he doused along his jaw as he winked into the camera. "Get the champion's edge," the narrator exhorted in sportscaster intonations. "Finish Line Products. For a man."

The room exploded with applause, cheers, and laughter. Dad took a modest half bow, then shouted over the clamor, "Hey, I was just the talent." He joined in the applause, saying, "There are a ton of people here who did the real work to make this thing possible. Thanks to everyone! Now, there won't be another Finish Line commercial for a while, so let's keep rockin', folks!"

Well, whoop-tee-do, a fancy dress party to watch male perfume commercials. I knew Dad had flown to LA for a couple of quick "business" trips but hadn't heard a thing about these slick TV ads actually being ready to broadcast. I couldn't believe how out of touch Dad and I had been for the past few weeks.

Dad, approaching with his arm around a willowy blonde I hadn't yet noticed, seemed to sense my thoughts. He chucked my upper arm. "I'm glad you condescended to attend our little affair, Guy Adrian Dimchek." He leaned back to regard me. "Yep, I see you even wore your best jeans and sneakers."

"And my favorite T-shirt," I said, pulling the hem to model the words splashed across a dizzy, sick-looking cartoon crab: Clean Up the Damn Bay If You Want to Keep Eatin' Me! "Which is lucky, Dad, since I just wandered into your party by accident. I wasn't invited, okay? I just dropped some plans to hang out with Randy. Came home to find the house under siege by overdressed middle-aged people."

The blonde, whom I recognized now, laughed. But Dad didn't even crack a smile. "Come on, Guy." He scrunched his eyebrows and stared at me. "Didn't I tell you all about this last week? Soon as I found out the ads were airing tonight."

"Well, the only thing I had on the calendar today was a visit to Motor Vehicles after school. Anyhow, nice party." I held up my half-chomped celery stick. "Classy eats too."

"Yes, we are going to have to work on Paul's party concepts," the blonde said, touching my arm and laughing. "It is wonderful to see you again, Guy."

Her very slight German accent took me back to that morning in February.

"I voted for fondue," she said. "But I seem to have little influence. I told him these rooms were too small for so many guests. My suggestion for fixing the stairway was also ignored." The blonde flashed me a warm glance, as if she already took our mutual sidelining for granted. Then she arched her brow. "Paul, you know, I have not had the official pleasure."

My dad slapped his forehead and apologized. "I'd forgotten you and Liz hadn't been introduced."

Liz. I finally placed that voice, which belonged to the accent on the phone at Penni's modeling school, the woman who'd salvaged the whole operation from bankruptcy and liberated Penni from the demands of capitalism. In the months leading up to the commercial shoots, Dad had been in contact with Aspirations Limited in search of pretty young "talent" and scene extras for Finish Line.

Liz shook my hand, quick and firm. "Guy, I have heard all the stories, all the great accomplishments of your charmed life. I have even seen the baby pictures."

"Don't blush, Guy." Dad laughed. "You had the cutest little tush."

Geez, already with the cute tush. Maybe they'd been dating even longer than I figured, which explained most of his nightly absences for months now. I didn't think Dad had gotten to anywhere near the baby-pictures stage with any of his earlier, postseparation bedmates. When would there have been time between all-night grunting and rutting and the sunrise departures? Dad and Liz obviously had something deeper going on, something he cared enough to keep private.

For sure, I hadn't been around much myself. I'd kind of planned to tell my dad about my confusing thing with Randy. But now that my non-love affair had dribbled to a pathetic end, I was glad I could just shut up about it.

Liz seemed so amazing to me, filling a simple white summer dress. Taller than Penni and less of a voluntary skeleton, Liz showed off what Adrian would call "dangerous curvature." She had a wide smile that seemed to show all of her fine, strong teeth. Close to Dad, she radiated cool—the opposite of clumsy, self-slamming Penni, who could only muster that kind of self-possession for the cameras. Liz's eyes bedazzled, so steely blue I was sure they could generate enough energy to electrify some third world police state.

As the three of us bantered, Liz kept the compliments coming: "Paul, he looks just as handsome as you looked in those shots from the Olympics," and "Guy, you must have all the girls at Walt Whitman chasing you."

I just grinned. I let her believe that I, queer lab rat, mascot of the AP Amazons and tennis team disgrace, had an ounce of my father's charisma. Dad just stood there grinning. He wore the prideful expression he'd have in the good old days after one of Penni's accomplishments, like when she finished a battery-powered napkin holder commercial on the fourth take.

Now Dad was asking me what I thought of the Finish Line ad.

I shrugged. "It'll probably sell a lot of cologne."

"Then it was a great commercial, huh?"

"It was well done, yeah. I liked the cutting back and forth in time. But I do kind of wonder if your Olympics stardom has enough juice anymore."

Dad sipped his drink, raising a brow. "Really?" I could tell he didn't like that comment. "Well, I guess '64 seems like a long way back to someone your age."

"Yeah, but I mean, you're more famous as a Claimjumper now."

"That is an interesting point," Liz said, nudging my dad. "Guy might be right, at least for the younger viewers."

I smiled, basking in Liz's approval.

"Look," Dad said, squeezing the plastic tumbler as if it were my neck, "you're the one who's going to benefit if this stuff sells. So stop being so smug."

Leon and his girlfriend pulled Dad away, drawing Liz aside too. Out of nowhere, Penni and Lester moved into the pause, as if they'd been hiding nearby.

Penni squealed, hugging me. Nowadays I could rest my chin on top of her head. "How tall you're getting, Guy! It can't be that long since I saw you."

"Who knows?" I said, shaking Lester's hand.

"We're all changing," Lester said, patting the place over his bald pate where his hair had once crowned his long, hawkish face.

"I think Mom's shrinking," I told him. "That's my theory."

Penni laughed, a forced, staccato barrage to show what a good sport she could be. "Maybe, but you are shooting up, honey." In a fakey, chummy voice, she added, "Isn't he the tallest sixteen-year-old you've ever seen, Lester?"

I just couldn't stand her like this, so I zeroed in. "I'm seventeen, Mom. Today."

She covered her mouth with her hand and looked at Lester wide-eyed, clasping his arm to brace herself. It was too much. Even for Penni, this pantomime was third rate.

"Oh, Guy! I knew there was something about today. Didn't I say that this morning, Lester?"

"Yes, you sure did," old Lester put in. "Then you remembered we had this party. It was the only thing on our calendar. So I guess we forgot all about the main event of the day."

After enduring Penni's muttered, overdone apologies, I felt bad I'd gone on this cheap guilt trip. I said I was too old for cake and candles anyway, though I didn't really mean it. I kind of missed how no one except Randy even mentioned my seventeenth. And for the love of Jesus, Randy had chosen the occasion to kiss-off *the boy*. But with poor Penni falling all over herself with regret, I just wanted to erase the whole deal. The past year had been such a bummer for all of us. No wonder my parents forgot my damn birthday.

As if on the cue of that thought, somebody reached to turn down the TV movie, and someone else killed the lights while the strains of "Happy Birthday to You" were taken up, first in the kitchen, then throughout the hallway and up the whole stairwell. The group sing-along followed Liz into the living room as she and Dad carried each end of a platter, topped with a cake too huge for its measly seventeen candles. They balanced it on the coffee table in front of me, with kisses and hugs all around.

My attempt to think up a birthday wish came up empty. I was long past hoping for a reunion between Penni and Paul. I sure couldn't wish to get Randy's love back without wishing misery upon poor pregnant Janine, so I faked a thoughtful pause. Then I blew out the candles to applause almost as raucous as for the Foul Line commercial. (If I couldn't dream up a wish, I came up with a devious birthday scheme, to torture Finish Line investors by calling it "Foul Line.")

Penni smiled sheepishly, and I realized how generous she'd been, putting her weak acting skills to work in order to sustain the surprise. She even let Liz soak up the limelight.

Liz continued to bathe in it. As we munched on cake and the partying started up again, she took Penni's hand, flattering her boss with her best modeling-school decorum.

"Penni, that shade of indigo is definitely your color. It ignites all your blonde highlights. And Lester, I just saw your latest watercolors at the High Tide. So sensitive."

Lester and Penni grinned at her, though under all this politeness, I knew it had to be tough for Penni that her business manager was dating the husband she'd ditched for art school and Oakland. "Didn't our Aspirations Unlimited girls do wonderfully in the commercial?" Penni asked. Even this small talk sounded strained. "Thanks again for arranging all that."

"I just do what I'm told, Penni," Liz said. "You know me." She touched Penni's arm, patted my shoulder, and eased herself into the adjacent group that had formed around Dad. I noticed the Red-Dress Woman and her husband, the silky LA couple, Adrian and the Foul Line accountant all closing the circle just as Liz sidled into it, beside my father.

Penni whispered something to Lester. In a second, Lester turned to me. "Good luck, Guy, navigating your seventeenth year."

"I'll need it, thanks," I said. "Luck. And a compass."

Lester smiled. "Tell your father thanks for having us over."

"Why don't you tell my dad yourself? He's right—"

"I didn't want to interrupt the, uh, conference." Lester pointed to the cluster around Dad. Just then, I felt sorry for old Lester. He'd done his best to look jaunty in a leather vest, flared jeans, and Mexican sandals, but seemed so out of place. This crowd, mostly cleaned-up jocks and public-relations types, probably thought fine art was a scenic check of a silver dollar rising over the Sierras.

When Penni stretched up to kiss me, I understood they were already leaving. "Mom, thanks for the cake. I knew you didn't forget," I lied, feeling sorry for her.

"Well, you're a better actor than I am, Guy. It was just so hard to pretend this date—of all dates—had skipped my mind! It's blazed into my memory for all time. I'll never forget how nervous your dad was. He dragged Adrian to the hospital with us in case I had you in the car. I don't know what he expected. Something about Adrian being good with a Swiss Army knife, for God's sake."

Though I'd heard this saga 4,489 times, it really hit me how young Paul and Penni had been when they had me, just kids, no older than Randy and Janine. "Why don't you stick around for a while longer, Mom? There's sure to be another of those wonderful Foul Line commercials any minute now."

"We'd love to," Penni said, heading out behind Lester. "But we've got another engagement tonight. I want you to come across the Bay this weekend so Lester and I can toast your birthday with a little champagne."

What engagement wasn't important enough for their calendar, I wondered, but I just smiled, sure, sure. Penni and I were always making these imaginary appointments to spend time together in Oakland.

I dropped into the love seat just abandoned by Dad's associates. On the screen, Marilyn Monroe's character was making an idiot of herself because she was too vain to wear her glasses. I knew the movie's happy ending had the money-crazed bachelorettes marrying their handsome millionaires only after they'd learned the value of True Love. That was Hollywood's cheesy faith, Risk Your Heart and Love Will Follow. Movies never ended on some Panhandle park bench with a Go-to-Hell Kiss-off.

I glanced around for distraction. Red-Dress Woman proclaimed that her thirtieth anniversary was only four days away. When all the assembled straight folks toasted this adulterated marriage, I suppressed a snicker. What did I know? I was just a boy.

Did I feel so estranged from the crowd because nobody had brought any sons or daughters my age, or because, as far as I knew, I was the only queer in the room?

"I will not let you sit here alone," Liz said, suddenly beside me on the love seat. She drew her knees up under her and settled her drink along the seat back. "Not on your birthday."

"Thanks," I said. "That cake was a great surprise."

"I heard that carrot cake was your favorite." She nodded at the "Save the Bay" slogan on my T-shirt. "I associate carrot cake with ecology types and hippies. Are you a radical, Guy?"

"Nah. I just like the crunch, the nuts and cream cheese."

She smiled. "You're just as clever as your father always implies. It is no wonder, considering your parents. What genes you must have."

"Uh—"

"It really pays to give attention to genetics, if you are thinking of having children."

"Do you—?"

"Kids? No, not yet."

Now that I consider how things turned out, our genetic conversation was one hell of a forecast. Her compliments continued: "I have not met many American boys ready to question their fathers the way you did."

"Yeah, but I never know what counterargument to make when it all comes down to money. And I'm going to need it for college."

Liz shrugged. "I grew up in a time and place when money was scarce. Prospects were grim. I have never questioned the value of wealth ever since."

"Germany, right?"

"Yes, Munich. During and after the war."

"Did you ever see Hitler?" It was an infantile question, and I regretted it as soon as I asked. But I was fascinated. I didn't know if I'd ever spoken to anyone who'd actually been alive during the Nazi rule of Germany.

"Only on newsreels, and then only years after he was already dead. I was much too young to remember him, you know. I barely remember the Allied bombings."

She told me her young father had "...the profession of war artist, which allowed him to draw and paint battles instead of fight. Still, my father was shot right in the heart while the German army retreated through Belorussia."

I looked at the remains of my cake, its battleship-sized proportions outlined by ridges of frosting. The candles lay askew, smeared in cream cheese frosting. I asked Liz how she came to America.

"I always dreamed about the States. I felt nothing for Germany." She explained, squeezed in before the next commercial, that while still in school, she'd met an American soldier. "Whether I was really in love with him or with the idea of America, I'll probably never know. We married in secret, because I was only sixteen, and with papers falsifying my age, we crossed to America as soon as his overseas service terminated. When we arrived at our little room in his family's house in West Oakland, I didn't know whether to laugh or cry. They were so poor, for Americans, in a wrecked neighborhood. Just like the one I had left."

Liz patted me on the cheek before she joined my dad in the circle of guests who'd gathered to watch the same Foul Line commercial over again. Not wanting to miss any nuances of the art form, I stood beside them once again to witness my dad transform from twenty-three-year-old Olympic gold medalist to thirty-seven-year-old commercial pitchman.

Liz turned to me after the applause for the commercial's second screening. "Your father was practically designed for the public eye,

Guy," Liz said. "He projects masculinity and competence. Effortlessly. Imagine what he could accomplish with that charisma. For example, imagine if we could nudge him further into politics."

Imagine that mysterious "we." I didn't say anything. I figured, as a politician, my father made an excellent volleyball player. I just told Liz I'd like to hear more about her life in postwar Germany sometime.

"We will have many chances, Guy. Just be thankful you were born here, when you were, to such wonderful parents. You're a lucky boy."

I nodded, familiar with the conclusion.

Chapter 4

LESS THAN two months after that party, right after spring semester finals in early June, I followed Dad's orders from the night before and woke early to help with the packing.

The plush carpet on the steps still felt alien to my bare feet, but it helped mute Dad and Liz's bedroom banshee love cries. Even though I'd done most of the dismantling myself, the living room shocked my groggy eyes, bay windows stripped of curtains, bookshelves bare. Imprints in the carpet traced the ghosts of vanished lamps.

Before I could reach the kitchen for a caffeine fix, the phone rang atop a big packing box labeled "Books—Paul's study."

So the new place actually had a "study"? Holy Pete. After three rings, I decided to answer. So early, it had to be big, bad news. Someone had died in the night, or remarried. But it was just Adrian, trying to reach my dad.

"He's still, uh, sleeping."

"When he, uh, wakes up, tell him I decided to catch the early flight for LA after all. Some contract details for Finish Line I've got to review before our meeting. He'll know."

"Which is a lot more than I do. I thought Dad was gonna help me finish the packing."

"He will. He's got an afternoon flight."

"So he's still going?"

"Hell yes. Why do you say it like that?"

"Guess who I get to spend the weekend alone with."

"Dear old stepmommy, huh? Is she showing classic signs of wickedness yet?"

"She's not that bad, Adrian."

"So you're off to your brand-new house! You'll see a lot more of Liz when you're stranded in the suburbs. Lucky boy."

"Know what, Godfather? I'm already homesick. I've lived on Lola Montes Terrace my whole life."

"Like I don't know? I held Paul's trembling hand while he signed the mortgage. That crazy house. Hell, I practically grew up on Lola Montes myself."

"We don't see much of you these days, Adrian."

"Finish Line, the investment company, and now this damn political campaign, they're keeping me pretty hyper. To think I said capitalism would be a nice break from my law practice. Be glad you're still... seventeen."

"Why? What comes next?"

"LA. If you're a sinner like me. See you, Guy."

I concentrated on the dial tone, half hoping Dial-A-Prayer would break in, offering a platitude to survive by. Everything familiar seemed to have reversed or been sold out from under me.

SOON AFTER that Foul Line launch party, my high opinion of Liz had disappeared as fast as that well-timed birthday cake, though I wasn't as sour on her as Adrian seemed to be. I don't think it was just her novelty that wore off either, because I wanted to keep on adoring her. I just couldn't make my adoration last.

When she and Dad were heavy into their new alliance, Liz almost seemed to be courting me. Once, when Dad was in LA, she invited me to dinner and a German flick at the Surf. Running into an old acquaintance in the lobby, Liz locked her arm in mine and introduced me as her "date." With pride. And I was proud to be seen with her. Stylish, slender, flaxen blonde Liz was the type other women called "striking." Wherever we went, there were stricken men in her wake stealing a long second glance.

Liz flattered me with long talks, dredging up my opinions on books, politics, American culture in general. As Liz stayed more and more at Montes Terrace with us—even though she constantly criticized the small rooms, unfinished stairwell project, and our prehistoric kitchen—I was infatuated with her too. Enough to forget the wartime German blitzkrieg on us Slavic subhumans.

By the time Liz's wardrobe was crammed into Penni's old closet and her hardbacks squashed our paperbacks, Liz even looked different. Tight, cinched dresses were stashed away while Liz disguised her rounded edges in severe business jackets and long skirts—dark rust-colored outfits Adrian compared to "the hue of dried blood and wounded flesh." She had her free-flowing blonde hair chopped to a shorter length than mine or Dad's.

Now that she was part of the household, it was natural that I was demoted from off-night date to stepchild.

"Guy, are you certain you want to wear those worn-out jeans when you go out with us?"

Though I was pretty damn certain, to keep things mellow, I'd change into slacks or khakis. I figured things would get better as Liz enjoyed her success in managing Penni's modeling school. Liz's winning strategy at Aspirations Unlimited had been to ignore all of Penni's suggestions.

Meanwhile, Dad stayed queer on Liz. He bragged about her brains and deferred to her "European" outlook, though she'd been American far longer than I'd been alive.

Foul Line's success swept Dad off to LA for deeper involvement in the expanded cosmetics product line, including SpotChek, a male powder puff, CryFoul, a dye to cover gray hair, and AgeErase, a wrinkle cream. Now Dad posed as Foul Line's primary TV pitchman, with macho, dignified "personal endorsements" on commercials for goop he wouldn't touch in real life. The real promotional decisions were made by a creative team in LA. ("The artists," Adrian called them. "Con artists?" I asked politely.) They referred to Dad as an "executive consultant," but he mostly consulted by smiling in TV ads and over traffic jams from four-color billboards.

Though Paul Dimchek was now more well-known as a commercial pitchman than he ever was as a high-jumping Olympian or pro volleyball star, I knew the cheesy source of all this easy money and fame embarrassed my dad. As an original investor, he complained that everything seemed to be decided in advance. It struck me that after all Dad's efforts to strike out on his own, he'd ended up where Penni Wise had been, a good-looking face marketing useless products.

That's probably why, despite the crazy pace of his life, hopping jets to flex a dimple for the cameras in LA, he doubled up his efforts to scout properties in "emerging" East Bay real estate with Adrian. They were both still involved in West Oakland slums but expanding into trailer parks, ancient apartment houses, and dumpy rentals. For some tax advantage, Dad and Adrian actually marooned themselves in a Diablo Valley

Boulevard "home" office to establish their official residence. When Dad started to write his home address as "Walnut Creek," I should have seen our future in neon graffiti: THE END IS NEAR.

The suburban address meant he had to give up his prized role as Democratic captain for our San Francisco precinct. But Dad soon made new East Bay connections, which led to much bigger politics. Adrian's friend from law school, Bart Morgan, the golden boy of the Democratic Party out there, was running for the state assembly. Dad and Bart Morgan were old college friends, and by January, Bart asked Dad to be his campaign manager. Since Bart had great left-wing credentials, having been an antiwar activist and Save the Bay hero, Dad got jazzed. He would lead the fight for Bart Morgan to beat the current wacko-conservative assemblyman.

Between business deals, slumlording, sex, and politics, Dad and Liz were so preoccupied I could usually avoid them. As a homosexual-in-waiting, I had a whole 'nother set of obsessions.

For starters, I didn't see Randy Blanding much after my seventeenth birthday. Faithful to my promise to myself when I walked home from the DMV. I ditched the Saturday clinics. I spent the rest of tennis season ignoring Randy off the courts, just as Rob Pescatore kept avoiding me.

On an April weekend field trip in the Sierra foothills as part of my biology teacher's conservation group, studying water quality in streams around abandoned mines, we were so busy hiking around drainages and counting bugs that I managed to keep my feelings for Randy buried.

But the grave was shallow. When the group visited Sutter Creek on a supply run, I swore I saw Randy walking out of a hardware store and cried his name down the main drag. When the tall, broad-shouldered, small-waisted hunk turned around, he looked at me with distaste. "You must have the wrong guy, kid." When all the teenagers on the project circled the campfire to reminisce about their boyfriends and girlfriends or to make out under the stars, I found myself hustling down a jeep trail, ambushed by envy, to sulk alone.

But as tennis season wrapped up, Randy still wanted to pick up our friendship, as if nothing but an endless summer of making out in a VW Beetle waited for us. "Geez, Guy, don't stay so mad at me."

"But I'm still a *boy*," I sneered. "As long as I stay one, why the hell are you interested?"

"I know I shouldn't have said that, okay? But I'm stuck, Guy. I had to do the right thing by Janine, didn't I?"

I knew he did, just like I knew my freak-out and jealousy were infantile. His rejection still hurt, but there was a real infant on the way, and Randy and Janine were broke.

So after I cooled down, I invited Randy to join me making a few bucks in my weekend job with Dad and Adrian's investment company. We cleared poor people's discards out of vacated slums so units could be "renovated." That meant we sprayed cheap paint on the battered walls so that a new batch of poor people could move in. To each other's amazement, Randy and I worked well together and laughed about everything. We were usually so rank with sweat, so hungover from lacquer thinner highs and crusted in dried latex paint that our old attraction wasn't even stirred in the mix.

Besides my weekend job, I kept my connection with Janine. We'd study in the quiet of our biology lab. Sometimes I strolled side by side with her to an after-school, college-level extension microbiology class she was taking at State. In Janine's good company, I could indulge my secret life of fascination with tiny water-dwelling critters without feeling like a geek.

As far as my secret love life, well, what did I have to reveal? My fantasies about a cute classmate in front of me in Geography for a Threatened Planet, how I wanted to lick the nape of his neck? Or the sweet bulges in Levi's that cruised by as I transferred to the bus at Seventeenth and Castro? Still a virgin, I enjoyed telling Janine about my aborted love life when Randy happened to be joining us for an off-campus pizza. "But I haven't really had sex yet," I told her, eyeing Randy just to torment him. "Just messed around with this college guy on a dock. Once."

"He didn't have any right to take advantage of a high school kid," Janine said. "What a creep!"

Randy just leaned back, nodding, silent, chugging an illegal Bud.

The tabloid liberation papers I picked up on Castro Street all exhorted homos to come out to family and friends. They were like evangelicals for unlimited sex. With my own and the world's salvation at stake, I waited for the best opportunity to raise the Topic with Dad.

Not that many opportunities came my way. After those night classes with Janine, whenever I slipped upstairs, I followed a trail of discarded clothes, like poor ol' Hansel in an updated porno flick. Dad's boxers draped on the railing. Liz's bra caught under their bedroom door.

Meanwhile, Foul Line profits were exceeding all projections, while Dad's new celebrity was reaching that turning heads at the checkout line point. Once, during a kitchen-table business meeting between Dad and Adrian, Liz rattled off the investment company's income versus debts with drop-dead accuracy.

As horny as she was with Dad in my presence, soul kissing and butt squeezing him as if I were as mute and heedless as the family dog, they had acted decent in public. By May, though, Liz became clingy, scooting to his side in restaurant booths and locking his arm at parties. When some chick chatted with Liz, calling my dad "your husband," she didn't correct her.

So when they flew to Las Vegas in mid-May for a Foul Line promotion, I should have seen it coming. While neither the Church nor city hall were holy enough to bless their union, Vegas could provide sacred ground.

Man, that was fast. They'd barely known each other for six months. When I answered the doorbell, Dad presented Liz as a bundle in his arms, carrying her over the threshold for a formal introduction: "Guy, say hello to your stepmother."

No Hansel-chomping witch in a gingerbread house—I was sure—ever looked as gorgeous and happy as Liz, who leaned to kiss me on the cheek. Released from Dad's arms, she'd danced me around the foyer. But my toes, always clairvoyant, felt cramped by certain doom.

Their marriage wasn't the only big switch yanked behind my back. The way we "decided" to move to the far eastern suburban fringe in the Diablo Valley was about as democratic as a Bolivian coup d'état. Right after the newlyweds returned from Las Vegas, one of the investors threw a reception for Liz and Dad at his home near Mount Diablo. Liz was impressed by his manzanita hillside, sunny redwood deck, and country club membership and went into Bavarian rhapsodies over the "clean, modern, gleaning kitchen." Liz pointed out how few of the other couples they knew, even Dad's Claimjumper teammates, lived in the city anymore.

"We are completely marooned here, Paul!" Liz cried. "There is not even a liquor store in this neighborhood that does not require an armed escort to get us safely in and out." For Liz, the City had suddenly become too dirty, too crowded, too full of poor people. "Maybe I see the neighborhood's decline with sharper eyes," she'd argued. "When I came out of the wine shop yesterday, I almost tripped on a man. When I stooped to see what was wrong, the shopkeeper laughed at me. He told me he would call the cops, that I should leave the man be. And I did, Paul, I just walked away. It reminded me of Munich after the war. The nuts and drunks and refugees who wandered the streets day and night without a *pfennig* to their names. The adults became expert at ignoring the misery around them."

"Liz, there have been drunks and crazies and lost souls lying prone on Haight Street since 1849," Dad said. "It's San Francisco, for God's sake!"

"But you must admit it is getting worse. Prostitutes prowl closer and closer. High school kids exchange plastic bags full of white powder at bus stops. And I saw two young men kissing in broad daylight on the corner of Haight and Masonic. It is nothing new, I agree. But it is more intense and blatant." Exasperated with Dad's lack of alarm, she turned to me. "Guy, do you agree?"

Me? "Liz," I said, "wait. How do the kissing guys fit in the same sentence with hookers and drug dealers?"

"Guy, please. All I am trying to say is how this city is going straight to hell."

So Liz's casual homo bashing added a new twist to my self-strangled coming out to Dad. I called a truce within myself, deciding I'd wait until I had something worth enduring Liz's cool disapproval for. I'd tell them both when I finally had a real boyfriend.

As far as Liz's suburban siren song, Dad still sounded like he would resist. He'd convince Liz that none of those big empty boxes on slippery hillsides in the 'burbs were worth the blackmail prices. He'd remind her of the long commute to work. Most of all, I knew how much he loved our house, the Haight-Ashbury, and every other square inch of San Francisco.

Yeah, my toes might be clairvoyant, but my brain was delusional. Dad must have been humoring me, or he really was of two minds. And his other mind, mentored by Liz, plotted the phony Walnut Creek address for his political future. Naturally, his city loyalty was trumped by a cushy business deal. The kicker was when he signed on as a spokesman for a "new concept" hilltop subdivision, Mount Olympus.

With a massive discount on a split-level monstrosity, a promotional contract, and a god's ransom of upgrades and goodies, Dad signed on as Olympian-in-Residence on the ticky-tacky mountain.

He and Liz closed on the place by the end of May. For a mellow white liberal dude, Dad could sure be a shrewd operator. For quite a while, I treated him like an intimate traitor.

THAT MORNING of the big move, Dial-A-Prayer did not come through. When I set the phone where an old table used to stand, I nearly dropped it on the floor.

I moped around the kitchen, praying to the ghosts of Penni's kitchen gods. I wanted their help to compose the final Lola Montes Terrace breakfast from the last of our food—dill pickles, english muffins, and moldy yogurt. In those last hours before I began serving my East Bay exile, it began to dawn on me everything I took for granted as a city kid, especially a queer one. Not only was I losing my happy, microscopic social pond at Walt Whitman High, I was also being severed from those scenic daily transfers at Castro and Seventeenth. No matter how I'd dreaded the clones, now I was going to miss them, along with their crotches, their butts, and their leering smiles. Those wild packs of lewd guys might have been too much for a schoolboy, but I always thought of them as a kind of sexual bank account, safely stored and gathering interest while I grew older and braver.

Out of nowhere, Liz appeared in her robe, sleepily investigating the food supply. She ran her hand down my spine, wished me good morning, and wondered if the muffins were still edible.

"Yeah. But maybe we should donate the yogurt to science. It's flecked with hairy blue colonies."

"Appetizing." Liz scrunched her nose, then held up one of the two muffins and reached for a knife. "We could cut them into equal parts, of course."

"Nah. You and Dad can have 'em. I've already indulged," I lied. I wasn't being generous. For the first time in my life, I felt too freaked-out to eat. The stomach that had once triumphed over Penni's kelp and frog liver flambé was too jumpy for a muffin.

To steady myself, I started to carry small furnishings out to the foyer. When I returned to the living room, the phone rang. I stretched to the floor for the receiver and heard Penni wishing me good morning. "Wow," I told her. "We just witnessed the transformation of yogurt, so I'm open to miracles. You actually called your only child!"

"Guy, are they feeding you properly?" she asked, suddenly stern.

I loved Penni's eternal concern that "they" who ruled my custody were starving me or torturing me with weird food, like that was something new. "Naw, just the usual improper type," I said. "It's to keep me from missing you too much."

Penni laughed. I liked her for being a good sport but suspected she even cheered Dad and Liz on, since it took her off the hook for deserting me. Then Penni turned serious, saying, "I've been worried about you. I know leaving Montes Terrace isn't what you wanted. But I'm excited for the big changes lying ahead. I hope your senior year is as wonderful as mine was."

I groaned at the thought of starting over in a suburban school staffed by Stepford Wives. "I swear, Mom, I keep hearing from people your age about how great it is to be my age. Makes me wonder, what happens after this? Do we just shrivel up at thirty and suffer through the rest of our lives?"

"No, of course not. Things do get better, but they're not as unencumbered. Adults take on more responsibilities, families to raise—"

"Like you did."

"Exactly. And speaking of responsibilities, did I tell you? It's so exciting. I got hired yesterday to do illustrations for a big commercial project. My first commission, Guy! Aren't you proud?"

"Sure. What's the deal?"

"This land developer Lester knows saw some of my sketches and wants me to draw a series for his real estate ads. They'll be in the Sunday Homes section later this month."

"I got it. Mount Olympus, right?"

"Right! In fact, Lester's connection was what led Paul to get involved in the promotion. And look what it led to. A wonderful new home for you and Paul. And Liz."

I felt strung from a rope of adult conspiracy that seemed to noose the entire Bay. "I'm so thrilled I can't spit."

"Guy, aren't you being just a little stubborn? Paul told me you wouldn't even go look at the new house."

"Mom, come on. You know Montes Terrace is more than just a house to me. I never thought we'd leave for good. So I was hoping the new place didn't exist."

"You're going to be surprised, baby. It's a gorgeous development."

Just what I always wanted, to be banished to a "development," which sounded like scuzzy germs left too long in a petri dish. Or some Pentagon euphemism for losing another pointless war. "So," I said, just to change the subject, "you're switching from fine art to commercial art?"

"What's wrong with commercial art?"

"I was just ask—"

"You're embarrassed now? That your mother isn't going to be some great artist?"

"I never said—"

"Guy, let's get real, okay? You've seen most of my art projects." She sighed into a long pause. "I've given it a lot of thought. Listened to a thousand critiques in studio classes. Endured savage evaluations. Not to mention what's worse, faint praise, from most of my instructors." She took another long breath. This couldn't be easy, but at last she found the courage to say it. "I'm just not good enough to be an artist."

It knocked the breath out of me too. "You might get there, though, Mom. You've sure got the determination."

"But not the talent. So when this project fell in my lap, I thought maybe this was meant to be. And before you say anything cynical, Guy, just remember, it might be advertising, but at least it's creative."

Coming from the erstwhile girl who'd posed on the burro twenty years ago to pitch tortilla warmers, this might not be as pitiful as it sounded.

But I half listened, a little ticked off, as Penni launched into her reminder that if I really was going to be so unhappy on Mount Olympus, I could claim "my" room at her place. When I'd just visited for my birthday dinner (blackened snails on sea grass), the extra room was wall to wall with her and Lester's excess art supplies, sketch pads, and abandoned canvases. While she droned on about self-fulfillment, I felt cheated. Art had been her supposed reason for leaving Dad and me in the first place. Now Penni's career in Oakland suddenly sank to scribbles for the real estate pages?

As soon as we finished with our bright "Love ya's," the receiver's hollow thud surprised me in the emptied silence. Liz and Dad were scuffling upstairs, unmaking that overheated waterbed for the last time.

Dad appeared on the landing, wearing a business suit and bearing a small suitcase. "Hey, Guy, you off the phone?"

"Yep. That was Mom."

"Oh yeah." A pause, two thuds on the steps. "You ready to roll?"

I nodded, planning the most painless strategy for leaving the house. My stomach was ragged. I grabbed a box of Liz's clothes as I fumbled toward the front steps. Out of the corner of my eye, though, I spotted that damn red For Sale sign puncturing Penni's ice plant.

AFTER WE dropped Dad off at the airfield, it was just Liz and me and the big new Volvo station wagon. Oh yeah, they weren't doing any of their suburban image-making half-assed. I steered this clunky Swedish oaf onto a manicured cloverleaf south of Walnut Creek, sprinklers ch-chugging around a perfect garden for cars.

On a commercial strip I liked to call Burrito Boulevard, we lurched through heavy traffic with nothing to contemplate but TacoTimes, Burrito Grandes, and Tostada Expresses clustered between drive-up banks and drive-thru cleaners. At strip's end, a weedy drive-in movie's cracked marquee still announced its zombied, three-year run of *One Flew Over the Cuckoo's Nest*.

Gazing off in the direction of a concrete conduit called Arroyo Seco, Liz smiled. "It is so lovely out here."

I studied a trio of shirtless guys jogging a school track beside the captive creek bed. "Yeah," I answered, enjoying their taut, tanned stomachs, "lovely." Beyond the track, a high school sprawled helter-skelter along the dusty floodplain, where my own captivity would begin in a few short months. East of the school, the boulevard narrowed to two lanes. Cattle ranches still clung to stark, bleached hills skirting the base of Mount Diablo.

Rising into the oak-studded hilltops, we started up the mountain at a junction strung with banners:

RESIDENCES AT MOUNT OLYMPUS
LUXURY HOMES FOR THE NEW CALIFORNIA

An arrow directed us Straight Ahead, the first of Mount Olympus's fake-outs, since the rutted lane started to buck around severe switchbacks.

Ancient barns collapsed into hillsides. Nasturtium and poppies covered them like funeral flowers for the Old California.

Atop the ridge, a whitewashed walled city appeared on bulldozed terraces, square houses advertised "to evoke a Greek village." We climbed up a series of hairpin turns, the most treacherous so far. Liz clutched the door handle, her white-knuckled homage to my driving, and muttered, "Careful-careful-careful-now." Near the top, the riskiest curve of all edged a pioneer grave and a single live oak. A historical marker even proclaimed it Casket Curve.

Immediately, where the developer's land began, the road widened, smoothed, and leveled, like a concrete plank to the gates of Olympus. Stopping at a cross-arm barrier, I shied when an armed guard popped out of a glass booth.

"What do you want, son?" Before I could answer, he recognized Liz. "Oh, hello, Mrs. Dimchek. Movin' in today, aren't you? Welcome to Mount Olympus!"

I about freaked. I swore the check station was an exact replica of the one we'd crossed on a ninth grade field trip to San Quentin. Outside of prisons, the only "gated community" was a retirement subdivision over the hill in Moraga, a laughingstock for its full-time sentries, rifles poised to protect old folks from pesky field mice and butterflies.

Beyond the gates, I followed Liz's complex directions through winding streets without sidewalks or front yards, just a blinding white maze of walls, driveways, and garage doors. No trees. No green at all besides a few stubby junipers. Not a single mortal wandered this concrete paradise on foot.

At the dead end of Circe Circle, one of three garage doors opened, by a flick of Liz's remote, ready to swallow the Volvo. Liz's new Porsche gleamed in the middle slot, an overpowered reminder that she'd parked herself in our lives for good.

"Here we are, Guy, home at last." She sighed with satisfaction, then shot me a killer smile. "Everything so new and clean and safe."

I could taste how bad I wanted to shout the obvious, that we'd moved to the boonies only to be more confined than we'd been in her "dirty, dangerous" city. But something in Liz's smile warned me off—she hadn't been smiling that much lately—and I figured this high-tech dwelling was a pretty big deal for my ex-refugee stepmother.

After all, the good life was a fairly new concept for Liz. I knew when she was little she'd been hustled on a forced march across the Bavarian countryside when the Allies bombed her Munich neighborhood to smithereens. I knew food had been scarce, every moldy scrap shared with cousins who resented her as a fatherless interloper, an extra mouth. I knew she'd landed in West Oakland's slums as a teenaged bride, before she realized the American soldier she'd married was completely broke. While she studied to become an American citizen and improve her English, her husband, missing the Army's discipline, showed more and more of his true good-time Charlie colors, drifting in and out of two-bit jobs, just enough to support his booze habit. Meanwhile, West Oakland had traded its poor whites for poorer blacks, who, released from the military, sought shipyard paychecks. Liz only redoubled her determination, working days as a hotel chambermaid and taking night classes in accounting and management. More than once, she miscarried due to "stress." Not long after that, she left Good-Time Charlie to his pink elephants and the streets. Out of this scramble, Liz had arrived, ridiculously attractive and perfected in American business manners, to rescue Aspirations Limited and claim Penni's ex-husband.

Now, with another click, the garage door sealed us from the sunlight. Getting out, she inhaled the garage air.

"Ah! Nothing so bracing as fresh paint." Liz unlocked the thick, iron-banded plank door and ushered me into my new life.

My first impression was White Plaster Everywhere. Plush beige carpet smooshed all footfalls in the shivering silence. The main room was a vast open space ("Perfect for big public receptions") where all the other rooms seemed to converge. In the kitchen, Liz urged me to run my hand over the tiles, random pieces meant to suggest fragments from a Grecian urn. "So tasteful," Liz proclaimed. "Perfect for catered events."

She saved me from more tile fingering by leading me upstairs to the tour's end. She and Dad would occupy the Grand Master Temple. Just its dressing-room-closet-combo deal could swallow Dad's entire bedroom at Montes Terrace. The bedroom itself, complete with "ruined" Doric columns, was as snug as an amphitheater. The entire *Oedipus Cycle* could be performed there, all at once, with the chorus chanting from a balcony over the swimming pool.

The bedroom Liz offered me also overlooked the still-empty pool, as far away from her and Dad's room as possible. For the first time all day, I felt… not happy, but aware that happiness still existed, hoping I could finally dream without their fornicating howlings intruding on my sound track.

"I wanted this to be a fresh start for you, as well as for us, Guy," Liz announced. "I've picked out a new bedspread for you, with matching curtains."

"Thanks a lot. But I'll just use my old stuff."

"Really?" She shoved off from the wall and backed to the doorway as if cooties from my old room might crawl from the boxes. "I am just surprised, sometimes, that a boy of your class is so content to be… what do you say, *scruffy*?"

"Yeah, that's right…."

"You must start thinking of projecting a certain image. Especially if Paul is going to be more and more in the public eye as Bart Morgan's campaign manager. It may not be fair, Guy, but they will judge Paul by your deportment."

Deportment? It had to be a fugitive word from an Aspirations Unlimited brochure. I didn't really understand yet why Liz gave a rip about the "public eye," receptions, and catered events, much less how state assembly politics could possibly involve me.

But I was clear that we didn't have to continue this stern-stepmother, doltish-stepson routine, not when we'd started out so well. "Liz," I called as she turned to leave, "do you remember the first morning I made you coffee? And the night we talked at Dad's Finish Line party? The night Dad introduced us? Remember how you took my side?"

"Guy, our relationship had to change when I married Paul. You are a responsibility of mine now, not a boy I met at a party." Her big blue eyes crinkled with mutual understanding; then she was off to the Master Temple.

Unpacking my scruffy crap, I realized it was already getting dark. When I stepped out the sliding door to shake the cooties out of my bedspread, Liz appeared in the bright frame of the Grand Temple's upper window, across the dry pool. She'd changed to work clothes and tied her hair in a plain scarf. Making up the enormous new bed, she might've been the Lisabeth of West Oakland, the chambermaid who'd finally gained admission to the palace.

Chapter 5

"WHAT YOU doin', Guy?" a deep voice called, the next weekend. "What the hell you reading the paper for on a day like this, man? There's major bikini action out here!"

No, the major bikini action was bounding up the brick steps and into my room. It was Leon, my favorite handsome ex-Claimjumper, now manager for the investment company's new offices. His trim Afro haloed by the sunlight bouncing in from the just-filled pool, he toweled off, towering over me. I tried to avoid staring at the interesting bulges squeezed fore and aft into his red racing suit. This was perverted—I'd known Leon since I was ten—lusting over a straight man who was practically my uncle.

"I've gotta find a job, Leon." While Dad's friends splashed, squealed, and belly-flopped ten feet from my sliding bedroom door, I buried myself under classified ads. I read the most hopeful one out loud to Leon: "Need window clerk at Don't Wok Drive-Thru Noodles. Will train."

He snapped my ankle with the towel and slid next to me. "Man, you don't want to work there," Leon said, spying the ad I'd circled. He leaned so close, smoothing out the paper to peer at the ad, that I could feel his breath on my neck. "I don't mean to sound racist, but I heard they serve puppy dogs in the sweet-and-sour so-called pork."

"It does sound racist," Adrian said, leaning in the doorway, dripping wet in his baggy surfriders. "And you've got the story all twisted, Leon. It was a drive-through kennel before a white guy opened it as Don't Wok."

Leon laughed, then skimmed through everything I'd crossed out, drumming his long fingers on my head. As my entire nervous system congregated under his touch, he swatted the back of my skull and hopped off the bed. "We've gotta get this boy a job."

I tried to imagine wasting the entire summer handing out greasy noodles to people who'd retrieved their poodles from the same window. Leon disappeared as quickly as he'd come, slipping by Adrian, who folded his skinny arms. "So you don't feel like playing with the grown-ups?"

Though the grown-ups howled every time some hunk tossed Adrian's latest squeeze, a shapely brunette, into the deep end, I knew it wasn't really all play. Most of the guests were Democratic insiders working for Bart Morgan's campaign. The June primary was only weeks away, and this pool party celebrated the latest polls giving Bart a huge lead over his closest Democratic rival.

As campaign manager, Dad basked in his success. Bart Morgan was spending the final weekend hiking at Point Reyes for a photo op in the coastal wilderness. Dad expected Bart to swing by the party late. So except for the chance to steal more glances at Leon, I wasn't thrilled about getting wet with a bunch of middle-aged politicos.

"I need to get a job before I can play," I told Adrian. "I've got to save enough for a car."

"Right. So who's the girl you've been spending all your slum-painting money on?"

"Adrian, believe me, there is no girl."

"Lonely up here, huh?" He leaned in farther. "You're just pent up. Your hormones are raging, and you're trapped on this mountaintop." Adrian smiled, wicked. "Find yourself some pretty *chiquita* at the local malt shop, then share a straw."

I was ready to tell Adrian why I wouldn't be sharing straws with any *chiquitas*, even if I could find a malt shop. Building up my nerve, I stared at him. "Adrian, I've been meaning to tell you…," I began, when Dad appeared beside him, shaking the water dog-style from his long blond hair.

"Yeah, I know. Spoiled suburban kid needs his own car," Adrian said to Dad. "Apparently his father is kinda tight with his millions."

Dad tried not to laugh, still shaking out his mane on the steps before coming in. "Sounds like a damn good father. Maybe he'll teach the spoiled boy that a man has to earn what he gets." Dad tossed his towel on my bed and hovered over me. "Guy, you've been doing great work for us on Saturdays." He patted my shoulder and rose to stand side by side with Adrian, two bare-chested businessmen now proposing the deal. "So, weekdays, we'd like for you to work with us at our new office. It's official now," Dad said, like he was splaying the words across an imaginary sign, CJ Properties. "There's new equipment to be hauled and installed. And when you're done with that, we'll always need your grunt work moving furniture and painting the, uh, residential units."

"But not just grunt work," Adrian said, still locked shoulder to shoulder with Dad. "Leon's going to need help with clerical stuff. And God knows we've got errands to run all over the East Bay."

"Yep, you'll have enough for a car in no time," Dad said. "You'll see how CJ Properties pampers its employees."

I tried to hide the idiot smile I felt forming, especially at the prospect of being their "employee." It sounded better than "spoiled boy" and had the ring of car ownership.

Adrian winked at me when the brunette squealed again, this time a bloody gasp that had no fun in it. And no splash.

We hurried out to the poolside to find everyone gathered around a late arrival who'd just heard the news on her car radio. During that photo opportunity on the steep headlands of Point Reyes, Bart Morgan had misheard the photographer's directions in the slapping wind. He took one backward step too many. In seconds, three hundred feet below the wild bluff, Bart's body surged against sea rocks.

"THIS IS it, Guy," Adrian told me. From across Madrone Street, we peered at a corner apartment house in West Oakland. It stood lonesome in the rubble of its demolished neighbors. "Our fresh investment prospect. The next site of the Oakland Miracle."

"This neighborhood's gonna need divine intervention." Leaning against Adrian's new black Jaguar sedan, I felt ridiculous in the scratchy suit Dad loaned me for the day, dark and somber for Bart Morgan's funeral. It was only my third day on the job for CJ Properties. I'd spent half my time making calls to rearrange Dad's and Adrian's appointments so we could all attend the service that morning.

But Adrian wanted to keep this noon appointment with the property's agent. While we waited for Dad and Liz to rendezvous with us here for a late lunch following the funeral, Adrian planned to tour the property for himself.

I wondered if Adrian was red-eyed behind his silver, reflective sunglasses. Choked up during the memorial service, Adrian fought to finish his tribute to Bart. "...one college buddy who never lost an ounce of his idealism or humanity." Several women, overcome, were ushered from the stuffy chapel by men who couldn't quite control their own sobbing. I barely knew Bart Morgan, but the grief of the overflowing crowd swept me away.

"We're moral pygmies," Adrian had blurted in the Jag, after we'd eluded the small clutch of reporters in the chapel parking lot. "Grubbing for lead nickels. You know, Bart really lived to make California golden again."

Now I stared at a patch of California that had sunk to baser metal. Old bricks heaped in a side lot surrounded by jagged debris and broken glass. A yellow rubber glove seemed to thumb the nose of a twisted vent. Stuck in the pile, signs promised Affordable Housing for a New Generation in chipped, fading paint.

Adrian pushed himself from the car. He wrestled out of his suit jacket and threw it onto the Jag's leather seat. I did the same. At least in shirtsleeves, we wouldn't look so much like mafiosi come to collect our protection money.

Before crossing the street, Adrian paused to point out features on the apartment house's facade. "Notice the stonework along the cornice," he said, raising his arms. "See how the pattern's echoed in the design of the frieze just underneath?"

"Notice the cardboard in the window just under the frieze."

Adrian ignored my sarcasm completely. "The skilled hands that could shape those brackets don't even exist today, Guy. It's up to us to restore a treasure like this."

The agent pulled up in front of the treasure in a big silver Mercedes. Smoothing his tie, he hailed us, shook our hands, and directed us inside the foyer with a denture-clicking smile. The agent led us into a piss-smelling hallway. "All these units bring in steady income right now, and you could raise rents any time without a complaint."

While Adrian took notes, I walked ahead, up the groaning steps, then into a dim hall splashed with crayon obscenities. A black girl my age in a white blouse, plaid jumper, and patent leather loafers passed me, smiling. Her beatific face and Catholic schoolgirl presence were so startling in this dump that I hardly noticed the shorter girl she led by the hand, as if reluctant, toward the stairs. The short girl peered around the immaculate schoolgirl, snarling at me, her mouth drawn in a cartoonish grimace, her walk listing sideways. When Adrian and the agent tried to sidle by in the narrow hall, the shorter girl hissed, "Yeah, you both buy it on the street! Don't fool me, no sir! I seen both of you before!"

Adrian looked sheepish in the wake of the disabled girl's reprimand. The agent tried to smooth it over. "Yes, it can be rough around here, no doubt. But the beauty is, this property is always at full occupancy." He fumbled with the key at the hallway's final, puke yellow door.

Inside, I inhaled an inviting scent of rancid tuna fish and broken sewer lines. I released a crooked shade to find a view of loose telephone wires and a lone chimney rising from a demolished ruin. The agent was telling Adrian, "The last tenant used that big pantry off the kitchen as sleeping quarters for his baby daughters."

The "big" pantry had rotten planks and a burn hole in the ceiling. Just perfect. After all the dumps I'd seen slaving for Adrian and Dad on weekends, all the stinking, worthless furniture I'd carted to the dump, all the cheap paint I'd applied to sloping walls, this was the lowest of the low. Fighting off an impulse to puke, I told Adrian I'd meet him outside and bolted to the street for some oxygen.

I sat on the front stoop. Two guys in their twenties strolled by in leather jackets and black berets, their slacks' hems stuffed into black jackboots. The nearest glared at me, brazen and tight-lipped, his handsome blue-black face screwed into contempt. Okay, so I was a squirrelly white boy in shirt and tie on the front step of a ghetto slum. So shoot me.

Adrian appeared in the foyer, taking notes on a clipboard as he quizzed the agent trailing at his side. Soon they shook hands, and I rose to wave off the agent, who smiled and gestured at the apartment house.

"You can't go wrong, Mr. Myers. The history's in the craftsmanship. The future's in these wide-open lots." The agent smiled at me, calling as he cruised away in the Mercedes, "Tell your dad, son, he just can't go wrong."

"You can't go wrong," I told Adrian. "Father Myers."

"If you really were my son, Guy," he said, still scribbling numbers onto a legal pad, "you'd be a nice, quiet, sincere lad. Not an ever-erupting Vesuvius of sarcasm."

I gestured toward the ruins. "For this," I said, leading the way past an ancient wringer washer stuffed with exploded foam pillows, "you gave up lawyering?"

"'Law' is the term," Adrian said, quickening his pace down the block. "Which I still practice, on behalf of Finish Line and CJ. Both of which keep you in candy and toys."

"Are you guys really serious about buying that slum, Adrian?"

"I wouldn't mind having a hand in restoring that place." We crossed a busy four-lane, DuBois Avenue. "See? Once you get one block north, it's a different story."

It was. Across DuBois, Madrone Street wandered among small, neat stucco houses shaded by palms and sycamores in tidy front yards. "Imagine how that building will stand out if we restore it," Adrian said. "Connect that bombed-out block with this nice one."

"Wow, Adrian. You really do give a damn about this place, don't you? Your commie-pinko student past isn't as dead as I thought."

We rounded the corner. An old supermarket with painted-over plate glass windows and double glass doors had been converted to The Brethren Community Church, announced by a small, neat eye-level sign. At a side door, the pretty girl in the plaid jumper knocked, then waited with her scowling, half-paralyzed companion. A nunlike woman in a gray dress and black scarf embraced the disabled girl, then led her indoors. The Catholic girl waved, then bounded across the street to catch an idling bus.

When the bus pulled away with a whoosh of diesel, it revealed two small houses directly across the street linked by a single sign over their porches:

OPEN TO THE PEOPLE! THE MARXIST MATRIX.

"And speaking of commies...." I told Adrian. Just as I said it, one of the young Panthers I'd seen emerged on the porch under the sign, shaking hands with an older black man who also wore a black beret.

"Isn't that kind of passé?" Adrian said, leading us back the way we'd come. "Black Panthers and Marxist community centers? It's all so 1972."

"While here in 1978, we have CJ Properties." I used my hand to splay my own imaginary sign across the sky: "Adrian Myers Resurrects West Oakland."

"Now you're talking, Guy." Adrian headed back down Madrone Street, swatting his hip with his clipboard as if he caught some backbeat in the keening sirens only he could hear.

Across from the apartment house, Dad was leaning against the Volvo wagon, arms folded. Looking shell-shocked, he nodded at our approach, as impassive as he'd been during Bart's funeral. "Where you guys been?"

"Assessing the environs," Adrian said, joining him, side by side, against the Volvo. They stared at the apartment house. "Nothing but potential, hey, Paul?"

"That's one way of putting it," Dad said, grim. "Where do you suppose Liz is wandering off to now?"

"Like I know?" Adrian said, glancing around.

Liz took determined steps farther down the narrow street that skirted the apartment house. As Dad and Adrian discussed the numbers on Adrian's clipboard, I decided to trail Liz from a distance. I was kind of worried about her as she marched toward the next corner, clutching her purse, alone in her navy blue funeral suit.

When I caught up with her, Liz was staring at a sign over a closed-down business, Golden Palm Lounge. Glass bricks curved toward a black door, locked behind a steel grate: Keep Out. As if she expected me, she turned to ask, "Did you notice the name of this street, Guy? Was it Manzanita?"

"I don't know. The street sign's missing. Is this close to where you used to live?"

"It has changed so much. I was surprised to find this bar here. It used to be across the street from a busy little shopping area. Look at it now."

A low-slung storefront ran from the Golden Palm to the corner, nothing but a plyboard expanse scrawled with spray-painted advisories: Jesus Gives Everlasting Life. Bernita Gives Head. Across the street two little boys chased a tabby cat over pulverized plaster. I crossed the narrow street to inspect the ghostly stoop that linked the sidewalk to the foundation. Steps to nowhere.

"The address is inscribed in the concrete," I called to Liz, who turned toward me.

"I see." But she didn't cross the street. Adjusting her purse strap, she nodded toward the direction we'd come. "Enough of memory avenue. Guy, what's that on your trousers?"

"Oh." I glanced at my back creases. "Must be from sitting on the stoop."

"Show some respect for fine fabric, would you? Now come over here." She actually produced a tiny brush from her purse. When I sidled beside her, she leaned to swat the powdery dust off my slacks. "I'd like you to look somewhat presentable if you're joining us for a business luncheon."

I pointed toward the apartment house on Madrone. "I'm lucky I didn't pick up anything more deadly from that dump. Like cholera."

Stepmotherly, she batted stray cobwebs off my forelocks with her fingers. "There. Good. Now, we will get out of here before you pick up any more of Oakland's filth."

AT THE business luncheon, Liz peppered Adrian with hard questions about the apartment house's cash flow. Armed with a stiff scotch, Dad just glanced from face to face as if it were a slo-mo tennis match. I tried to ignore all three of them, glancing around my upraised menu to the sun-drenched view of Oakland's waterways and docks. Then the waiter took my order and the menu, so I had nowhere to hide.

Liz was saying, "I don't see why we should hesitate to raise the rents."

Adrian sighed, stirring his cocktail with a tiny straw. "It's all pretty substandard. Let's fix 'em up before we play Snidely Whiplash."

"Please, Adrian! Those tenants have housing subsidies. I lived in that neighborhood for five years, after all. I know how the system works."

"It's not the same system it was then. You saw that war zone."

"Adrian, I lived in a war zone too. A real one, not one caused by too many drunks loafing around."

Adrian coughed, the shrimp appetizer caught in his craw. He washed it down with a big gulp of whiskey, staring at me over his glass.

What did he expect me to do? Raise my fist and shout Power to the People? I did feel for Adrian, though. In less than an hour, his Oakland Dreaming woke up to Liz's Loafing Drunks.

"Know what I think?" I finally addressed the endless stalemate. "That place is a godforsaken pit. You guys should think about *lowering* the rents."

"Please be serious, Guy." Liz lowered her voice. "Adrian, you are an intelligent man, and you know how much we trust your judgment. But we would be fools not to take advantage of this market."

"Not fools. No," Adrian said. He turned to Dad. "If you plan to raise the rents, Paul, you'll have to count me out. But I do intend to discuss this. With you, Paul, this afternoon, at the office." He dropped several bills on the table, rose, and hurried out.

Liz stood, calling after him, "Please, Adrian...." A few heads turned at other tables, and for the first time Liz actually seemed embarrassed. She sank to her seat, pretending to be absorbed by her crumpled napkin. When the waiter brought her order, she stared at the salad as if it were crawling with maggots.

Dad fumbled with his silverware, dropping a knife he didn't bother to retrieve. Finally he said, "I guess Adrian's been working too hard on this deal."

"I am beginning to wonder if Adrian is unstable, Paul."

"But Adrian's pretty steady," I said. "He just really cares about improving that place." I wondered why I bothered.

Liz gave me a patient look. She sighed, pushing her salad away. "We all do, Guy. But we have to be realistic about our finances."

Realistic, I thought. With all of the investors driving their sleek European power horses, erecting castles high into the hills with pools the size of Botswana, it wasn't hard to understand Adrian's frustration.

"We may also need deeper pockets," Liz went on, her voice lowered, less assured, "if we are ever going to get serious about the political... situation."

"What political situation?" I asked, but Liz was already standing, strapping purse over shoulder, and shoving in her chair.

"Your father will bring you up to date. Will you, Paul? Excuse me, gentlemen. I have a meeting in the city." She kissed Dad, pecked my cheek, and vanished, leaving a pristine pile of greens and shellfish beside the cooling prawns the waiter had left at Adrian's empty place.

"Help yourself," Dad said, following my stare to their full plates. "God knows I'm paying for it all."

"So what was Liz talking about?"

"It's nothing definite. After the funeral, the campaign folks approached me about some details. That's why we were late."

"What's going to happen to Bart Morgan's candidacy?"

"Party lawyers have to look at election law. It's not every day a thirty-seven-year-old candidate dies a week before the primary." He pushed his salmon aside, leaned back, and folded his arms. "Jesus, I've never been to a funeral for someone my age. Bart took one lousy step in the wrong direction. It's like everything good in politics fell to its death with Bart. Against those damn rocks."

It was enough to make me stop picking at the crab. "You okay, Dad?"

"Just kind of thirsty." Dad reached for his scotch. "Imagine what I was thinking, Guy, staring at that friggin' apartment house. When the hell did I turn in the wrong direction myself? When did the high jumper turn into a slumlord?"

Dad asked the waiter to box up our neglected feast and told me we had an errand to run for Foul Line. It involved a struggling commercial artist here in Oakland, he said, "Who could use three or four square meals."

WHEN WE ended up tracing a familiar route to the winding, sunny streets of Rockridge, I figured out the "artist" was Penni. "It's nice of you to spread the work around," I told Dad on her front steps, "but do you really think she's up to it?"

"Hey, her work for Mount Olympus wasn't so bad. Besides, if I didn't keep work in the family, you'd be boxing noodles, bud."

He snickered, going up the exterior stairway, proud of his logic. I smiled just because nobody had mentioned Penni as a member of the family in quite a while.

Her rented apartment perched atop her landlord's flat-roofed house, a Spanish-style rambling along a hillside. Penni's perch was a newer wooden addition with big sliding doors opening onto a wraparound deck. The long staircase to her front door had become an obstacle course of potted flowers, a jumbled, color-crazed hanging garden. In a paint-splattered denim shirt and cutoffs, Penni waited for us on the top step, deadheading geraniums.

She effused over my ever-startling stratospheric gains in height—"Guy's about to top you, any day now, old man"—effused over our fancy duds until she remembered—"I'm so sorry for your loss, Paul"—then effused over the offered Styrofoam boxes of seafood.

While she and Dad discussed Bart Morgan's demise, I was instructed to find room in the fridge for the grub. Lester's no-meat, nondairy, nonwheat, abiotic "food" jostled with Penni's usual array of amphibian slugs in lite formaldehyde. What would these two want with plain old salmon or prawns?

Out on the deck, Dad and Penni leaned toward each other, Penni patting Dad's arm, shaking her head in sympathy. In the living room, I found a new collection mounted, all the original sketches she'd done for Mount Olympus ads. No worse than the other stuff in the Saturday real estate supplement, they took all the usual liberties with reality. Giant oaks shaded streets full of chatting neighbors. Children scampered, jump roping and skating as a portly postman smiled. More action in a single drawing than the sterile streets of our subdivision would see in a year. It hit me all of a sudden that Penni's drawings actually rendered our old block in the city, which wasn't as cutesy and clean but just as juiced with life. In pencil and pastels, she'd relocated Montes Terrace to humanize Mount Olympus Custom Show Homes.

When Penni took a phone call inside, I sidled up beside Dad at the railing. Penni had a choice view of the smoggy flatlands of West Oakland and the Bay Bridge disappearing into Yerba Buena Island. "So what's up, Dad? Were you and Mom discussing Bart Morgan all that time?"

"Well...." He stared off west. "I was also telling Penni about the role I'm likely to play in the new campaign."

"Wow! Couldn't the campaign wait for the poor guy's corpse to get cold?"

"One week, Guy. Without Bart, we'll run a weak candidate against Will Peters. We might as well send the devil himself back to Sacramento."

Penni reappeared in the open doorway. "Paul, don't we have some sketches to get done?"

Penni led Dad inside. I stayed where I was, leaning on the rail, but could hear the clatter of sketchbook and easel, then Penni's voice as she posed Dad.

"That scowl's making wrinkles. I'm afraid you're not going to sell much AgeErase looking that way."

"Penni, you can take ten years off with your eraser."

"Hell, if you want Paul Dimchek at twenty-seven, I could draw you from memory."

I didn't really want to hear any more of their hostile-affectionate banter. It reminded me too much of the good old days, so I decided to take the garden tour. Stairs led from the rear of the deck to the land behind the landlord's house.

Last fall, when Penni moved here, this had been an ugly scab of stickers, weeds, and bare earth. Her landlord had granted her free rein of the weed patch, and she'd rewarded him by recreating the best of our little garden from Montes Terrace here. The scale of her success shocked me. All of her favorites clustered in alternating shade and sunlight along mossy flagstone paths. I've got to admit it kind of killed me to think it had been so long—three seasons, enough to alter a whole landscape—since Penni had split for her new life.

A few weeks back, when I'd asked Lester for the truth about his former student's talent, he'd led me to the rear deck overlooking Penni's garden.

"See how she's arranged every clump of color to heighten and harmonize each effect?" He pointed out the patterns below. "And what you can't see is how she's plotted the whole palette with a sense for the play of light and shadow throughout the spring, summer, and fall. It changes hour to hour, Guy, season to season. Her sense of color is unfailing. What would you call this but the work of an artist?"

When I went back up to Penni's perch, the artist and her subject were still teasing each other. At the easel, she asked Dad whether, "...this AgeErase stuff really does one bit of good."

"About like Mount Olympus really looks like your sketches up there, Penni."

"I'm glad to know men's wrinkle cream is just as phony as women's."

"Sometimes I think all this investing is putting more wrinkles on."

Penni smiled ruefully. "Remember how high finance was all you'd ever need to make you happy?"

"Oh, are we gonna start on that? How about if I remind you how you were going to be the next Georgia O'Keeffe? You think Georgia is busy now, recreating her ex-husband's image so he'll sell more worthless garbage?"

Penni turned to me, working her pastels madly. "I'd love to sketch you sometime, Guy, if you'd ever sit still long enough."

"Yeah, Guy." Dad jumped in. "You ought to do it now, while you're still young and good-lookin'."

"You are a handsome devil," Penni said, "if I do say so myself."

"And you have lots of credibility, Mom. I can't wait to tell all my little friends that my mother thinks I look okay."

"Speaking of your little friends…," Penni began.

"Yeah. We were talking about that earlier, Guy," Dad said. "Anything up with the girlfriend situation?"

"What girlfriend situation?"

"Paul says you're going over to the city occasionally."

"That's just to see Randy and Janine and other friends from Walt Whitman. I don't have a girlfriend."

"It's only a matter of time," Penni said. "Believe me, when you start back to school as a senior, those suburban girls are going to be in raptures."

"No, Mom. Please."

"I don't mean to embarrass you, baby. It's just—"

"It's just…," I mocked. Then, superannoyed, it just came out. "I'm gay, for God's sake! Don't you get it? Isn't gonna be any girlfriend. Ever, okay?"

Penni stopped sketching. Dad dropped his pose. They stared at me, then averted their eyes as if I were naked. Always so relentlessly talkative, for once they were as exposed and vulnerable as I felt. Silenced. Flabbergasted. They stared at each other, then back to me.

I dumped it in their paths, so I guessed I had to help clear away the debris. "It's okay, you guys. It's cool. I'm happy. Don't freak out on me, okay?"

"Okay," Dad said.

"Okay," Penni said. "But how can you be so sure, baby? You're only seventeen."

"But I figured it out when I was fourteen. Around my Confirmation Day. When you were a teenager, Mom, were you *sure* you were straight?"

"Well, that was natural."

"Don't say that, Penni!" Dad cried.

"I'm sorry, Guy! I mean, I just knew. I dreamed about boys. Like every girl."

"Like *most* girls, Mom. And guess what? I dream about boys."

"Okay," Penni said.

"Okay, then," Dad said. He took a breath. I knew he was longing for a nice, fat scotch on the rocks. "Do you have a… boyfriend?"

"No. I'm kind of a virgin, okay?"

"Good," Penni said, exhaling. "Good."

"Why? Why 'good'? I don't want be some sexless monk the rest of my life, Mom!"

"I didn't mean it that way, baby. You know I didn't." She knocked over half of her art supplies when she crossed the room to force me into an embrace. "I feel stupid. I know I'm saying stupid things."

My dad stood up too, and it became one of those damn three-way hugs.

"I am too. This is a shock, okay? We know we sound asinine, Guy. Bear with us. We could never figure out where you got your brains."

"If I had any brains," I said, "I'd have something intelligent to say right now."

"I just thought of something," Penni said, her head resting on my shoulder. "Amazingly intelligent. How about, 'I love you'?"

The phone, still on the floor by the door, rang mercifully. It was Liz, who told Dad that the state Democrats, unable to reach him, had called her with their decision. Just as they expected, the party decided to endorse one candidate to run in Bart Morgan's place in the California primary next week. His name was Paul Dimchek.

THE FIFTEEN-MINUTE drive from Penni's to Walnut Creek that afternoon, alone in the Volvo with Dad, threatened to stretch into the longest silence we'd shared since I learned to talk. All the weight of unspoken topics massed, as dense as the Caldecott Tunnel's blasted walls. When we came out of it into Orinda's overheated sunshine, Dad finally spoke. "Feels weird to be the lead Democratic candidate. I don't even have a campaign."

"Haven't you been running that campaign since January?"

"I guess. But I was behind the scenes. I just feel exposed, you know. What the hell am I doing?"

I laughed, pointing at a Foul Line ad billboard. A decidedly female hand reached to caress Paul Dimchek's jutting chin. SpotChek—JUST THE TRICK FOR SMOOTHER SKIN! "I think you're already exposed, Dad."

"Yep, as a mute face on a signboard. For a powder puff! Now I've got to prove my real self. My better self, I hope, has just been in the closet all this time. Waiting for this chance."

"I know exactly what you mean."

"I'll bet you do."

"Talk about feeling exposed," I said. "But I'm glad I told you. I'm glad it's over."

"I'm glad you told me too. To tell you the truth, I was a little concerned about the girlfriend deficit."

"Then why didn't you ask me?"

"Maybe I was afraid to hear your answer."

"Yikes." I took a breath. "I guess it's no big thrill, having your only son turn out to be a homo."

"I didn't bring you into this world to thrill me, buddy. I wanted you to be your own man. Okay?"

"Okay."

"I'm just scanning my brain for any asinine remarks I've made over the years."

"About gays? I can't remember any. I do remember times when some clown hanging out with the Claimjumpers told a fag joke, but you never joined in the fun."

"Good. Good. 'Cause to tell you the truth, there are things I said, when I was just another clown in the locker room, that I'm glad you never heard."

I thought about that as the yellow hills of Lafayette went humping by. "But I've done that too, Dad. Remember Darren Kennedy, from my class at Most Precious Suffering? How everyone teased the hell out of him because he was such a little sissy?"

"Wasn't he on your tennis team last spring?"

"Yeah. We're fine now, but I remember taunting him, too, as part of this big fascist mass of Catholic boys, until the poor kid went crying to Sister Fred." Flushed, I turned the AC to maximum. "Remember how you and Mom laid into me about that? I was all ears, you know, all that time you and Mom preached about being respectful of everyone. That made it easier for me to come out. To myself, years ago, when I barely understood sex. Let alone gay sex."

Dad nodded, pushing his Ray-Bans farther up his nose. "I'll tell you the truth, though. What worries me is that if you're too open about it, you're going to expose yourself to worse than taunting. There are thugs out there, Guy."

"I'm not going to wear this on my sleeve, Dad." I steered the Volvo toward the little converted house that served as world headquarters for CJ

Properties. "Anyway, I'm sorry about Bart Morgan, but it's total bullshit that he's the last humanist who'll ever walk the Earth. They just don't know you as well as I do."

Dad didn't say anything, nor did he hurry out of the car. He fingered the back of my head, like he used to when I was a little guy, smoothing down my curls and caressing the nape of my neck with his fingers.

From the curb, a burly guy in short sleeves, a broad tie, and black-rimmed glasses leaned toward the passenger window. I recalled him as one of the reporters who'd lain in ambush for Adrian after the funeral. Now he flashed his press card at Dad. Then he gazed with a smirk as Dad kept his hand on my neck.

"I hope I'm not interrupting anything, Mr. Dimchek."

"To be honest, yes." Dad eyed the guy, then settled back against his headrest. "Private conversation, you know."

"I do know. It looks *very* private." The burly reporter kept smirking, half wolf, half prick. "Even intimate, you might say."

"No moment could be more intimate."

The reporter turned his attention on me. "You're under eighteen, right? Are you feeling forced into this, young man?"

Dad sighed. He squeezed my neck harder. "This is my son."

I extended my hand through the window. The guy was built like a linebacker and acted too macho, somehow, for a journalist type. He looked at my hand like it was scabrous, then clasped it for the shortest possible second, as if touching lepers like me were another hazard of journalism.

Dad asked him, "What can I do for you, Mr. *Oakland Tribune* Political Reporter?" Despite his outward cool, Dad's neck squeeze turned to a clamp, as if clinging to my neck could halt some deadly plunge.

Chapter 6

BY THE end of summer vacation, I'd saved enough to buy a car. Of all possible beat-up rust buckets on the planet, I ended up buying the Beast from Rob Pescatore's family.

My savings could only buy something from the undead corner of the used car market, oil-burning junkers available for just the price of fifteen record albums or twenty movies or thirty Big Burritos. I checked out bald-tire station wagons from the late fifties with dented fins and push-button transmissions that always had a missing gear, or pickups born around World War II, their cab floors rusted straight through so you could watch the passing potholes between your feet. Adrian suggested an ancient Plymouth with knifelike wounds in the seats, probably the getaway car in a bank bombing during the Vietnam War protests in Berkeley in the sixties. I wanted that one, not even close to my 240Z dream, but at least it might have been famous in crimes against the state. It was snapped up fast, though, before I could even put in my thirty-burrito-sized offer, probably by one of Adrian's ex-revolutionary clients.

Dad ended up coming through, telling me he got a message from his answering service that "Rob wanted to sell me the Beast," that elderly 1961 Ford Galaxie his mom had already driven to near extinction back when Rob and I were still cowering under the dictatorship of Most Precious Suffering School, terrified tykes still stricken by Sister Fred's ruler.

So I called back, getting Rob's mother, then took BART across the Bay that evening, plus a couple Muni transfers, to the Pescatore house on Hayes Street. The old joke was that Rob lived on the "wrong" side of the Panhandle and that I had to lower myself, literally, to drop a few blocks from our godly hilltop on Ashbury Heights to sink to his scruffy street. But it was weird now, making the journey to my old stomping grounds from the sanitized East Bay suburbia of Mt. Olympus itself. The truth was that I loved Rob's block and how he and I schemed and goofed, back and forth and up and down across the park's Panhandle through all of our school days, as if the entire Haight-Ashbury was our private playground. It excited the hell out of me, just getting off the bus near the Pescatores', their small house squeezed between tall grand-but-shabby Victorians. I was blissing out on a thousand memories of the block. And especially that Rob was back in touch.

Rob's sister met me at the door, hugging me and dancing me inside to the radio blaring "Short People," the tiny tribe of which she definitely belonged, being only eleven. The whole house, as usual, smelled savory-sweet from garlic in the pasta sauce. Celeste Pescatore met me in the hallway off the kitchen, wielding her marinara-dipping wooden spoon in my direction. "Guy! Where the hell have you been, baby?"

"*Mamma mia!*" I cried out, then wrapped her in my arms. She'd insisted I call her anything but "Mrs. Pescatore" since I was about seven, so I'd settled on "Celeste" and sometimes "Mamma mia." It was weird that all the distractions of the past couple seasons had made me forget how much I missed her. (Best friends' moms are in a special category. They don't have to correct you, and be All Responsible, so being around them is just mutual admiration and pure love. And if they can cook real Italian, it's even better.)

I eased into the kitchen while she stirred the marinara, asking, "So why isn't Rob inheriting the Beast?"

"He doesn't want it, Guy. You mean you didn't know about his motorcycle?"

"Not a thing."

"He's very proud of it. A Honda CB750. It's been way too long since you've been in touch, now that you're over in the Diablo Valley," Celeste said. "I can't believe Paul wanted to move out there. We've all been wondering what became of you."

So Celeste had called my dad about the Beast, not Rob. I studied the little altar in a kitchen corner, which started off dedicated to Pope John XXIII, a color portrait of the Good Pope smiling at us. The altar long ago expanded with photos of the Kennedy brothers, then Martin Luther King. The added pictures made me think of all the years I'd been part of the Pescatore family, watching the Catholic shrine grow to include the wide smile of President Jimmy Carter, a Baptist peanut farmer.

In a way, I practically owed Celeste Pescatore my life. For most of my hungry existence, I had an open invitation to her scrumptious

Italian dinners. It was always the same for Rob at our house on Lola Montes, though I think he got the worse end of the deal, with Penni fixing squid guts on a seabed of crenulated kelp.

So it didn't really surprise me when Celeste insisted I sit down for a bowl of spaghetti before I traded a wad of bills for the Beast and drove it, shimmying up the hills, back to Mt. Olympus. Rob's dad was out at his night shift slinging luggage at the airport, so Celeste insisted I take his place at the head of the table. "*Mamma mia!*" I cried, "my first edible meal in months...."

I looked up to see Rob staring at me, dead quiet, from the doorway. I admired his new sideburns and leather motorcycle jacket. Now he had a cool, macho Italian-hoodlum look. He clung to his helmet, glaring back when I smiled. He turned down Celeste's offer to join me in scarfing spaghetti and about-faced in the hallway, heading back outside.

I got up from the table without taking a bite from the bowl, steaming and tempting as it was, and followed Rob out.

On the porch, Rob stopped before the top step. "Head of our table, Guy, really?"

"You know your mom. She always treats me like a prince. I think she's always liked me because I've always liked you."

"And I like you too, Guy. You've always been a prince of a friend. I know I was a jackass that day you told me. So I tried to keep quiet ever since."

"You succeeded. Big time. You've been a stranger for like, six months."

"Man, you blindsided me."

"Sorry. But we're still brothers, right?"

"You're an only child. Your parents didn't even have a dog, for God's sake. I'm not your brother, Guy. I never was."

"You don't mean that."

"That brother shit? It was kid stuff. It's time we grew up, Guy."

"Then I don't want to grow up."

"Maybe that's what it means to be gay, huh? Being like Peter Pan your whole fucking life. But we've gotta move on." He bounded down the front steps. "New plans, new friends."

After Rob exploded away on his new motorcycle, I went back inside and stared at my cooling pasta.

Rob's sister stared at me. "How come your eyes are all red and puffy, Guy?"

Celeste asked if I was okay. "What on earth is going on between you and Rob?"

"I better get going." I shrugged, telling her. "It's messing up my allergies, I guess, being on this side of the Bay."

"What allergies, Guy? You never had allergies."

I tried to think of something that bloomed around Labor Day, but I couldn't. Then I remembered news of some brush fires down the Peninsula. I got up, thanking Celeste for the food I hadn't touched. "The burning eucalyptus branches," I told her, "must be sending out combustible oils."

IN THE light of the next day, I could see how much rust erupted through the Beast's red and white metal flesh like terminal acne. Grass blades sprouted from huge, soil-caked holes in the rear bumper. To keep the last square inches of chrome intact, I plastered on Dad's campaign sticker, CHECK DIMCHEK FOR A GREENER CALIFORNIA.

Dad liked that. "Just mow the bumper every now and then, Guy."

Even though trying to connect with Rob kept misfiring, everything had gone pretty well after my blurted coming out at Penni's. I just had to survive dinners with each of the supercouples. In a noisy steakhouse, Dad helped me break the news to Liz by mentioning a former teammate and the high price he'd paid for staying in the closet. Then Dad whisked my stepmother to a campaign event before she could interrogate me. Penni served yak-milk quiche and apologized for never having had a lesbian adventure. Lester had hugged me awkwardly, muttered something about the Kinsey Report, and left early for some self-improvement seminar.

Then Dad cakewalked through the primary. One Democratic rival even dropped out on election eve, urging her loyalists to cast votes for Paul Dimchek. My summer job spun into a whirlwind. I worked for the campaign when I wasn't running errands for CJ Properties. When Dad needed to read research or rehearse speeches on the way, I drove him to evening fundraisers or party meetings in Sacramento—with stopovers there to inhale Granny's cooking.

Adrian briefly flirted with the idea of managing Dad's campaign, but when Liz stepped in as unofficial Queen of Political Wisdom and

European Know-How, Adrian decided to keep his role behind the scenes. The young guys who'd served as Dad's staff on the campaign stayed on after Bart Morgan's fatal fall. When Liz showed up at the campaign office in a tight T-shirt, CHECK DIMCHEK jiggling across her bazooka breasts, their typewriters silenced. The boys almost drooled on their ink spools, paralyzed, waiting for her next correction as if it were a honeyed kiss.

Through it all, we kept hearing from old-timers that those weeks of speech making, hand shaking, and press releasing were "the fun part." They said it would get ugly before October, when the opposition would fire all their nukes to keep Will Peters in Sacramento. Because Peters was an icon at the Capitol, "Bible-thumpers and right-wingers" would discharge money from all over California to save his assembly seat. Dad kept reminding us that the November showdown threatened to be a bloody massacre.

I had no idea how much of that blood would spurt on me. Just before fun ended after Labor Day, I was preoccupied by the start of my senior year at the ugly high school down on Burrito Boulevard. Luckily, it was all downhill, so that if the Beast died en route, I could coast down Casket Curve and roll right into the huge parking lot.

The good news came first. Because of my AP courses, I had enough credits to graduate in January. The counselor helped me apply to Cal Berkeley for spring semester. It blew my mind. One fine day in January, I'd be the same seventeen-year-old high school punk, and the next, a college man at Berzerkley. But something even better was waiting for me on my first day at Diablo Vista High School, something I'd been dreaming of all summer.

A new friend.

Just being among several hundred kids my age on a late August morning put me in a great mood. Where the hell had they all hidden themselves during the long suburban summer? Toward the end of the senior orientation circus, they had a student-organizations fair in the gym. Long lines snaked for the Prom Committee, Campus Crusade for Jesus, and the Athletic Supporters. Even the literary magazine was swamped with skinny boys and girls in granny glasses. But one booth was left alone, despite the electric blue eyes, shapely shoulders, and formfitting jeans of the guy manning it.

"Hi," I said, jostled toward the booth without the chance to read the taped-on sign.

"Hi," he said, suppressing a smile. "I just want to tell you before you ask, it's not really a religious thing, and it doesn't matter what religion you are. Or aren't, okay?"

"Okay," I said, unable to suppress my own grin. I'd been so isolated in suburbia and busy with CJ Properties, it was a shock to be face to face with a good-lookin' boy my age and height. This was like a whole new phenomenon on planet Earth, the long neck, the cute ears that stuck out from brown hair cut short at the temples, the full, trimmed sideburns… and those eyes, sapphire, deep set, with dark, thick lashes. They fluttered as he avoided my stare by looking down at his pamphlets.

Wow.

Okay. "So…," I fumbled, "have you had a lot of questions about that religious thing?"

"Man, I haven't had that many questions at all. Just a few smartass comments in passing. I guess I should've known."

I was standing right against the sign and didn't want to step any farther back just in case I never had another view of those eyes at such close range. His white T-shirt read "From Our Acorns Grow Mighty Oaks in Oakland," letters arrayed around a cartoonish seedling. "So it's more of an inner-city improvement project?"

"Yeah. It just happens to be based at the church. But it's not really church like *church*, you know?"

Somehow I knew, or if I didn't, I didn't care. I just wanted to watch those lips keep moving, hear that deep, inviting, ironic tone, and feel the sting of those sapphire eye darts. But before he could go on, a shorter guy in warm-ups pinned him from behind.

"Come on, Wade. Leave your sign-up sheet for the juniors tomorrow. We've got practice in five minutes."

"Sorry," Wade said. "Gotta go. My tennis coach will cut me if I'm late one more time. Here"—he handed me a pamphlet—"see ya around. Let me know if you're interested in coming."

Tennis. I watched Wade retreat, his perfect butt scooped in those jeans. *Tennis?* Was it already too late to sign up? Could I make varsity out here, in this giant school, with my pygmy talent? *Let me know if you're interested in coming…* to the practice? To join the team? To fall in love? No, to do the acorn thing, planting seedlings along blighted blocks. Yeah, the pamphlet… that's what he meant. I turned it over. A

Mighty Oak Grows in Oakland: The Story of the Brethren Community Church. Inside, a grainy photo of that familiar storefront church.

Under the heading "Interested in More Info?", I wrote my name and phone number on his virgin sign-up sheet.

DAD, WHOSE greatest virtue as far as I was concerned was his hands-off parenthood, suddenly grasped a strange new theme. "Guy, please don't go out for tennis. Okay? We'll need your help at the office just about every afternoon. And you've gotta be on call for the campaign every weekend."

Adrian, who'd overheard my plans at the office after I finished senior orientation, chimed in. "You've done everything with tennis you're ever going to do, kid."

"Yeah, except get good."

"So what's it gonna take? A raise?"

While it felt good to be courted by CJ Properties, and while the raise would help with the Beast's car insurance, I agreed only after long regrets. So much for my fantasies of meeting Wade every day at practice, riding to tournaments, then hitting the locker room together. I kept hoping he'd call about my signature on the sheet, but in the back of my mind, I figured I'd seen all of Wade I was ever going to see.

I tried to concentrate on enduring my semester in suburbia with a minimum of backbreaking schoolwork and without more heartbreaking messes involving an attractive tennis player who was probably hard at work impregnating some damn girl. I'd just labor for CJ and the campaign. Then, after election day, it was a short slide through the holidays to land, a free man, at Berkeley.

Credits assured, I could lighten up now. Except for science, I stayed clear of advanced placement and the higher math. Alone in a turbulent punch-card sea in the gym, I snagged slots in Bachelor Living, Field Hockey and Lawn Bowling I, and The Big Dig: Alive in Dead Cultures. I had to take one English class, so I settled on Senior Drama Survey in hopes we'd act out secretly homo-flavored Tennessee Williams and Edward Albee plays the whole semester.

"Don't get the idea we're going to sit around acting out plays the whole semester," Ms. Lillian Pullman said before she even took roll on the first day of class. "We're going to spend most of our time cussing, discussing, struggling with the very soul of our culture. And having a hell of a good time, if any of you thirteen seniors has a brain in your head."

We were only twelve, though, our student desks arrayed around Pullman in a semicircle.

"I'm going to tell you a little about myself, and then I want to hear from each of you. As you can see, I'm forty-three, prematurely gray, and still beautiful. Okay, I'm fifty-one, but who'd believe it?"

Since I was directly across the circle from her, she asked me to introduce myself first, and her eyebrows rose when I spoke my name. A girl beside Pullman asked if Paul Dimchek—the Foul Line Man— was actually my dad. "I heard he's living up on Mount Olympus with a gorgeous German model."

I wasn't sure what Liz was a model of, but I corrected her. "My stepmother just runs a modeling school. My dad just sells wrinkle cream. It's no big deal."

"Is no one going to mention that young Mr. Dimchek's father is our state assembly candidate?" Pullman asked. "No Democrats among you cheering for our district's good fortune? Will no one erupt in joy for having this dazzling Olympian run against the Neolithic cretin we've sent to the Capitol for six straight terms? No?"

Pullman stopped to aim her attention on a late arrival, a tall, shambling, well-built guy loaded down with a cardboard box. It was Wade, who grabbed an empty desk and caught his breath. "Sorry, Miz P." Flushed, he dropped the box at his feet. I could see it was full of Brethren Community Church pamphlets. "I had to collect this after freshman orientation."

"So, Wade," Ms. Pullman asked, laughing, "they allowed you to brainwash the little ones too, about your Maoist-front, so-called church?"

Wade laughed back, a hoarse bark. Then, with recognition dawning, he called to me, "Hey, hi!" and waved across the circle. Holy Pete, this guy was too much! "Well," he went on, turning to Pullman, "I didn't get a chance to brainwash anybody. Not a single freshman showed any interest whatsoever."

"There may be wisdom in the freshman psyche after all," Pullman said, "but I have yet to see any other signs of it. Well, class, we already know that Mr. Guy Dimchek has family connections to legitimate Democratic politics, while Mr. Wade Hart remains in the thrall of the People's Republic of Oakland, so let's hear from the rest of you."

After class, which ended the day, I asked Wade when our group would be meeting.

"What group?" He set the box down by his locker, pulling out his tennis racket, a bulky canvas book bag with sneakers tied on, and a huge volume of art prints. "Oh, the church? It's just a group of two. Me and you."

"So are we gonna open a ministry here?" I asked. "This place could use a few mighty oaks."

Wade turned, flashing me a big grin. "Something like that, if you're interested."

"The truth is, I don't know anything about radical churches. I just felt bad that nobody signed up."

"Man, that's pretty radical. What the hell, you wanna give me a hand?"

So I carried the box while Wade hurried with his books and equipment. I let him slip ahead as we made our way out of the maze of breezeways and concrete courtyards to the parking lot. I enjoyed the back of his long neck immensely, the way his hair was cut close to the nape. It made me realize that, for most of my conscious life, males had grown collar-length hair and hid this amazing erogenous zone. Today, Wade seemed more jock-like in his V-neck T-shirt with athletic stripes. Still stumbling behind him bearing the heavy box, I ached to nibble on his funky ears, out-turned like an Okie boy's.

Did the poor guy have any idea that his only partner in Marxist Christianity only prayed to lick every inch of his naked body? We wandered through the student lot, chatting about Pullman. "She was just amazing last year with *The Grapes of Wrath*," Wade said, speaking of Okies. "Really changed my whole outlook toward society. She's sly too. Jokes about everything, then you realize she's dead serious."

"Yeah, she's not what I expected from a place like this."

"Must be tough to transfer in your senior year. You must miss your old school, huh?"

I did; I sorely did. It had flashed in my mind all day, my old cohorts starting up classes and teams without me, that Pacific fogbank spread over Walt Whitman High like a worn security blanket. But here, in the hot bright sun, in Wade's company, I just couldn't dwell on that. He was parked beside the concrete drainage that skirted the school. His tiny gray Datsun had a crumpled fender, its entire rear end plastered with the whole decade's classic bumper stickers: Stop the ABM Treaty, Honk If You Love a Woman's Right to Choose, Jerry Brown for Governor, Nuke the Murder Machine at Lawrence-Livermore, Save a Golden State: Vote Bart Morgan. Next to it was plastered CHECK DIMCHEK FOR A GREENER CALIFORNIA. I smiled at that.

After I set the box on his front seat, I leaned against the chain-link fence. Wade surprised me by doing the same, right at my side. Then he turned to seize the links in his fingers and face the dry concrete conduit. "Walt Whitman is right near Ocean Beach, right? All we've got is this pathetic drainage ditch."

I dared to grab the links so that my little finger grazed his. He either didn't notice or care, so I kept it there while gazing down at the slowly dying slime.

Maybe it was my imagination, but Wade's pinkie seemed to slide closer to mine, sawing back and forth slightly, flesh to flesh.

"Sometimes I hate to think what crimes against nature we're committing all over Diablo Valley," he said, glancing at his watch. "Man, I gotta get goin'."

Damn. Couldn't we touch appendages other than pinkie fingers? I let go of the fence and turned to the acres of cars and beige-stucco school buildings. The ridge above, now dominated by Mount Olympus Residences, blocked the view of Mount Diablo.

As Wade hopped around me and squeezed into the Datsun, I asked, "Unless we're looking at the very devil himself, why do they call this place Diablo View High? Where the hell's the view?"

Driving off, Wade cried, "Where the hell's the high?"

SEMILOST IN Wade's neighborhood the following Sunday morning, I realized I was headed to a church service for the first time in the three years since Rob the Pest and I kissed off religion on Confirmation Day. I also wondered if this counted as my first "date" since Randy hauled me off to that island in the Delta, and whether it would be just as nerve-racking.

All that Wade had done was to let his little finger graze against mine for an extra few seconds while we talked. Then, because I'd signed his sheet, he'd invited me to the "celebration" at the Brethren Community Church. Not much evidence that my crush was reciprocated. I could relate to Rob and other old buddies at Walt

Whitman, all their mooning over some unattainable girl. The secret, vulnerable way they felt. The highs over little attentions returned, the downers over being ignored.

Camino Gordo was an older, exclusive area sprawled around a golf course in a woody canyon. There in Fat Road, the streets were skinny and most homes hidden behind pepper trees, oleander, and chaparral. The Harts' house was a formless ranch style spread beyond a yellow, weedy lawn. A tall, big-bellied bald man bearing a golf bag met me on the driveway. Mr. Hart shook my hand before he hurried into a new Mercury sedan, a showboat so massive that when he pulled away, I realized it had completely concealed Wade's little Datsun.

Inside it, Wade was dusting off the dashboard, singing along with Elvis Costello's album *My Aim Is True*. He crooned until he noticed me. "Hey, Guy! Just in time, man! Let's get the hell out of here."

"Not so fast, buster," croaked a female voice through the wide, screened windows beside the garage. I could make out a red scarf, tied upward in rabbit ears, wagging over the kitchen sink. "Bring your friend inside. I've made some extra cinnamon toast."

"We gotta get goin', Ma!" Wade cried. "Really."

"Don't be rude. Don't embarrass your mother in front of a boy who is obviously from a better class of people."

"No doubt," Wade sighed, snapping off the radio and slamming the Datsun's door. He rolled his eyes for my benefit. "Do you mind, Guy? I'll make this as brief and painless as possible."

I shrugged. "Cinnamon toast sounds good." I still imagined that Wade came from a normal, intact suburban family like the ones on sitcoms and wondered if Wade appreciated his family's normal foods and normal mealtimes.

In the kitchen, I accepted a cooling piece of toast. Mrs. Hart adjusted the red scarf binding her gray-brown hair. Tightening her bathrobe, she cast me an appraising look. "You don't look like a religious fanatic, Guy."

"I'm not, Mrs. Hart. I'm just curious about the church's social work."

"You'll fit right in around here. We all begin as do-gooders, then end up in cults. I'm not exactly thrilled Wade is attending Mass with Black Panthers in Oakland."

Wade belted back orange juice but exhaled in chokes. I took the opportunity to pat his back.

"Thanks," Wade said, recovering his breath and his cool. "They're not Black Panthers, and they don't serve Mass. If you start in, Mom, I'm going to do a hari-kari."

"You can't *do* a hari-kari," Mrs. Hart pronounced, "any more than you can *do* a masturbation."

"Thanks for the grammar lesson, Mom. Guy, we really gotta hit the road."

When we were headed west in Wade's Datsun, I tried to lighten his frustration. "You should see my family."

"I do, Guy. I see your Dad on every other billboard. I see him sponsoring *All in the Family* reruns. I see his sparkling California family having hot dogs around the ol' backyard barbeque."

"That's all Hollywood. Fake wife and kids."

"Well, now that he's running for office, maybe he'll have to use his actual son in his campaign commercials."

"Wow. I hadn't thought of that." I really hadn't. The whole idea gave me the heebie-jeebies, so I shifted the subject. "It's cool that you have one of my dad's bumper stickers."

"Yeah. Most of 'em came with the car, but your father's is the only one I put on myself."

Wade's big blue eyes were so vivid under his long lashes. When we reached the Caldecott Tunnel, I ached to touch the back of his head or massage his arm, so I sat on my hands and stared straight ahead through the dark bore.

Out of the tunnel, Wade spoke up. "You wouldn't know it to look at her now, but my mom was a religious revolutionary when she was in college. She and my dad did missionary work in Kenya in the fifties. Then they got involved in Berkeley politics. They brought me to Free Speech rallies in my baby carriage. That's why I was born so late. My parents had to save the world first, then settle down and have me when they were almost forty. But how they ended up this way, man, I shudder to wonder."

"What way?"

"Dad sells Mercurys. Mom's getting her real estate license. Neither of 'em have darkened the doors of a church since I was in grade school."

What could I say? I hadn't either.

When we reached West Oakland, and Wade nabbed a space in the church's former supermarket parking lot, he led me at a brisk pace through the crowd milling around the entranceway. He exchanged hellos with several folks as we sidled through the foyer. Amid bright flyers for food banks, street theater groups, antinuke events, and strikes against racism, a troop of young black men in black berets and dark suits lined the entry. After passing through their stone-faced gauntlet, we emerged into the gigantic, gutted space, once occupied by the supermarket.

Among the sea of folding chairs, Wade hustled us to a middle row. Older black men in Sunday suits nudged elbows with young white couples in blue jeans. Under the happy noise of a thousand greetings and scraps of gossip, the church felt supercharged, as if a miracle were expected. Wade already had a beatific expression as he took his seat, hands folded in his lap.

We stared at a mural stretching wall to wall behind the podium and choir. In bright reds and yellows, like a West Oakland version of Red Chinese poster art, a group of women in scarves and overalls restored a falling-down house. Not exactly the cold white marble statues at the Catholic Kremlin. The Virgin Mary of the Brethren Community Church was a black teenager cradling a baby in one arm and a power saw in the other.

I asked Wade, "So how did you find out about this place?"

"My mom and dad used to shop here when it was still a market. We lived just up Grove Street. Reverend Gladstone and my dad worked for the same church organization in Kenya. I went to kindergarten with some of the kids who are here today."

"So your mom was joking about the Panthers?"

"Kinda… hey." He nudged me. "There's Gladstone."

A tall, beautiful, gray-haired black man in a black robe stepped up to the podium, arms slowly upraised. The choir kicked into a slam-banging, rhythmic chant, and the entire assembly joined in, all hands clapping to the beat. As Gladstone's arms reached full length, the choir immediately silenced and all clapping ceased. "Brothers and sisters!" he incanted. "We come again to celebrate and rejoice! Not in the broken faith of Sunday hypocrites but in… what?" He cupped his hand theatrically to his ear.

"*Love!*" came the cascading roar from every corner. "*Love!*"

"What, my brothers and sisters?" Again the cupped hand, with Gladstone laughing, then assuming the shrunken posture of a deaf old man. "What? What is the message of the com-mun-ity?"

"*L-L-Loooove!*" crooned the swooning congregation, with Wade yelling it in full volume inches from my eardrums.

Now the Reverend Gladstone smiled like a pleased conductor. "Oh, my word, yes. *Love!* What power in that word. Now stand, brothers and sisters, to join hands with your neighbors and proclaim your love."

Everyone followed his instructions quickly, without embarrassment, an old routine. The tiny old woman beside me clasped my arm and squeezed it, muttering, "Love ya, brother."

Wade finished his proclamation to the rotund man on his right, then put his hands on my shoulders. Then he pulled me into a tight embrace. "Thanks for coming, Guy," he whispered, patting my back.

"Love ya, brother," I whispered back, forcing myself not to chew on his earlobe as we slowly slipped from our hug. As we faced forward again, though, our hands linked, fingers sliding into a tight lock. We and the entire congregation swayed to a rising, rocking hymn. Up and up into a shouted refrain, the song's passion enflamed us all. I tried to maintain my cool and concentrate on the clasp of Wade's hand in mine, the wet, rough heft of his palm. But I was tossed into the burning mood like kindling in a bonfire. The rock hymn dissolved into an endless loop of "Glor-or-or-or-orrrrr-ia...." and I began to sing along, too, against my will.

Wade, singing, turned to break into a smile for my benefit. I dared to squeeze his hand even tighter, glad that religious hysteria hid my lusty grasp. When the little old lady yanked on my other, limper hand, Gladstone again raised his arms, the choir cued to another sudden drop of silence.

We all let go of one another's hands as if by signal and sat for the sermon. Gladstone proceeded to sell us on the good deeds of the Brethren Community Church, making a pitch for that "wonderful affiliate fellowship, our brothers and sisters of the Marxist Matrix," especially their free breakfasts and education program for disabled children. As he linked the Matrix to other Christian projects, the choir came up softly, a sweet counterpoint to Gladstone's advertisements. Baskets were passed down the rows, heaped full with dollars, checks, and food stamps.

After the money gathering, Gladstone surrendered the podium to a speaker from the International Committee, a professorial, fiftyish white woman in thick glasses who exhorted us to support the "burgeoning freedom movement in Cambodia and their people's leader, Pol Pot."

To underscore international unity, little girls from the church's primary school staged a tribute to "the new Mao of Kampuchea." Their little ballet in Southeast Asian costumes ended with plastic tommy guns raised in solidarity. Gladstone re-commandeered the stage, taking the girls under his robe's black wings to deliver the closing poetics. "And so we join with peoples worldwide, as Christians of Jesus the beggar, Jesus the Ethiopian, Jesus the lonely, Jesus the suffering, Jesus the quiet revolutionary. Let's plant with our blood, bread, and love a new age. Brothers and sisters, what is the message of the com-mun-ity?"

"*Love!*"

"So… embrace your neighbors!"

Again the tiny woman grabbed me, pulling me into a sideways hug, then abandoned me for the little boy to her left while Wade reached for me, his arm around my shoulders as the choir roared a rocking reprise of "Gloria!" Gladstone implored us once again to drop our dollars as we exited. He slipped into line with the choir himself, rocking and swaying as people drifted out.

Wade and I found ourselves drifting on a euphoric cloud, but outside we suddenly unclasped our arms, as if Gladstone's spell had lost its grip. As the exiting crowd swirled around us, carrying the chorus of hymns to their cars, I drank gulps of fresh air.

Wade exclaimed, "Whew! Wish that feeling would always stay with me. Like I belong to everyone else."

I didn't say anything. I thought I recognized a big bruiser in black-rimmed glasses clutching a camera. His face swam out of the crowd for a flickering moment, then sank in the tide of people. He seemed so familiar, yet… maybe he was somebody I'd met through CJ Properties? Or a campaign volunteer? Lots of lefties in the Party probably lapped up Gladstone's social sermon every Sunday.

"Guy? Hey, did ya hear what I asked you?"

"Sorry, Wade."

"Well, what did you think? Did you like it?"

"Yeah. Yeah, I felt that unity you were talking about."

"Really? You don't sound so sure."

"Let me put it this way. It was a huge improvement over any Mass I ever attended."

"Hah!" shot from behind me. I turned to find another semifamiliar face. The Catholic schoolgirl from the Madrone Street apartments led the shorter, hobbling girl with the paralyzed scowl through the crowd. "You'll have to excuse us, boys."

"Pardon me," I said as Wade and I made room for them. As she passed, I asked her, "And what do you think? How does Mass compare?"

She stared at me, solemn, eyes narrowed in suspicion. Then her smile broke the tension, her pearly whites sparkling. "Well, Mass is the real thing. This is just politics. But I'll tell you one thing, the Catholic Church never offered my family any help with my sister. These folks gave us a leg brace and help with her schooling."

Meanwhile, her sister started fussing, yelling out something incomprehensible, then pointed at me. "I know you! I seen you prowlin' our stairwell, boy!"

The Catholic schoolgirl looked heavenward, then smoothed her sister's hair. "It's okay, honey. They're nice boys." She ushered her sister away, through the thinning crowd gathered on the corner, then laughed, turning back for our benefit before she disappeared. "Maybe. For Christian commies."

I smiled at Wade. "So does a nice boy like you really belong to the Marxist Matrix?"

"No. Just the church."

"Is there a difference?" I pointed at the steady stream of church folks pouring back and forth between the twinned Matrix houses across the street.

"Yeah. The Matrix serves free pancakes. Want some?"

It was too crowded for us even to attempt the sit-down breakfast in the little buildings, but Wade managed to score two pancakes on one paper plate. We strolled down Madrone Street along that block of tidy gardens, dipping into a shared smear of syrup. "It must be lonely, Wade," I said, "being the only Christian commie on your block."

"Yeah, but it's not lonely on Sunday. I wish you'd enjoyed it more, Guy. I really liked having someone my age along."

I remembered his whole motive, the information booth in the gym, the unwanted stack of pamphlets, and regretted my whole "lonely" crack. Then I compared it to my motive for attending church, my depraved craving for this beautiful boy. Wade's sincerity stabbed me, along with his attachment to this charismatic so-called church. "I did enjoy it, I swear," I said, trying to salvage our good feeling without overt lying. "Almost too much. Mass emotions kinda scare me. They're easy to get caught up in, and I'm as susceptible as anyone."

"Bullshit, Guy!" He slapped up more syrup and inhaled the rest of his pancake. "I get the feeling you're not susceptible to believing in anything."

"I'm just cautious. I'm surrounded by people who believe in things so passionately. Whether it's a certain kind of diet, or watercolors, or saving the slums, or even"—I thought of Liz—"their own ambitions for other people. Even the goddamn Democratic party!"

"Man, how would you like it if all your dad believed in was a Mercury dealership? And eighteen holes on Sunday morning?"

"There are worse things, Wade. Like believing too much. Like that guest speaker lady in there. How long would she have lasted under the real Mao? She'd be the first person the Red Guard sent to the rice paddies for ten years of hard labor."

"See what I mean? You're a total cynic."

Farther down Madrone, beyond the junk-heaped empty lots, I could see the Catholic schoolgirl help her sister struggle up the apartment house steps. I'd never really thought of myself as such a big cynic before, and I felt jealous of Wade's faith. "I may not be religious," I said, "but I do believe in things. I'm big on nature, for one thing. In fact, I think I'm going to study watershed restoration. Or something. Yep, I worship nature." I stole a glance at Wade's little rear end, shapely even in his baggy khakis. "In all its forms."

Wade's glance followed my gaze's direction, and I wondered if he figured out that I was not only cynical but a lewd homosexual as well. But his expression didn't reveal anything. He tossed the paper plate in a bright plastic trash can marked with the slogan, "FROM EVERY ACORN... A MIGHTY OAK GROWS IN OAKLAND... Clean It Up With The Brethren Community Church." Wade pointed out the contrast between the two halves of Madrone Street, the neat and maintained blocks surrounding the church, benefiting from all its social programs, and the demolished sector beyond. The crappy block where my people, the godless capitalists of CJ Properties, reigned as absentee slumlords.

As we walked on into the wasteland, I told Wade about CJ's involvement. Adrian and Dad had decided to put off the restoration project at their apartment house. The mutineers among the investors, led by Liz, objected to anything more than a cheap coat of paint. So now the apartment house sat in its trashed-out limbo, generating cash flow for CJ while some little kid slept in that damn firetrap pantry.

We wasted the rest of the afternoon prowling college bookstores along Telegraph Avenue. After that, with Cal Berkeley just opening for fall semester, we capitalized on our height and the crush of confusion in a dark basement pizzeria and managed to snag beers. We talked for hours about music, movies, and parents. The shortest part of our conversation was about girls.

"You going out with anyone?" Wade asked me.

"A girlfriend, like?" I said. I sipped my beer with manly indifference. "No. You?"

"No," he said, forthright. "No."

But being in reality minors still shackled to our parents' schedules, we had to head back to the 'burbs by evening. Maybe it was the beer, but I felt hunted by time itself, the September sun shot down too soon.

When we pulled up in the Harts' driveway, Wade killed the engine but sat still. Dizzy, I responded by sitting on my hands again, staring straight ahead. To ease my nervousness, I focused on the living room window, lit up like a drive-in movie screen. Wade's parents seemed to be shouting angry words, squared off across the wide room while the television flickered between them. The scene played against Wade's face, reflecting all his disgust. "It's almost as inevitable as the Sunday Disney show," Wade said. "Only it isn't cute."

"It's a drag when they fight," I said, nervously stating the obvious. "Well." I reached to grip the door handle. "My own happy family is waiting for me. There's actually going to be a meal on the table, so it's a special event."

"I'm glad you came along today, Guy. Too bad you're not more susceptible."

"Oh, I am," I said, "more susceptible than you'd ever believe." I grasped the door handle without opening it. "To be honest, I just wanted to hang out with you."

Wade squeezed my thigh, just above the knee. "Come on. I'll walk you to your car."

So at the Beast's door while I fumbled with the keys, it happened. Wade placed his hand over mine, pulling it away from the lock while he pressed himself against my back, his other hand pressed against my belt buckle, his lips grazing the back of my neck. I turned around, glad his lips were the same height as mine, easy to seek in the deep suburban dark.

MY UPLIFT over kissing Wade for the first time lasted about as long as the set of Pointer Sisters songs that played between Wade's house and mine.

En route I wondered about sharing my good news with Dad. I also steadied myself for Liz's reprimands about being late for dinner, but I prepared for the wrong thing. When I pulled into Circe Circle, Adrian's Jag was pulling out of our driveway.

He stopped, rolling down the window when I approached. "God bless us all, Guy. Careful, it's ugly in there."

"What happened?" I looked around the cul-de-sac, empty of cars. "I thought there were going to be a bunch of political people for dinner. Liz said Governor Jerry Brown might even stop by for dessert." I half hoped to meet his open-secret lady friend, singer Linda Ronstadt.

"The governor couldn't leave Sacramento. He's at an emergency strategy meeting tonight. All the campaign folks are huddling up to the capital tonight too."

I thought maybe another Democrat had fallen into the Pacific Ocean, but Adrian didn't say anything more about that. He was looking at me as if for signs of some infection I might be bearing, pox marks or stinking lesions.

I leaned closer, putting my hand on his door panel. "What's up, Adrian?"

"What's up with you, Guy Adrian Dimchek? How was church?"

"Radical."

"Good. Anything you want to tell your old godfather?"

"They told you?"

"It came up naturally, in conversation."

"Damn. I wanted to let you know myself. I almost told you first."

"I'm glad to hear that." He put his hand over mine, a brief pat. "I'd like to hear all about it. I'll buy you lunch. You'll tell me how careful you're going to be."

"Why does everyone keep saying that? Would you say that if I were going out with girls?"

Starting his car, Adrian laughed. "Hell yes!"

In the entry, I could hear Dad and Liz, their voices raised. They were on opposite ends of the kitchen island, Dad refilling his scotch, Liz taking apart a tray of appetizers.

"Paul, you have to be realistic about Adrian. I'm not sure his advice is always in our best interest."

"He's my best friend, Liz. Our best interests are the same."

"That is exactly what I fear. Adrian lets his judgment get clouded by sentiment. I am glad he is idealistic—"

"Liz, what are you saying?"

"But this is politics. This is softball."

"I think you mean *hardball*, Liz." I tried to smile. "Sorry I'm late."

"Yes, *hardball*. Exactly. Guy, tell your father."

"It's *hardball*, Father."

Dad swigged his freshened scotch. "We're not talking about anything as fun as playing ball."

"What are you talking about? What happened to dinner?"

Liz and Dad actually fell silent. Now I noticed the electric torches lit around the pool, festive but lonesome, mirrored in its placid surface. A few other hors d'oeuvre trays were scattered, untouched, around the sunken living room.

"I'm sorry to say," Liz finally said, "that we had to cancel dinner. We called the caterer just in time."

"A few campaign people showed up," Dad said, "but they had to join the Democratic Party folks in Sacramento when we got word this afternoon."

"And the word was…?" I asked.

"You know, I am not feeling well," Liz said. "Maybe it was something in these appetizers? Just a little stomachache, but I had better lie down."

"Go ahead," Dad said. "I'll put the rest of this in the fridge."

"Just leave some out for Guy." She drifted upstairs. "He must be starving."

"Thanks, Liz," I said, thinking, *just please let me know which of these delicacies made you sick.*

Dad reached for a full tray from one of the living room end tables, placed it in front of me, and urged to me to make dinner out of broccoli, crackers, and cold little coagulated meatballs.

"You'll be fine, boy, with that stomach of steel." Then he held up a plain white sheet, full of single-spaced paragraphs. "This press release was leaked from Will Peters's campaign. We got word of it late this morning. Due out at a press conference tomorrow. Yep, it's hardball time."

I tried to digest the press release, which disgusted me more than the meatballs' dry fat flecks. Without asking, after reading it halfway through, I poured myself a glass of red wine.

"Go easy," Dad said.

The Peters campaign announced its sponsorship of a major new bill, Save Our Schools, modeled on its Florida equivalent, made famous by ex-beauty queen, now orange juice pitchwoman, Anita Bryant. There was a reason for the supposed "decline of our public schools—a slump in SAT scores, the abandonment of discipline, the rise in youth violence." It was all the result of "unrepentant practicing homosexuals" teaching school statewide.

The middle paragraphs outlined a plan to restore "morality and the basics" back to California classrooms. The new code would fire homosexuals, abolish sex ed, and establish a "moral education" curriculum.

The final paragraphs bragged on Will Peters's moral character, his many Christian supporters, an honor roll of Bible-thumpers from San Diego all the way to the Oregon border. Then Will Peters named the enemies of common decency, our laid-back governor, the swarm of homosexual sympathizers among San Francisco's Democrats, and above all, his own opponent.

In the only direct quote from Peters himself, he pitched the final hardball: "Paul Dimchek has no experience whatsoever with the state's most pressing issue, the sad state of our public schools. So without any voting record, we are left to look for clues in his personal life. And what do we find? This divorced playboy, this spokesman for men's cosmetics, would likely advocate the same permissive philosophy he's lived as a male model. What can Paul Dimchek possibly offer to save our blighted schools? To cover their moral wounds with his powder puff?"

"No wonder Liz got sick," I said. "I think I'm gonna puke, myself." I asked him what the campaign was going to do.

"Well, the party is planning a press conference of their own to counter Peters's position. The Democrats are going to denounce the bill, expecting it will die in committee."

"Die of stupidity?"

"I wish. But it's gonna be popular with a lot of voters. That's why they're having the emergency meeting tonight."

"Why aren't you there, Dad?"

"They don't want the candidates involved. They want us to sit tight and wait for the cue from Sacramento. Then I'll hammer out my own press release, I guess."

I guess. As much as it scared the hell out of me, I sympathized with Dad's inexperience. I sat there, in the company of my libertine father, remembering how, during the Pointer Sisters' songs, I'd fantasized that I might tell him about the boy I'd just kissed. I sipped my illegal wine—enemy of common decency that I was—looking into Dad's worried eyes and decided to keep my good news to myself.

Chapter 7

IN SACRAMENTO the next Sunday, I picked tomatoes beside my dad in Granny's garden, thinking about Wade.

All that week, school had conspired to keep us apart. In our dramatic lit class, Pullman broke up our "free choice pairs" with "study groups of Lillian Pullman's choice." A big tennis tourney kept Wade in extra practice after school, then hijacked him to Monterey for the weekend. I'd invited him to Dad's next big banquet fundraiser just to stake one claim on his time. I was beginning to wonder if we'd ever really kissed and ever would again.

"Yep, really juicy," Dad said, biting into a fat tomato.

I carried my pickings up the back steps to Granny's kitchen. She was starting a salad to go with her specialty, *kapus*, a Croatian cabbage soup. To deflect Peters's "moral" hardball about how immoral he was, Dad had a campaign meeting in Sacramento Monday morning. Granny had gathered the whole tribe, including Penni and Lester, for *kapus*.

"Nina," Liz said, peeking into the simmering pot, "your sauerkraut looks wonderful."

"It's just peasant food, you know," Granny said, upending garlic cloves from her scooped apron onto the countertop. "From the old country. My mother's own recipe."

"My God," Dad said, shoveling tomatoes onto the counter. "Do I ever miss the taste of these in the summers, now."

"Really, Pee Dee?" Stirring the pot, Granny swatted Dad upside the head with an oven mitt. "If you miss fresh garden food, why did you move to that concrete place?"

I laughed. "Good question, Gran!" I loved her for despising Mount Olympus as much as I did.

"Penni always raised wonderful tomatoes," Granny added, chopping a garlic clove, "even in San Francisco fog."

This unexpected fractured-family sleepover promised all my favorite things (other than Wade): Granny and home cooking; the good vibe that usually hummed when Penni and Dad joshed each other in Granny's company; and good ol' Sacramento, with its massive trees shading funky, timeworn houses. That I'd have to miss my Monday morning class—Bachelor Living—probably wouldn't ruin my intellectual development.

I smiled at the sharp contrast between Granny and Liz. Granny was plump, broad in the hips. The top of her head barely reached Liz's shoulders. Her housedress, apron, and slip-on canvas sneakers shrieked "Sacramento grandma," while Liz's designer jeans were so pressed she could've diced the garlic with those creases.

Granny elaborately rinsed off the chopping knife and stashed it out of Liz's reach. "Now, why don't you all take a nice walk and leave me be while I get dinner ready, before Penni and Lester get here? Paul, show Liz the flowerbeds in Capitol Park. They're perfect right now."

"Yeah, let's do that, guys," Dad said, raising his brows.

When they waited for me, I waved them off, then poured a half jelly-jar glass of cold white jug wine for myself and a full one for Granny. She scolded me for drinking the wine—"So, you're a big shot grown-up now?"—but accepted the glass and swigged it heartily. "Why don't you go too? Shoo, Guy. Get out of my hair."

"Crabby as you are, I'd rather stay here. I've been cooped up in that Volvo with those two all afternoon."

I asked if I could help. She didn't want any. I offered to slice the tomatoes. She didn't like the way I sliced things. Then I asked what the matter was.

"Nothing. I'm just nervous about the *kapus*."

"Yeah, right. You could make *kapus* in your sleep."

"All right, big shot. I believe some things can't be forgiven. Ever."

"Come on. You'll never forgive Liz for calling it *sauerkraut*?"

"You talk big, Guy. Just like your father. But you don't understand anything. And why should you? I'm glad you never had to live through what we did. So I'll tell you the truth. It's still not easy for me to have a German, a real, native-born German in my house." Leaning against the stove, idly stirring, she sipped her wine and pointed to the simmering pot. "But if you say anything, you're finally going to know what my wooden spoon feels like on your butt."

"Come on, Gran. Liz was just a little girl."

"Nits grow to lice."

I should have known it was going to come to nits and lice. Germany was the one subject my little Gran was completely irrational about. The widow Nina Dimchek spent her days as a teacher's aide at a mostly minority elementary school, marched with her son for civil rights, volunteered for the Democratic party, and led the Altar Society at her Catholic parish. She also practiced another rock-solid faith, in the Inherent Evil of Germans.

When Granny connived a visit to Yugoslavia in 1947, there wasn't much family to see except in graveyards. Her sister-in-law had been slaughtered in a death camp. Her grandmother had died from pneumonia complicated by malnutrition. Her godfather, a Partisan in the fight against the Nazis, died of typhus in a detention camp two weeks before World War II ended. I tried to imagine Granny at about Penni's age now, wandering in the ruins of her parents' family, swearing to despise forever all the good Germans who had allowed the Nazis to blitz their beliefs all over Europe.

"Give Liz a little credit, Gran. Her family wasn't doing so great before the war. After her father was killed, her mother turned tricks to put bread on the table."

"Yes, and my cooking's not even fit for a whore's daughter," Granny cried. Now she mocked Liz in *Hogan's Heroes* German, "But hurr fahther vas un ahrtist! Ein vahr ahrtist! Painting lovely pictures of the subhuman Slavs the Germans massacred like animals in the field."

I just looked at her and poured us each more wine, this time topping off my glass.

Granny didn't object but set her own glass aside. "I guess I should've prepared something fancy for your father's elegant bride." She glanced at the simmering pot. "But when she breaks bread with subhumans, she should know she's going to have to share our swill. Guy, keep your eye on the *kapus*. Stir it every now and then. I'm going out to the garden for more onions."

I stirred the pot, then took my wine to the kitchen table. I heard a familiar voice calling through the front screen door: "Nina? Paul? Is anyone home?"

"Yes," I called to Penni, "but I was given strict instructions to guard the *kapus* from any intruder."

"Intruder!" She met me halfway across the kitchen, opening her arms to me. "Is that how you think of your old mother?"

Penni didn't look old or very motherly, nor was there much of her to hold. Her skeleton was wrapped in a loose sundress, Hare Krishna orange. She stepped back, flouncing, to show off her transformation.

"I think highly of my old mother," I said. Then I lied. "You look great."

"Thanks. I lost a little weight. I owe it all to SELF, Guy."

SELF or Seminar: Earning Life Fulfillment, Inc. was the outfit Lester had become ensnared in. For a few thousand bucks, its disciples learned "to earn the responsibility for their own wholeness."

I smiled at my mother like a lunatic, a frozen grin to hide behind while I gagged back snotty comments. I'd had plenty of practice when adults told me, straight-faced, they were exploring astrology or past life regression. Why not "explore" the Tooth Fairy too? SELF was even worse. It didn't leave cash under the pillow but snatched it away.

"So you've joined SELF too? Where's Lester?"

"Oh, Guy, the weekend retreat was an amazing breakthrough for both of us. But I'll have to try to stop—" She stopped herself, remembering some SELF psychobabble. "If you *get* it you just *do* it, you know?" Noticing my confused stare, Penni stopped again. "Okay, it may be bullshit, Guy, but I have lost ten pounds!"

"Great, Mom. And where did you say Lester was?"

She took a breath. "Well, he needed to get back to Oakland. So he caught a ride with another couple. Can I have some of that Chablis, Guy?"

I poured her a glass, and after thanking me, she wanted to know why I was drinking wine, especially alone. "Where's Nina?"

"Out in the garden. She's kind of upset. We got to talking about her family in Yugoslavia."

"Oh, sentiment and regret, right?" Penni bristled like a student proud to recite what she'd learned, I suppose, from SELF: "Sentiment is the booby prize. And regret is just worrying backwards. I just wish I could communicate that with Nina."

I led my mother outside to head off Penni's next assault on the English language. On her knees in the garden, Granny tossed aside whatever she'd been picking and hurried to embrace her ex-daughter-in-law. Flimsy Penni oozed into plump Granny.

When I was little, I actually thought Granny was *both* my parents' mother, an incestuous but understandable mistake. When Penni was only eighteen, her folks moved to Florida to manage a trailer park. With my mom secretly pregnant with me and just starting her Penni Wise career, Granny had stepped in as Penni's surrogate mom.

Great September yields rose all around, yellow corn on sky-scraping stalks and sunflowers casting long shadows on jungles of tomato and squash. Now that I'd lost Montes Terrace, Granny's was the only place that felt like home.

When we went back inside, the kitchen got raucous with Granny and Penni's usual bustle. I downed another glass of wine by the time Liz and Dad appeared from the hallway's shadows. Leaning back into Dad's clasped embrace, Liz announced, "On our walk, Nina, I told Paul that we should think about living up here in Sacramento someday. Especially if Paul actually wins!"

"Pee Dee's not only going to win, he's going on to be Governor someday," Granny said, gesturing with her wooden spoon. "Mark my words!"

"This neighborhood is beautiful, but it gets a little rough just a few streets away." Liz smiled tightly. "I have to admit I was a little surprised by what we saw in Capitol Park. A drug deal, right in broad daylight, not twenty yards from the Capitol itself. And what looked like a meeting place for predatory homosexuals."

Granny tsk-tsked and returned to the sink. Penni glanced at me, embarrassed. Dad stared at Liz, aghast.

I sighed. "Whaddaya gonna do?" The wine made me even more sarcastic than usual. "All the nonpredatory homosexuals are busy rescuing puppies, teaching school, and running the state government."

Liz was undaunted. "You know what I meant to say. Nothing against gays, just the type that flaunt themselves, right there in the park, with so many children around. It is just as bad with all the streetwalkers."

"I feel sorry for those girls," Granny said with an aggressive slam of cooking metal. "I'm sure they're just selling themselves to feed their little daughters."

The wine whirled my brain. I'd lost track... was it my third glass? When had I last eaten?

"Liz and I were just talking about how quickly these old neighborhoods can slip," Dad said. "It's still beautiful and homey here, but before you know it, neighbors rent to people who might be... less than desirable."

"Oh, undesirables," I said. What a politician Dad was becoming, I thought, under Liz's influence. "Like homos, or a bunch of *kapus*-smackin' bohunks?"

"Hey, that's enough, Guy," Dad said. "You're not nearly as funny as you think you are."

Now that pissed me off. "You and Liz don't seem to mind charging high rents to 'undesirables' in West Oakland."

Instead of the drunken debate I'd hoped to ignite, silence dropped over the kitchen. It was as if Dad's slum-investments business was taboo because it was funding his "golden boy on a white steed" political campaign. I chugged deeply. In the quiet, I could feel my heart pumping pure alcohol into my frontal lobes.

Penni finally broke the silence at my expense. "Maybe Guy's had enough wine."

They all chuckled, and now I was a specimen, a third person—*oh, these darn teenagers today.*

"Anyway, Nina, we only meant a thought for the future," Liz said. "If you ever want to move to a safer area, we'd be happy to do what we could."

"Well, I do appreciate that," Granny said without a vowel or consonant of appreciation in her voice. She presented a tray of cold cuts, then stood beside Dad. "Here," she said. "Everybody eat something, and maybe we'll all be in a better mood."

"Thanks, Ma. But what do you think, really?"

"About moving? Pee Dee, I would be so lonely anywhere else."

"But this house is probably at its peak of market value," Liz said. "There are speculators who would make a killing for you on this place."

A killing. I watched Liz inhale a cold cut, fatty pink stuff with green olive slices stuck inside. Hungry as I should have been, the antipasto tray repulsed me. The peppers seemed to squirm, baby-shit green, beside all the fleshy meat slices. My stomach rose into my lungs, vile juices squeezing my oxygen supply. In fact, the whole damn room was swirling, and before I could figure out why, I was running like hell for the toilet off the back porch.

My barf was scented with the subtle bouquet of Safeway Chablis rising on stomach bile.

ADRIFT ON the glacial North Atlantic, I clung to a bulbous tureen, vomited into the sea from *Titanic*'s sinking kitchen.

No, don't even mention vomit.

It was somehow after nightfall now, and side lamps lit the living room, though I was in the dark, crashed on the couch in the den, my head stuck to a cushion. The TV silently flickered the local news. Still queasy, I fixed my gaze on the scene in the living room.

Liz, Dad, and Penni sat on the sofa, directly under Granny's gallery of family photos, which included, huge and prominent, a framed photo of Paul and Penni at their 1960 shotgun wedding. Behind Penni, on adjacent shelves, spread the Great Olympic Shrine, with Dad's gold medal in a special cherrywood case, along with framed clippings and photos from the news and sports pages, including a cover of the *Sacramento Bee*'s Sunday magazine with Dad atop the medalists' dais, Golden Hero From the Golden State. He smiled in new photo masters for his Foul Line magazine ads and beside June's front-page headline, Dimchek Slams East Bay Primary for Dems.

Liz smiled, snuggling up to Dad's shoulder, an old yearbook sliding off her lap. I could smell Paul and Penni's drinks, brown alcohol in frosty tumblers, and swore I would never touch the demented poison of Bacchus ever again. Liz sipped fizzy stuff, 7Up maybe, and muttered a comment about how silly Paul looked in his fifties butch cut, and how, with his goofy, boyish, toothy, formless face, he looked "exactly like Guy."

"Is he still out?" Penni asked. I quickly shut my eyes and groaned softly. They all giggled.

As consciousness drifted away again, I heard Granny call Penni to set the table. Meanwhile, Dad turned up the TV slightly to catch a news snippet about Will Peters taking his Save Our Schools campaign to an Orange County fundraiser. "Good," Dad said, "let him spend all his time down there with the whackos. I'll win the district while he preaches hate in Disneyland."

Someone—Penni?—tried to rouse me for dinner, tossing a life jacket into the briny waters, but out of her reach, I only sank deeper.

BEYOND THE muted video drone, silverware and unintelligible dinner talk clattered as *Titanic* went under. Then black Atlantic waters dotted by icebergs. Distant screams of the drowning. Wade, bare-chested in the icy night, rowed a billiard table toward where I floundered.

Granny's TV tinkled cheesy patriotic music. "Welcome back to *On the Right Side*, Sacramento's only Sunday forum for conservative voices." Now a muffled but distinctive voice from the dim past, along another waterway. "This interview with Will Peters is of interest to all Californians because, as our most powerful moral voice, his assembly seat is seriously threatened by a celebrity opponent."

Out of my face-planted muddle, I cocked an eye toward the screen. The rotund, balding, middle-aged man looked so familiar. Why was I thinking propane? What brought to mind fried chicken? Why Randy's hard body pressing next to mine on a river dock, the Delta waters lapping under us in rhythm with our kisses?

I was jolted off the couch and propelled into the living room by the revelation. The show's host was the Reverend Harold Pruedhoe. Gas 'n' Jesus himself!

I crouched in front of the television, Granny's afghan snuggled around my shoulders like a security blanket.

"Sounds like you'll usher in the California Dream once and for all, Will," Gas 'n' Jesus was saying. "Now, if only they'd let you address our problems with illegal freeloaders and homosexuals in our schools."

Will Peters smiled, catching the easy lob. "That's exactly what Save Our Schools is all about, Harold. It ensures that no California child is imprisoned in an immoral classroom."

"So your supporters are concerned," Gas 'n' Jesus commented, "that Paul Dimchek is a negative role model."

"Some volunteers on my campaign have uncovered disturbing new evidence that Dimchek isn't quite the golden boy he pretends to be. They'll be releasing some documents later this week."

"Can you clue us in on the nature of these documents, Will?"

"Scary stuff, Harold. Dimchek's own family members may be linked to both the Marxist and the homosexual underground."

Dad was standing in the doorway, licking his fingers. "Guy, I'm glad you're up. You've got to join us for dinner. The *kapus* is unbelievable."

"Yeah, Dad, but you've got to see this—"

"No, bud, you've got to get your butt in here. Liz wants to share some good news with the family."

I would've insisted, but Gas 'n' Jesus went to a commercial, so I followed Dad into the kitchen, wondering how in hell I was going to break the news about Will Peters's secret documents. What if Dad freaked out and I ended up ruining the rest of the evening all over again?

Everyone at the table turned to me with a smile. Dad was fighting with a champagne cork while Liz poured sparkling cider for herself and me.

"Oh, poor Guy," Penni said, "you must be starving."

"I'm just a little groggy," I said, studying the demolished meal, the scraps of ham fat on plates, the empty bowls of *kapus*, the remnants of salad. I accepted the cider while Dad popped the cork and poured the bubbly.

"We have an announcement," Dad said, raising his glass. "We were waiting for you, Guy."

"Yes," Liz said, raising her goblet of cider with a movie-star smile. She squeezed Dad's hand. "We wanted to let each of you know that we're expecting a baby. We have tried to keep it a secret, with so much else going on. But soon everyone would have seen for themselves. I am in my fifth month!"

After a toast, Penni clapped and cooed. Granny's mouth dropped open. Then she caught herself and joined the applause. Dad glanced at me, raising his eyebrows and smiling.

Liz bowed, accepting the best wishes. "Yes, yes! Imagine, a child of our own!"

I'd tried to put on my best face, not easy when my stomach was still flip-flopping and my forehead felt pounded by crucifixion nails. I realized I had missed much more than one of Granny's homey meals. I'd missed a whole private drama all summer, Dad and Liz's whole future-building, Mount Olympus-climbing, household-expanding bonding. Okay, I got it. Liz and Dad's push for investments, their fantasizing about safe havens for themselves and Granny here in Sacramento made more sense. Bart Morgan's sudden death and Dad's nomination must have been a double shock. It thrust Dad into a new arena of risk just when they'd first absorbed that fact of a "child of their own."

Would I have to douse the baby news with the sick story Will Peters was about to tell, that there was a homosexual Marxist in the family and it was me? Were they all going to freak out now if I told them about Wade?

I scanned the table, to spy a chunk of that pink baloney laced with green olives. I found myself running for the toilet again, barfing in dry, emptied heaves while the adults laughed.

Chapter 8

"So you think Oedipus overreacted?" Ms. Pullman asked Wade, arching a brow and shaking his essay. "You wouldn't gouge out your eyes if you you'd accidentally married your mother?"

"*My* mother? No, ma'am. I'd disembowel myself."

Pullman smiled as she allowed the class "a strict lifetime limit of three sick Oedipus jokes." My attention kept floating away to a different piece of ancient Greece. On some gay isle, Wade lounged naked in wet sand, his gorgeous butt lapped by the wine-dark sea.

"Ladies and gentlemen, do you think it's possible to discuss this classic without descending into puerile bedroom humor? Or am I alone in combat against teenaged lust?"

Lust… what a perfect word to describe this surge of new craving for Wade. Its sound even matched its meaning, the languid "l" tugged under by the surging, tidal, mindless "uhhh…."

I tried to survive my afternoon classes that Monday, stupefied, fresh from my weekend hangover. All the way from Sacramento, my head ached, stuck in a cruise-control stupor. I wondered when to tell Dad about the anti-gay-Dimchek attack on Gas 'n' Jesus's program. Meanwhile, Dad and Liz cooed in the Volvo's backseat, chatting about shopping for an antique crib, "first thing after our Election Day victory party."

Not the right time for baby's big brother to spill the sorry news.

Now I sat in Pullman's class beside Wade, just back from his tennis tourney victory in Monterey. My headache vanished the minute I saw him, but I still couldn't make any sense of the day's lesson. For all I knew, Pullman was speaking in some dead Macedonian dialect. Was she really drawing a goat on the board to embellish her point?

While the class cracked up, I stole glances at the golden hairs on Wade's forearm. I studied where the denim tugged tightly between his legs.

As if coaxing me from a dream, Pullman was calling out my name. "Anybody home, Mr. Dimchek? Would you care to comment on that last point about the tragic destiny?"

"I'm sorry, Ms. Pullman. I got lost among the Macedonian goats."

Pullman smiled while the circle snorted derisive laughter. "You've been thinking about something much more compelling, Guy. Class, I've never seen such a bad collective case of spring fever, especially in September."

She dismissed us with the bell. While most of the class hurried to the parking lot or playing fields, Wade tugged me the other way, toward where the breezeway dead-ended. Behind a stack of discarded desks and file cabinets, Wade had discovered a dark alcove full of broken vending machines. By jimmying a metal shutter, we sidled easily inside.

"Pretty cool, huh?" Wade clutched my shoulders.

I clasped my arms around his back and pulled him closer. He collapsed against me, his face grazing mine. I petted his hair and smooched his funny out-sticking ear. "I missed you, Wade, last week and the whole time I was in Sacramento. And the whole drive down here."

"I thought about you the whole time I was in Monterey." He smiled, flinching at the tickle of my ear licking, then turned to catch my lips on his. "It seems like a month since we did this."

Since we'd kissed each other good night the previous Saturday, I'd relived it so many times. With one hand, I steadied myself against a rusty old Coke machine. Instead of letting me catch a breath, Wade pressed even closer and lunged for my mouth again. "God," I gasped. "You're good at this."

"I've been practicing in my sleep. And I've got another skill at my command." Pushing the end of my belt back toward the clasp, he'd just unfastened the buckle when, out of the freaking blue, I heard a deep voice calling my name, distinct and close.

It was my father. His yelling "Guy! Guy!" down the breezeway kind of broke the mood. I redid my belt, then stood perfectly still, staring into Wade's eyes. They mirrored my own disbelieving shock.

Now we heard Pullman's voice, farther off: "Any luck, Mr. Dimchek?"

"No. I guess we just missed him."

"Maybe I can have the office page him on the intercom?"

"It's worth a try."

Was Dad talking to Pullman at her classroom door?

"What the hell...?" Wade whispered.

"I don't know. But it's gotta be something big," I whispered back. "And bad." Since Dad hadn't set foot in any of my classrooms since a sixth grade open house at Most Precious Suffering, I immediately flashed to Liz and the baby. I eased around the metal shutter, peeking down the breezeway.

Jesus! Adrian was there too, whacking an oversized envelope against his hip. I slipped out between two snack machines, smoothing down my hair. Wade followed me, just as the three turned our way again. We might as well have whistled as we faked nonchalance, ambling the difficult yards toward the adults. "Hi, Adrian," I said. "What's up, Dad?"

"Where the hell have you been?" Dad said, arching an eyebrow at Wade. "I've been yelling your name all over the English wing, Guy."

"I was just...." I pointed back to the dead-end breezeway. "We...."

Wade was the cool one. "Sorry we were so clueless, Mr. Dimchek."

Wade's politeness spurred introductions, handshakes, and pleasantries. After squeezing Dad's hand, Pullman retreated to her classroom, urging him to, "Save us all from Save Our Schools, please."

"Dad," I said, "I'm not late for work or anything, am I? I was just on my way."

"No, everything's fine," Dad said.

"Except what's not fine," Adrian said, turning to Dad. "You know, the stuff that's so urgent?"

"Yeah, we're on our way into Oakland for a meeting, and we wanted to catch you before you drove all the way to the office."

"And I've gotta get to tennis practice," Wade said, heading down the breezeway. "Nice meeting ya, Mr. Myers, Mr. Dimchek. I'll call you, Guy."

"Nice kid," Adrian said, watching Wade's retreat. "Looks real familiar for some reason."

"Come on, Adrian," Dad said.

"Looks just like his photographs." Adrian swatted my head with the clasp envelope. "Let's blow this joint, gentlemen. High school was the scene of my earliest crimes, and we're in so much trouble now, we might have detention until Election Day."

"JUST IN time for Saturday's big fundraiser," Dad said, spilling the photographs across the table. He and Adrian chose a back booth at the

Bull Ring, a dark steak-and-whiskey restaurant near the school. They squeezed around me, close, like bodyguards. Dad belted back straight scotch.

With the cocktail waitress safely chatting with the only other customer at the bar, Adrian arranged each glossy black-and-white side by side for my benefit. I wished somebody would say something, even a smart crack at my expense. Struck as dumb as two freshmen clueless about their next move, Dad and Adrian just stared at me.

I sipped my ginger ale, biding time. I was getting over the weird panic of my father, my godfather, and my English teacher almost catching me kissing my boyfriend with my belt undone. But a new dread twisted my guts as I studied the photographs. Some creep had been circulating photographs of Wade and me attending the Brethren Community Church. There we stood on that first Sunday, shielding our eyes as we left church, laughing, arms locked around each other's shoulders.

Or, if you prefer, sharing a pancake from the Marxist Matrix.

Or toasting each other with illegal beer in the basement of a Berkeley bar.

I recalled the burly reporter who'd tried to get a comment from Dad that day after Bart Morgan's funeral. "So he was lying? He was really a spy for Will Peters?"

"Well, he really did write for the *Tribune*," Dad said. "But now he's 'on leave' while he 'consults' for the Peters campaign."

"He's the same journalistic professional who's been investigating your dad's past," Adrian said. "Paul's postdivorce, alleged love life."

"Alleged?" I asked. "Listen, so Dad had some interesting company on Montes Terrace. What's wrong with that? Remember Free Love? Doesn't it apply to everyone? Including me, myself, and my boyfriend?"

"Great," Adrian said. "Tell that to the next reporter who catches you and this Wade guy in compromising positions."

"So…," Dad started, pushing away his emptied glass. "You consider Wade your boyfriend?"

"I'd sure like for him to be."

"Okay," Adrian said, "but remember you're both underage. Wouldn't it be a good idea to save the boyfriend stuff until you're both eighteen?"

"Would you ask me that if Wade were a girl? Like, never in a hundred, never in a million years? You used to tease me, Adrian, because I was still a virgin. You were all ready to take me to a whorehouse, remember?"

"Okay, Guy. I'm a hypocrite. But now we've got to be cool. Discreet. Paul is pitted against the whole state's Bible-thumping power bloc."

I looked at the three photographs again. "Anyway, I really don't get what that power bloc gains by this. Is this ex-reporter blackmailing you?"

"In a way," Dad sighed. "He's blackmailing our campaign. Just the dirty tricks we should've expected."

Adrian filled me in. "It's through CREWP, the Committee to Re-Elect Will Peters. Nasty but perfectly legal. Unless we withdraw our opposition to Peters's Save Our Schools crusade, they'll release these photos to the press."

"CREWP is grooming Peters to take out the Democrats in 1982," Dad said. "Then they'll turn the Capitol into a Holy Roller revival tent."

"I still don't get it, though," I said, pointing to the photographs. "Except for the stupid beer, there's nothing here. Who's going to know Wade and I are gay? Just because we went to church together?"

"I don't think they're going to play the gay card yet," Adrian said, inventing a headline bracketed between both hands. "'Dimchek Son Having Breakfast With the Marxist Matrix' is enough for the anticommie hysterics."

"And for the prudes, your underage drinking is another fun scandal." Dad sipped his scotch, then coughed.

"Then, closer to the end of October, they'll slap down that gay wild card. So we got trouble," Adrian said. "Big trouble, as you can see. And we need for you to be a good boy, Guy."

"Please don't become a juvenile delinquent," Dad said, managing half a smile. "You've been a saint your whole life so far. Much more than I ever deserved, Guy. Just stay saintly until the first Tuesday in November, please?"

"But I haven't done anything yet, have I? Maybe getting drunk at Granny's wasn't my finest hour, but Jesus, what have I done that's so delinquent? Gone to church? Had a lousy beer? Met a nice boy?"

"We're dying here, Guy," Adrian said. "Please don't act the wide-eyed innocent. Just restrain your hormones for six more weeks. Maybe, for one example, you might avoid kissing Wade in public.

And make it a special point not to be photographed with the communist wing of the Black Panthers."

"So, Dad, I don't get to enjoy any of the personal freedoms your campaign is fighting for?"

Adrian jumped in. "Guy, save yourself a lot of torment over justice and fairness and look at it this way." He tried to smile. "You don't have any freedom. At least not until after Election Day."

Silence fell again, broken only when ice clinked. Adrian and Dad clutched those tumblers of scotch as if they were tiny glass life preservers. I was sure they were building up to the real bad news. Something worse than these photographs, some ugly ultimatum from CREWP. They were easing it to me, sipping while they searched for the words.

They both looked so beaten down and scared. Young-like too, both of them, college boys lost in the grown-ups' political wilderness.

"Okay," I finally found the wit to say, "I'll avoid kissing Black Panthers. In public at least, I promise. But what do you do about CREWP and Save our Schools' blackmail?"

"Nothing," Dad said, staring at me as if surprised I even asked.

"Huh?"

"Guy, Save Our Schools is a total abomination. It's a witch hunt. It robs every teacher's basic rights. It pisses me off that those self-righteous slimeballs dared to think I'd cave in to this."

"So this is what we're asking you, Guy," Adrian said. "Are you ready to have your picture in the paper?"

"Oh." I stared from face to face. "Well, hell, yeah. I'll ask Wade how he feels, but I've got nothing to hide."

"Give it some thought," Adrian said. "We don't want to leave you out there, twisting in the high school gossip storm."

"I don't care. So what if I went to Gladstone's church? And I'm only at this school for a few more months. And like I keep reminding you, I haven't done one thing I'm ashamed of. If you're okay with it, I'm okay with it."

"Are you sure, Guy?" Dad asked. "Because we don't want you out there, unprepared for whatever CREWP smears you with. These photographs should be the first and last of it, but it could get real ugly. I mean ugly like we haven't even seen."

I started to tell him about Gas 'n' Jesus, but he'd already seen a tape at that morning's meaning.

"The state campaign people told us there's a whole new breed of hysterics on TV and radio talkers on the AM dial. They have the personal morals of hyenas, but they hide behind the Bible. They're hungry to feast on my carcass. And I don't want them tasting even a bite of yours."

"With that said, Guy, we're hoping that all this backfires." Adrian looked at his watch, then collected the photographs. "If the photos do run, we're hoping the reaction is, maybe, sympathy. Maybe puzzlement and doubt. 'Why are they picking on a teenager? Doesn't the poor kid have any rights?'"

"Amen," I said. "I'm in. I'll try to be ready for whatever happens, okay?"

"Good boy," Adrian said, standing up. "You'll go to the fundraising banquet on Saturday night with your handsome Dad and gorgeous stepmother, ignoring whatever the press does with these." He waved the photographs before he slid them back into the envelope. "In your dinner jacket and a fresh haircut, kid, you'll give a big ol' confident all-American smile for the cameras."

"Great. I'll ask Wade to get a haircut too."

"Oh." Adrian grimaced. "You sure that's such a great idea? I was hoping, after our little talk—"

"Adrian, I already invited him. Besides, he's totally behind Dad's campaign. He had a 'Check Dimchek' bumper sticker before I even met him. I'm not going to disinvite Wade now."

Dad stood up, gently easing Adrian out of his way to exit the booth. "It's okay. There's no reason Guy can't appear at the event with one of his friends, right? We're not going to let these hyenas howl down our personal lives."

"Thanks, Dad."

"Okay, gents, let's remember it's only six weeks," Adrian said. When I sidled out of the booth, he grabbed me around the back and pulled me close. Then he jabbed my shoulder with his fist and shoved me away. "Now, get yer butt to work. You're late."

Outside, as Dad got into the Volvo wagon with Adrian, I asked him how he'd managed to keep quiet about the photographs all the way down from Sacramento.

"Liz...," he said, as if that were self-explanatory. "She wanted to talk about baby stuff. I didn't want to upset her, especially if nothing too bad comes of this."

Dad squeezed his tall frame behind the wheel and drove off with a wave. Though he looked kinda dumb in the clunky station wagon meant to symbolize his shiny new suburban life, I had to admit he was a man I admired. Pressed to the wall with a squad ready to fire, I would even admit that Paul Dimchek towered, in his casual, easy way, over a landscape of "moral pygmies." People thought he was a hero for his athletic prowess, his Olympian feats and commercial persona, maybe even his political convictions. But he was my hero because he always respected other human beings and their rights and prerogatives. That's why he'd volunteered in Mississippi and marched with the farm workers and side by side with Harvey Milk, stuff I'd always taken for granted, but I'd begun to see that most adults didn't give a damn the way my dad did. His respect for human rights was the foundation for most of his conduct. And when it wasn't, he had the grace to be embarrassed, like when he was screwing every available female in San Francisco or wheeling and dealing in West Oakland slums. I was embarrassed, myself, for having contradicted Adrian long ago when he'd told me Dad was only trying to become his own man, not a captive celebrity to pro volleyball or a pretty model for jock spray.

"Oh! I wish they wouldn't cover him over," one woman said to another in the parking lot. Turning to where I'd parked the Beast, I followed their gazes to the billboard across Burrito Boulevard. "He was sooo nice to look at."

There was Dad, staring down from an AgeErase ad I hardly noticed anymore. This blonde forever attacked his smiling face with her slender, painted nails. Letters large enough to be read from the freeway glowed:

FROM FINISH LINE. SLOW THE STRAIN OF THE GOOD LIFE.

Workmen swiped the surface with glue and slapped a fresh sheet over Paul Dimchek and his seductress. I leaned against the Beast and watched the process. The new billboard featured a smiling, relaxed Will Peters in front of a chalkboard covered in equations. He pointed toward a schoolgirl waving her hand. Above him glared the new message:

HERE'S THE FORMULA:
A VOTE FOR WILL PETERS =
A VOTE TO SAVE OUR SCHOOLS

SAVE OUR DAUGHTERS
SAVE OUR SONS

Chapter 9

THE FOLLOWING Saturday afternoon, instead of making an appearance with me at Dad's fundraiser, Janine and I studied by a babbling brook. Wade dozed next to Randy on a blanket on a mossy ledge above us. The two guys, who'd just met, had bantered about God all during our picnic, but now the great debate had ended in separate snores.

I liked being out in the boonies watching the creek ripple over rocks, the last sunlight dazzling everything. Taylor State Park had all kinds of streams and seeps, and we'd found a quiet bank all to ourselves, shaded by redwoods and firs. Paul and Penni loved this park when I was a kid and let me goof around in the stream, maybe at this very spot.

From her biology text open on the blanket, I was supposedly helping Janine study by quizzing her, but we kept being distracted by slow strands of conversation.

"I wish you'd apply to State next term," Janine said, smiling at our geeky conspiracy. "Just think, we could study like this any time we wanted."

"I know. I'm starting to regret my decision about Berkeley. It means I'm going to be stuck on the same side of the Bay as Dad and Liz."

"But maybe, after the election, there won't be so much tension. Plus, you'll have a baby brother to look after." On the thought, Janine patted her own bulging tummy.

By the end of that week, my plan to cooperate with Dad's campaign turned upside down, along with my high opinion of the candidate. Liz and her yes-boys on Dad's campaign team insisted "it would be for the best" if Wade "chose not to attend" the banquet. Or a thousand other mealymouthed variations on one: denying me my freedom of association, and two: taking back my invitation to Wade.

I waited and waited for Dad or Adrian to step in and squelch the yes-boys' doubletalk, but in the end I realized they were both just holding their breath. They wanted to disinvite my boyfriend too.

Dad's campaign workers, mostly inexperienced young volunteers, had spent the week cowering about possible news leaks from Will Peters's CREWP goons. The campaign guys were sure the *Oakland Tribune* would splash my picture across the front page any day. To hear them talk, that sneaky snapshot showed me feeling up Wade while gripping my Marxist submachine gun and howling down God and Family. By Thursday, when no photos had appeared anywhere, I shrugged it off, telling one volunteer, "It's a boring picture of two guys sharing a pancake after church."

The volunteer pointed out that it happened to be a *commie Black Panther* pancake and Wade was my *underage homosexual* love interest.

I told the guy that they'd become too good at making up what they thought the Committee to Re-Elect Will Peters would say. So good they could outdo CREWP at dreaming up *Bible-thumping right-wing* propaganda.

Besides, no one seemed to appreciate how Wade had been such a good sport about the photos. He even said, "Yeah, it stinks. But I'm just not as afraid of being exposed anymore. Since we got together, you know." I did know. With a real attachment to a guy like Wade, being gay transformed from secret lusting to open affection.

I hated that Wade's reward for letting his own privacy be violated was to be excluded at the door of Dad's fundraising banquet. So, instead of getting ready for Dad's event that Saturday afternoon, Wade and I joined Randy and Janine for this picnic in Marin County. I told Dad and Liz to sell my banquet plate to someone on the waiting list for an extra hundred-dollar donation, but Dad just stared at me with this numb, wounded expression. And to think, after that panicky after-school session at the Bull Ring, I'd gotten all gushy about how he was my hero.

I suppose I should have felt sympathetic, since it seemed like everybody was running Dad's campaign except him. But I didn't. I liked sticking it to him, I admit, and especially Liz, for being hypocrites and caving in to the antigay zealots. Besides, I just didn't feel like chomping on little sandwiches, Wade-less, in a roomful of back-slapping, middle-aged, white-bread, two-faced suburban Democrats.

Putting the biology text on a mossy rock, I stole a glance at Janine's swelling belly, pouching out her T-shirt. It made me smile, and I wondered if I'd ever feel as good about my half brother, the demon spawn about to spring from Liz's loins, as I would about Janine's baby. Both babies were due just before Christmas. "Right now," I told Janine, "Liz bounces between this loopy kind of mommy love and crazy empire building."

"Hasn't Liz had three miscarriages or something, though? She must be scared to death, Guy. And believe me, it's easy to get loopy when you're pregnant."

"I swear, for the first time, I'm more pissed off at Dad than Liz. He hid behind her skirts during all the baloney about Wade and the banquet."

"Maybe. But as far as I'm concerned, your Dad's a victim too."

"Come on, Janine. All he had to do was make a stand. It's not like he doesn't like Wade or wanted to hurt my feelings. He just did the easy thing and wimped out."

"But your dad's at the mercy of monsters, Guy. CREWP's got his campaign all distracted because you have a boyfriend. One who attends what they call a commie Black Panther Church. Meanwhile, Will Peters isn't going to be satisfied with firing every gay teacher in California. That's just the appetizer."

"Then what's the main course?"

"Gutting the whole public school system. CREWP won't stop until they've forced tax transfers to private Bible schools. Then they'll cut the universities, then public health. Then pollution controls. Good Lord, they might even close these state parks someday. I've heard enough from Gas 'n' Jesus to make my brain boil."

Sometimes I had to remind myself that Janine had an inside line on the campaign too. Harold Pruedhoe, old Gas 'n' Jesus himself, was her mother-in-law's new husband. Now Will Peters's biggest media cheerleader, Gas 'n' Jesus stared Janine down at Sunday family dinners before he drove to Sacramento to broadcast his talk show.

"I hope you won't be too tough on your dad, Guy." Janine pushed her wire-rimmed glasses to the bridge of her nose. "No matter how creepy the campaign gets, don't sacrifice what you and your dad have to politics."

An older woman of nineteen, the smartest person I knew, Janine seemed to navigate her passage through life better than anyone. If California seemed storm tossed by lunatic belief systems, Janine kept her balance. But she minded where the lifeboats were stowed. Stellar student, dedicated mother-to-be, Randy's backstage manager, she still lowered herself to counsel muddled high school boys. Once I thought she was lucky to have Randy, but now I knew it was the other way around.

A wolf whistle echoed above me on the high bank. Wade half hopped, half slid down a slope of redwood loam to join me streamside. I stood, excusing myself from Janine's perfect company, and took Wade's hand as he steadied to a halt upstream. He peered up the fern canyon, saying, "Man, it really is gorgeous around here."

I squeezed his hand and gazed into those big gem-quality sapphire eyes. "Yes, sir. Gorgeous."

Then we both got kind of embarrassed. We untangled our fingers and stood apart, looking upstream to where the creek cascaded over a granite ledge. Above that the creek disappeared into a jungle of ferns and madrone brush. We weren't used to being affectionate anywhere but that rank, dark ex-vending nook at Diablo View High School. This open-air paradise felt off-limits to our habit of secrecy between broken soda machines.

Pale rays filtered in through the redwood canopy, with the sun getting ready to set behind Drakes Bay and Point Reyes. Wade smiled and pulled me closer to him, his gaze searching my face as he said, "We've never kissed in broad daylight, bucko."

"Maybe we should try it. Just for laughs, pardner."

Ohhh yeah, I thought, our lips moving into each other's until Randy suddenly shouted from the top of the bank.

"Hey, boys, stop yer smooching." He laughed, hustling down the loamy slope. "This is a family park."

Yep, Randy Blanding, my First Big Love, could be a buffoon. I always tried to tune out that whole fuzzy period when Randy and I made out for hours, kiss-cheating on Janine until that day in April—my seventeenth birthday—when Randy told me she was pregnant. Ever since, he'd just been a friend and weekend work partner, a big, closeted, married gay goon.

"I've never had much interest in religion, myself," Randy was telling Wade, continuing their waking-from-nap conversation. "My mom always had to drag me kicking and whining to Sunday services."

"Makes me wonder," Wade told him, "how you can stand your stepfather's rantings."

"I've just drifted further and further from my mom and old Harold since they got married. 'Course I heard about Harold's Sunday show in Sacramento, but I never knew it was such a big deal. I thought it was a Bible babble thing."

"Yeah, Bible babble that's practically destroying Guy's father's campaign," Wade said, "and what's left of California."

"Yeah, Old Harold's totally out of control now," Randy said. "I hate what he's saying. But, geez, what am I gonna do?"

"Do you have any influence over him?" I asked. "Maybe through your mom?"

Randy laughed. "My mom? She's so blind in love with Harold Pruedhoe I barely know her these days. Did I tell you she's now bookkeeping for his radio and TV shows and his Holy Roller congregation? I've got almost nothing in common with her anymore."

"Still, if you're with the two of them, at Sunday dinner or whatever, you could speak your mind," I said. "He shouldn't be exploiting hatred of gay people, for starters."

"And you're going to be a family man, Randy," Wade said. "You have credibility."

"Geez...." Randy smiled, eyes crinkling. "Family man," he murmured. "It all feels so different when you're busy saving up for your baby and just getting the next meal on the table. I hate to say it, but I've hardly had a chance to follow politics this fall."

Funny that Janine didn't have any trouble following the news, I wanted to say, but I was determined to pursue something else. "Randy, come on, it's not like you're that removed from the gay world."

"What do you mean?"

"You're standing beside this stream," Wade said, "with two known homosexuals."

"At least two," I said. "Maybe more."

LATE SATURDAY evening, after I'd driven Wade home and was already back at Circe Circle atop Mount Olympus, the resident god and goddess arrived from the banquet I'd boycotted. As I headed downstairs for a midnight snack, I heard them unwinding in the sunken parlor. Dad tended to a fresh drink and undid his tie. Liz, in a killer pregnant-lady pantsuit and pearls, let her tea steep as she shuffled through a stack of junk mail that had been gathering on the coffee table. They were so absorbed in an ongoing conversation they didn't notice me. Still in no mood to engage with them, I was about to pad quietly back upstairs when I heard Liz say, "...and we should think about going to Mass tomorrow. And every Sunday."

That stopped me dead in midstep. *Mass?* I hadn't even heard the word mentioned by anyone in our family—except Granny—since the Early Pleistocene epoch.

Liz continued leafing through a glossy catalogue. "We could attend a different parish every week until Election Day. All around the district."

Dad just stared at her, then pressed the frosty tumbler of scotch against his forehead.

"That is what impressed me talking to some of the Catholic activists at the fundraiser tonight," Liz went on without looking up. "How perfect Sunday occasions are for casual campaign contacts. We could chat with new acquaintances on the church steps, when people are relaxed and feeling virtuous."

"I guess." Dad sighed. Now he massaged his temples with his forefingers. He must've had one of those deadly headaches brought on by a whole weekend of campaigning. "The only drawback about your plan to attend Mass is we'd have to attend Mass."

Liz finally looked at him. "Is that supposed to be a joke? Let me know when I should laugh."

"No, I mean it. At best, I always just endured Mass. Half the time what the priest said just made me mad. There were several years when Penni and I just went for Guy's sake. After his confirmation, when he called it quits, so did I. I was actually relieved."

"Aren't you the holy one."

"Give me a break, Liz! We'd both be lucky we were spared the Lord's lightning bolt if we crossed the church threshold tomorrow morning."

"I used to go to Mass in Munich."

"Yeah, about a quarter century ago."

"I have always felt church was more of a cultural activity, Paul. We should take advantage of our backgrounds. And religion is a political reality in this country."

Dad looked heavenward, his palms clasped. "Dear God, am I ever sick of political realities."

"I suppose it would take a miracle to persuade Guy to attend Mass with us."

I doubled back on the stairs, pretending I'd just started down. "Persuade me to do what?"

Liz turned in surprise, but Dad just smiled. Slightly, slightly, through a haze of ache.

"Play the good Catholic son," he said, "and go to Mass with Liz and me next Sunday."

"We have just been talking about how nice it would be if you attended with us, Guy."

Like usual in the wake of Liz's shamelessness, I stood there blindsided. "Sure. I'll see if Wade wants to come."

"Oh, please, Guy." Liz continued flipping through the mail. "But if CREWP has to spy on you, it would be better at a Catholic Mass instead of that fake Black Panther church."

It was all I could do to hold back the news that I'd finally kissed my boyfriend under the open sky. Sweet baby Jesus, where were *Tribune* photographers when you really needed them?

"And if you are able to sit through the Reverend Gladstone's rantings every Sunday," Liz droned on, "just to please Wade, could you do the same for your own father?"

"Are you actually going to start going to Mass again, Dad?"

He shrugged.

"Come off it, Dad. You too, Liz. You're the one who told me how the Catholics colluded with the Nazis in the war. And aren't you opposed to everything the Pope has to say about birth control and sex? The Pope thinks my soul's in a state of sin just by being true to my feelings."

"*Everyone* is in a state of sin, Guy," Liz said. "It has been true for eternity. According to the Church, we are born that way."

"Whoa! I take it back, Liz. I never could get enough of that good old-timey original sin."

Liz sipped her tea, staring at me as if I'd belched or something. Then she tore into an envelope, asking, "Guy, how long has it been since you've had a haircut?"

"An eternity." I was about to finish heading upstairs when Liz suddenly got up, her hand flying to the slight bulge in her stomach. In her other hand, she pressed the torn envelope against the folds of her blouse. She excused herself, assuring Dad she was all right, just a little nauseous, and hurried past me on the stairway.

Dad stood, wobbly, his tie wagging loose, his shirt's top buttons undone. He looked like an over-the-hill frat boy who needed to sleep off the party. "Okay, Guy, you can stand there and pass all the righteoussh judgments you want. It's your right. You're pure as the Sierra snow and you always have been. While dumb schlubs like me wallow in the sludge."

"What the hell did I say, Dad? What?"

He approached the foyer landing holding out his glass and taking each step slowly to avoid tottering. "I will go to goddamn Mass next Sunday and every damn Sunday until Election Day. I'll cut my goddamn hair and lock my goddamn gorgeoussh pregnant wife in my arm and smile for any camera I see. But just remember who I'm playing the goddamn hypocrite for. That part's not just a game, buddy." Heading upstairs past me, he used my shoulder for support. "It's not the high jump or volleyball or even party politics. Because the stakes are real. Think about what happens to gay rights in this state if I lose. Then laugh at me, okay?" He disappeared into the upstairs hall, in search of his gorgeoussh pregnant wife.

Dumbstruck, I stayed behind, stranded on the single step I'd made toward Paul and Liz's shag-carpet heaven above.

Chapter 10

Ms. Pullman passed out *Hamlet* toward the end of class. She smiled at our groans, then scrawled "Tragic Destiny" in huge letters on the board, her gray mop top shaking. "The tragic hero acts with determination, but he's undermined by forces beyond individual control." She turned to the class, pointing her chalk right at me. "It may surprise you that *Hamlet*—the famous masterpiece about a confused young prince scratching his head in a big castle—is not really about our own Guy Dimchek."

The other kids glanced at me with sympathetic smiles while Wade grumbled and pressed his knee against mine. Pullman had begun treating me to her satire as Dad's campaign heated up through October. Today, when she assigned our "free choice" student-led seminars, she told me I had a special prechosen topic: "Hamlet, True Son or Spoiled Brat?" But I didn't mind Pullman's torment, since the class was so small and close knit, and I knew she was rooting for Dad's victory.

After class, Wade and I ducked into the ex-vending nook's darkness. Wade slipped his arms around my waist and nuzzled my neck. "We shouldn't start anything," he whispered. "Especially since you have to run off to Oakland with your stepmother."

I nodded, bussing his ear.

"My dad's setting me up with this weekend hotel clerk job," he said. "I could start in a couple weeks. That means I'll be making room arrangements."

My *Hamlet* paperback dropped to the sticky concrete. Freed, I gripped Wade's jersey and yanked it from its tucked bondage in his jeans. Slipping under, I explored his warm, taut stomach. "Room arrangements," I murmured. "Please, arrange 'em, please?"

Wade shot back a hungry blue gaze. When I pressed him against a toppled snack machine, he started to unbutton my shirt.

I sighed. "We better not." I let go of his jersey and pulled away before he undid my lowest, most dangerous button. "I really do have to pick up Liz."

DAD HAD assigned me to accompany Liz to her appointment in Oakland right after school. She'd been summoned to identify confiscated Nazi art at the Army depot.

The letter she'd concealed and run upstairs with on Sunday evening was from the US Army Commission on War Art. When Liz was finally ready to explain, she just left the official memo on the kitchen countertop. The result of an accord with the West Germans, artists' American descendants would be allowed to choose one artwork and receive slides of the others. The display period for the entire West Coast would be a few afternoons in Oakland. The Army notified Lisabeth Binder Dimchek, as the only surviving member of the artist's family, to identify and review the portfolio, then make her choice before her father's artwork for the Nazis would be shipped to permanent storage in Pueblo, Colorado.

Dad didn't really explain why Liz needed an escort. I was instructed to be a gentleman, support my stepmother throughout the appointment, and usher Frau Binder Dimchek and her father's Nazi art back to Mount Olympus in the thick of rush hour. I'd stayed extra sour on Liz ever since Wade's banquet disinvitation. I knew it would be a pain just to be polite.

When I pulled into Circe Circle to pick her up, I was surprised to see the Porsche already out of the garage. The Porsche was parked at an angle across both garage openings, weird for meticulous Liz. I noticed a small dent right beside the driver's side headlight. The cornering lamp had suffered a puncture to its amber cover. Rust particles clung in the dent's crinkles.

This wouldn't have been any huge deal, except when I factored in a bizarre little moment from the night before. I'd avoided taking notes for my *Hamlet* presentation by watching the late news across from Liz. She napped deeply in neat, regulated breaths until a gunshot from a liquor store shootout news clip startled her. Still asleep, she muttered and shuffled. "It's dead, you know, Paul," she'd blurted, "I'm carrying death inside of me," then fell back to a full snooze.

Now, rather than finding Liz coifed and scented and appareled, tapping her toe in the foyer and ready to scold me for my tardiness, a second surprise. Liz, in jeans and a light sweater, barely looked up from the dining room table, where she wielded a pencil over a document. "Oh. Guy. Is it that time already?"

Yeah, I wanted to say, time stolen from my daily allotment of make-out minutes with my boyfriend. But I just asked, "You okay, Liz? What happened to the Porsche?"

She turned to stare at me, eyes magnified in her reading glasses, then turned back to her paperwork, waving her hand dismissively. "Some rusty car must have dinged it when I was parked at the Lucky super mart."

I waited for the rest of the story, especially for the legal and-or revenge fantasies she'd visit upon the anonymous weasel in the rust bucket who'd hit-and-run her precious roadster. But no, she kept twirlin' that busy pencil. She had her hair up in a ponytail, unevenly tied by a scarf, which wagged with every notation. "So...," I started, nonplussed. "Liz, are you sure you're all right?"

She chuckled without turning to me. "Guy, the car got dinged, not me. I am fine. And I will be ready to go in just a minute."

Reminding myself I was getting paid for the escort service, on CJ Properties' time clock, I grabbed a soda and tried to relax.

Liz sighed. "Sometimes I wish I had become pregnant at a more convenient time. This might be the right image for a candidate's wife, but it slows me down. Just when I need my energy for our campaign the most. Oh well." Now she shuffled the papers into a rough stack. "I have no hope of reviewing all this now. A lot of it is distressing. There is a terrible new twist. Our campaign needs to respond to Peters on Save Our Schools. And fast." Dropping the stack, she told me they were CREWP's forthcoming press releases that a volunteer had "obtained."

Whoa. Was that really kosher? Legal? Gripping my soda, I strained to remember my place—a mere employee, a mere stepchild— and gulped away the urge to speak.

NEITHER OF us was prepared for the humongous scale of the Army depot warehouse. We lined up beside huge cargo boxes, wearing plastic nametags draped over our necks like Catholic schoolkids' scapulars.

We'd already been patted down and ID'd and quizzed about our mothers' maiden names, then released through mesh metal walls. A narrow lane formed by the boxes squeezed maybe fifty invited families, some German-speaking, some mixing English and German, most speaking standard West Coast American. Most faces wore the same apprehensive, shell-shocked expression as Liz's. As we wandered closer toward a cage-like partition, soldiers with submachine guns stood guard at regular intervals.

Suddenly, in a burst of noise from the open warehouse doors, reporters maneuvered everywhere around the motionless soldiers and the family lineup, sometimes paired with camera operators. I saw tags for most local TV affiliates, the Bay Area and Sacramento dailies. In the rear of the crowd, I spotted the burly reporter who'd ambushed my dad. He caught my eye, narrowing his into a stony smirk.

"I had no expectation of this," Liz marveled. "I am not sure what is news here. The relatives of the painters, or the paintings, or both?"

"They're probably after mushy family moments and maybe tears."

I expected Liz to correct me and comment on how useful the media might be for the campaign. After all, a grown daughter seeing her dead father's confiscated art had to be at least as photogenic as Liz and Paul emerging from Sunday Mass clutching their missals. I steeled myself for the first reporter she would indulge. Instead, she said she wished she hadn't even come.

"The Army should have informed us of the true nature of this ridiculous circus." Liz actually traded places so she could hide between me and the wall, out of the media's sights. "I am glad you're getting so tall, Guy. Keep me blocked from view, all right? I am just not in the mood to be the Pregnant Lady Welling Tears Over German War Art."

What mood was she in, though? What was it like, her first sight of her father's paintings three decades after his death? He'd been a half-starved young artist on a Russian battlefield. Since Liz hardly knew him and was barely five when word reached Munich of his killing, she never had much to say about good ol' Conrad Binder.

"It is so difficult to keep in mind that my father was barely older than you, Guy, when he had to leave art school and serve in the Nazi war effort. He even looked like you in the old photos. Tall, slender. Too much wavy hair. Big toothy smile. Now that I'm older... thirteen, fourteen years older than he ever lived to be... and I look at you, I think how young he was. A schoolboy."

"Do you have any idea what he was like, Liz?"

"My mother, my relatives always pestered me with stories about his great aspirations. For his art and for me. So he was a dreamer. Not exactly the kind of soldier Germany needed. Meeting Russian fire with his paintbrushes." Her voice went low and hard with contempt. "Germany became a graveyard for dreamers and true believers."

Something spun out of balance in the universe, because I found myself half agreeing with Liz. She often said she had no use for "idealistic softness" and more and more cast herself in Dad's campaign as the "ruthless" one who would fight Will Peters's "brutes" in CREWP dirty trick for dirty trick. I understood her suspicion about true believers, all of 'em, the Moonies, the Panthers, the Maoists, the Bible-thumpers, the Nazis, and the con artists leading SELF. For the first time in months, I held common ground with my stepmother.

At last we'd reached the partition, where uniformed clerks ushered the press through a mesh metal doorway. The families too were herded into a presentation to learn the "epic story of Nazi War Art and the US Army's role in its rescue, restoration, and safe storage."

I started toward the presentation, but Liz balked, holding me back. She told a clerk, "I want to get out of here as quickly and painlessly as possible. I am a US citizen who's pregnant and tired and out of patience with waiting." She pointed toward the other doorway. "Are my father's paintings in there? Conrad Binder?"

So, along with a few other refuseniks, we were allowed "a preview" of what was behind door number two. Before I knew it, Liz was filling out forms while conversing in rapid-fire German with a curator, who handed her a portfolio and led us to an empty table. The curator explained that the Nazis originally wanted an artistic record of the war, a chronicle of victory in paint.

When Liz finally opened the portfolio and shuffled the watercolors between us, I could see immediately that this artist had defied his orders. Liz and I passed back and forth each hurried, masterful watercolor sketch in silence.

In blue-white drifts of blizzard, a haggard woman lay facedown, her bundle cast into another snowdrift. Blood trickled from the ear of a boy in uniform, prone in a frozen field, while a medic's wagon headed away, into a leafless woods. In a blur of snow, a soldier tottered forward at the point of collapse, shot from behind. Typical of them all, the composition was off center. Every wintry canvas cornered small, helpless figures.

We spent more long minutes, studying, shuffling, as the images coalesced and blurred. Solitary figures struggled without direction. Leftovers from lost battalions fled broken vehicles, mortal wounds, and abandoned corpses. A chronicle of absolute defeat. But amazing—as Penni once pointed out—how the artist's sense of beauty somehow salvaged what might have been gross horror. But Penni would have died of envy over Conrad Binder's watercolors. It made me kind of embarrassed that, here in comfortable peacetime, neither of my parents had recorded life with so much veracity. When truth and beauty came knocking at Penni and Paul's doors, they'd answered with hype, promos, and commercials.

The only exception to the landscapes of death was an oddly meticulous portrait of a little blond girl, about three, in a red dress. She had Liz's unmistakable big blue eyes. Liz regarded her image curiously, then set it aside. "How odd that this is mixed in with all these scenes of war. No one ever told me he had painted my portrait."

"Well, what do you think, Liz? Wasn't your father an amazing talent?"

She stared at the portrait. But she left it alone and reached for the staggering soldier in the blizzard. "Yes," she said, rising. "I expected draftsman-type pictures of tanks, and heavy equipment, and battlefield logistics. I had no idea. So he was a real artist, after all."

Liz completed more paperwork, signed more carbon papers in triplicate, claimed her single painting and slides of the others, and then, grabbing my elbow, urged me out. But the presentation had ended, and while families tried to enter the second gate, off-limits to the media, reporters harangued stray family members with questions.

Pressing our way down the corridor of storage boxes, I guarded Liz's chosen watercolor with my entire body and wove through the crowd like I was running offense in some new sport that finally blended art and football. At some point, though, when I was almost to the checkout beside the exit, I lost Liz.

I paced back to find her trapped in the company of the ex-*Tribune* reporter and current CREWP creep, along with a new character, another heavyset guy with press credentials, cameraman in tow.

"Hey," I called out to the ex-reporter, "aren't you working for Peters now? What are you doing here?"

"I still have my certification," he answered, shrugging. He signaled me aside with a nod. When I balked, he grabbed me by the arm, hard, but acted all chummy. His voice lowered, like we were old buddies, he explained, "I'm just here to cover the excitement for the campaign. Be sure to tell your stepmother how Will Peters was instrumental in working with the Army on releasing this art."

Like hell, I thought. But it was a good fake out, because now the other fake reporter had Liz's attention as he asked, "We keep hearing rumors, Mrs. Dimchek, that your husband is leading the opposition to Save Our Schools because your son is gay. Do you care to comment, clarify for us?" He pushed the mike in her face.

Panicked, I was about to yell to Liz that she didn't need to comment at all, but she looked at me imploringly, the roll of her eyes urging me away. Oh! That reporter didn't know I was there or who I was? Catching on, I decided to back away, behind the media equipment next to the checkout. Just as I slipped into my hiding place, all the other newshounds moved in to surround Liz. From there, my back to Liz's interrogation, I watched a bank of TV monitors from different stations transmit the interview, multiple images of Liz composing herself, clutching the transparent packet of slides, then hoisting her purse higher on her shoulder.

"First of all," she began, "my husband, Paul Dimchek, opposes the so-called Save Our Schools initiative because it is destructive of fairness and equality. This is another battle in the struggle for civil rights for every Californian."

"But what about your son? Opponents say Paul Dimchek is making this whole issue personal."

"It is personal, sir," Liz said. She began to walk away, while the reporter fought to keep the mike steady with her pace. "Our son is a student in high school, a minor. Nothing could be more important to us than his privacy and safety. Above all, sir, we want our boy to grow up in a California where every citizen has equal access to teaching and learning."

I watched Liz ignore the reporters' next questions, her composed figure receding away from the video screen. Then Liz reached for me, locked her arm in mine from behind, and hustled us through checkout before the cameras could follow. In a blitzkrieg of forward motion, Liz made sure her father's war art and her "boy," that tall wild-haired "son" of hers, safely reached the enormous doors.

Chapter 11

"GOOD FOR Liz," Leon said, watching a video clip of her Army depot performance for the cameras the following Saturday. "She couldn't have done any better if she'd been following a script."

Dad beamed, raising his beer to the screen. "Yep. Now everyone can see Liz's savvy for themselves. It's what I've said all along." He and Leon stood watching the TV in our family room while techies from the Foul Line film crew circulated in and out of the glass doors to the pool deck.

They were shooting two commercials around our pool that afternoon, "Pool Party," for Foul Line and "Father and Son" for the campaign. CJ office manager, Leon, would be an extra in both of them. Nothing like a handsome black guy to earn commercial goodie points and sex appeal. "Liz is incredibly astute," Dad told Leon, "when it comes to political marketing."

"It's downright scary," Leon said.

I was downright disappointed because the commercials' director had decided that Leon's little red Speedo was "too provocative" for the pool-party spot. He had Leon change into a pair of Dad's swimming trunks, dorky, baggy flower-print jams that concealed areas of extreme interest. To make matters worse, Leon was so naturally affectionate that he kept clasping his hand to my shoulder or swatting my butt to make a point. Someday after I'd escaped from Circe Circle and CJ Properties, I planned to return Leon's caresses—maybe in front of one of his girlfriends—with a big ol' soul kiss to establish that I wasn't in elementary school anymore. Anyway, the three of us stood there shirtless, watching the video loop of Liz defending my privacy and the Rights of All Californians for the fifth or sixth time. Meanwhile, Dad and Leon waited for the technical crew to finish preparing the cameras, sound, and lighting.

As surprised as I had been by Liz's forthright words that day at the Army depot, the surprises kept coming. Even though her on-camera opposition to Will Peters's Save Our Schools initiative got airplay on local news channels, the bigger story came out of right field. In weekend spreads featuring the War Art in Oakland event, the San Francisco and East Bay papers all seemed more fascinated by this "celebrity political neophyte's wife" whose "father painted propaganda for Hitler."

DIMCHEK WIFE REVISITS FAMILY'S NAZI PAST
ATTENDS ARMY DEPOT RELEASE OF GERMAN WAR ART

The state Democratic strategists were as stunned as we were, so much so that they hadn't figured out any official response. News people continued to call for comments or to probe for new angles on the story.

The next surprise was that Liz wouldn't be home at all for the filming. She'd already left for the city by the time Dad and I had coffee that morning, determined to spend quiet Saturday time getting caught up at Aspirations Limited, which no doubt was in discombobulation now that Penni managed things on Liz's days off. But that Liz would volunteer to miss the filming made an even bigger headline in my head. When had her old, controlling personality been body-snatched?

The third surprise truly baffled me. Despite the CREWP operatives' appearance at the Army depot and their plan to set off the Dimchek-gay-son alarm, no stories had appeared that hinted at my sexuality. Or my secret life as a white Black Panther, Marxist-Maoist Sunday cultist. Those negatives from my visit to Brethren Community Church stayed in CREWP's darkroom of scandal and blackmail, undeveloped. They were waiting, we figured, for the last weeks of the campaign. Blustering on TV news and paid ads, Will Peters turned up the antigay noise, stating that gay teachers were "a threat to every Californian's future" and were even "invading from the drug-infested, transvestite blocks of San Francisco into our safe suburbs." Will Peters had to find the photos of Wade and me irresistible. With CREWP willing to play dirty behind the scenes, I dreaded the day my inconvenient sexual orientation would be used to wound my father's body politic.

Especially because my "inconvenience" might go statewide. Most assembly campaigns didn't bother with TV ads since the broadcast areas were much larger than the districts. But Will Peters led state committees and had star quality as the next big conservative hopeful to replace funky Governor Jerry Brown. That meant Peters's big money antigay crusade reverberated from the Oregon border clear to Tijuana.

Peters not only had help from in-state screaming meanies like Gas 'n' Jesus but had CREWP's unholy alliance with Anita Bryant's antigay campaign in Florida, Save Our Children. His people had started running ads in all California media markets, promoting Save Our Schools. I cringed, imagining Peters's next round of ads would feature Wade and me, secretly filmed making out in our ex-vending alcove.

DIMCHEK SON CAUGHT
IN HIGH-SCHOOL-FAGGOTS' LOVE NEST
SUPPORT SAVE OUR SCHOOLS OR SURRENDER TO THE HOMOS!

Dad's campaign planned counterattacks. Using the same camera crew, actors, and extras, they were going to follow the Foul Line shoot with a political spot against Save Our Schools.

We followed Leon out for one last take of Foul Line's "Pool Party" commercial. One more time he'd mill around the pool deck, a beach ball crooked under one arm, a beverage in the other hand. He'd hover in the near background as the white actors in the foreground repeated their Shakespearian dialogue:

> WOMAN: They always say you can't buy happiness.
> MAN: They just haven't heard of Finish Line's new fall products.
> WOMAN: Come to think of it, darling, this SmoothChek lotion, with sunscreening emollients, makes my fingers feel very happy.

To be politic, Foul Line cut Dad from the new series of commercials, but it was funny as hell to see the lookalikes they hired to stand in for the candidate and his lovely wife—a tall, sandy-haired, blue-eyed hunk and a willowy, Nordic blonde. (*Her* dinky bikini, by the way, wasn't "too provocative.") Going for the national market, the new Foul Line theme sold the California Summer, how all North America could share Olympian Paul Dimchek's fabulous poolside lifestyle. With only two ingredients missing, the old Olympian himself and the California summer.

Since it was already October, the crew had to resort to tricks to make the slanting light and deep shadows seem like July. With the last take, they cut the yellow spotlights while prop guys removed the potted palms. It was time to film the campaign commercial in actual autumn light.

"Come on, Guy, we gotta hustle," Dad was calling from across the pool. "Get into your team shirt and comb your hair."

Though I'd been prepped in advance for my big scene, I didn't expect the political spot to follow so fast on the waving fronds of those vanishing palms. Suddenly the light was real, with harsh midafternoon shadows. Even though it was still warm, the Foul Line actors and extras covered their bathing suits under long pants and sweaters. Long tresses got pinned up in french twists or scrunched under caps. Their drinks got spirited away and replaced with teacups and coffee mugs so the extras could wander poolside, I guess, as sober prudes.

Dad joined me at the two tall director's chairs, with the house's balconies and castle doors as a backdrop but with the pool off camera. I treated him to one of my finest smirks.

"That Foul Line scene is a lot more true to your life. You know, drunken and half-naked around the pool."

"Har. Har. Hilarious, Guy." He reached over to smooth down my collar. "Everyone knows what a party animal I am. Amazing how I fit all that debauchery into fourteen-hour workdays."

A hair person assaulted us from behind, tamping down our too-wild manes. The sound checker wanted me to "Say anything" into the mike check.

"Okay. I feel dorky in this team jersey," I announced, hearing my words boom, amplified around the entire pool deck. "If it's meant to make me look like a jock, remember, it's *tennis*, the biggest fairy sport of all...."

Dad swatted my arm and tried to frown but laughed instead. "Now that you've got that out of your system, let's concentrate on our lines."

We'd both practiced the script earlier, and now, rehearsing with the teleprompter, I wasn't too concerned, except I didn't like our fake conversation much.

"FATHER AND SON"

FATHER: My son and I are glad to have this chance to say how indebted we both feel to California's public school teachers. I enjoyed the advantage of a great education in the Sacramento system. Not that I ever soaked up all the wisdom I was exposed to... but luckily my son, Guy, is a much better student than I was.

SON: I've been lucky too. As soon as I started public schools in San Francisco, I felt totally supported. And now as a senior, I've got excellent instructors at Diablo Vista High, especially in literature....

"And," I ad-libbed, "like, Bachelor Sewing Circle. And, you know, Conversational french Kissing. Okay, okay, you're right. It's not funny. I'm sorry. I won't say that when the cameras roll. I promise. Hey, Dad," I said, lowering my voice while the crew fiddled with sound equipment. "I've gotta tell you something. I promised Wade a long time ago I'd go to this fundraiser with him. At Gladstone's church. Tonight."

"What are they raising funds for? The Campaign to Torture Professors in Red China?"

"Yeah, that's my favorite. Plus, this fund to help little West Oakland girls study dance. They're going to perform this original ballet. We'll be in and out in less than an hour."

Dad rubbed his temples. "Guy... it's just so risky. You can go where you want, do what you will, but I can ask you to respect my judgment."

"Which is?"

"Understand that you're in a fishbowl for the next few weeks. Even if it's absolutely impossible that anyone is following you or snapping shots with a telephoto, conduct yourself as if it were possible. It's just a month, Guy. Then you're a free man."

"Not if you win."

"Nice problem to have, eh? Guy, isn't there some harmless excuse you can offer Wade? Can't you get together afterwards, go out for coffee?"

I didn't tell him we'd already been invited to stop by Penni's after the dance recital for dessert. "Not a beer?"

"Not funny. Heads up. It looks like the cameras are set to roll."
We redid our scene from the top, finishing with:

FATHER: It'd be a crime to deprive educators of
their rights.
SON: Not to mention students' rights. Firing some
of our favorite teachers won't "save our schools."

The second time we ran through it, while the cameras rolled and the houseful of coffee-swilling adults in the background smiled and nodded and muttered, Dad and I sounded more natural. I was developing a taste for performing feel-good propaganda.

A small man in a loosened tie and stained khakis showed up, looking haggard and bummed out. I thought he was a production manager unhappy with either the script or our line readings, but Dad called him by name and signaled him over. It turned out he was a state liaison to Dad's campaign, rumpled from a long meeting and the drive down from Sacramento.

"Paul," he said, squeezing in before the next take, "I'm afraid we've got more bad news."

"Worse than my wife being portrayed as a Nazi?"

"Well... we can clarify that, even turn it to our advantage, like I've told you, Paul. Play the hungry-war-orphan card, et cetera. Play up Liz's love for her adopted country, et cetera. But yeah, this is worse. Our sources told us about Peters's next move on Monday. CREWP's planning a big press event right in front of your son's school. He's asking every California legislator and every candidate from both parties to sign a pledge to protect the morality of all California school children."

"So what? I can sign that in a New York minute. I am so supportive of morality I can't spit."

"Naw, Paul, it's not that simple. There's detail buried in the pledge. 'Traditional, healthful expressions of human sexuality.' Not a word about homosexuality, but it's impossible to interpret except as a pledge to support Save Our Schools and dismiss gay teachers. I've got a copy of the full text in my briefcase."

"Well, if it's that asinine, none of the Democrats—and a good many Republicans—will sign it."

"Oh, Paul." The man's frown was pained, his brow furrowed deep. "We're sure," he went on, "that every sitting legislator and every candidate is going to put pen to paper as if this piece of crap were the Declaration of Independence."

Now I wondered if our paid political announcement would ever see the light of broadcast. Maybe it was all irrelevant now, Dad's whole candidacy. And why bother? Once we'd fired all the gay teachers, California would be golden again. Crime and urban squalor and poor parenting and pollution, along with bad cholesterol and toxic pesticides, would disappear if we banned the queers.

As we tried to absorb the strategist's news while attempting to give our best to the final take of "Father and Son," Liz must've entered at some point, leaning against an open glass door, observing our performance. In jeans and one of dad's shirts, tails out, tentlike on her curvy frame, she looked relaxed except for a spot on her forehead she kept dabbing with tissue.

When Dad noticed it was a fresh cut she tended, he pulled her aside, inspecting the wound.

"It is nothing," she emphasized, "nothing at all. There is a worse wound to the Porsche, Paul. Worse than that nick from before. This is a real dent, right over the front wheel."

"But what about you? Did you lurch forward, any whiplash?"

"Paul, I know you're worried about the baby. But I keep telling you, I am fine. The seat belt restrained me so that my forehead barely touched the steering wheel."

"Let's take you to the hospital just to be sure."

Liz laughed. "We must take the Porsche to a body shop instead."

As the crew struck the set and the extras drifted out, Dad had me nuke a cup of hot tea for Liz, whom he'd ushered to a sofa. She refused to lie down but allowed him to swab the cut with disinfectant. "It was that historical marker," she explained, as if anyone had asked. "I had to avoid an oncoming car. It dodged into my lane on the narrowest part of Casket Curve. I turned the other way and must have scraped the edge of that stone marker." She shrugged. "Maybe."

Maybe? I wondered, delivering her tea. Just as with the earlier "nick," she was oddly vague and calm. The Liz I knew would've gone for the other car in a high-speed chase.

"But until that, I had a wonderful day," Liz said, sipping her tea. "Very productive. I can get so much done at the office when no one else is around to recite self-help mottos." She actually winked at me. "And it looks like you've both had a productive day too. I enjoyed your last scene. It was very natural."

"I just hope it does some good," Dad said.

"I am sure it would have," Liz said, "but I am afraid this commercial might be beside the point now. I have just been waiting for Will Peters to try this stunt. His theater for the cameras. In front of Guy's school! What is it they say in card games, Paul? It is time to cut our losses."

"What losses?" I asked.

"Guy, we cannot let this pledge grow into an opportunity for Will Peters. The best thing to do is to let the whole issue die. Most people are not concerned about gay teachers one way or the other. It is all a ridiculous distraction, and we are playing into their hands."

I didn't know when Liz's mind had become so cluttered with poker metaphors, but I could see how Peters had upped the ante. Still, how was I supposed to reconcile Liz's new realpolitik with her fine, principled moment at the Oakland Army depot? When she said people's rights trumped *theater for the cameras*?

Dad clearly wasn't as struck by this as I. He leaned in beside Liz, smoothing back a stray hair and whispering something that made her smile.

I didn't want to flash, in anger, any of the objections I was holding close to my own poker face. I decided to follow Leon out to the garage and see what damage the Pioneer Monument could cause to German steel.

"HUNGER WAS the only serving at all the tables across our valley," intoned the schoolboy narrator. The stage lights glared across the stage at Brethren Community Church. They sharpened the contrast between his pointed Chinese peasant hat and dark brown face. "Doom blew as a frigid wind over our children."

After a Crop Failure dance, a Hunger dance, a Greet the Commie Officials dance, came my favorite, the Tractor dance. A cutout plyboard tractor slid on stage on schoolboys' shoulders. Dancing girls, grabbing red streamers from the steering wheel, did a farm-equipment maypole number, their pigtails taking flight as they skipped and high kicked. Then, using the crepe streamers as a goad, they led the tractor down furrows, which instantly produced delicious plastic corn.

So much for Socialist Realism. The stage went dark, and the plyboard tractor vanished with a few awkward thuds. When the lights came up, the little girls had exchanged their smiles for grim faces and their gay streamers for bayonets. The sharp ends were aimed straight at us. Being targets of fifth graders with wooden weapons inspired the audience to a hearty ovation. Wade smiled and nudged me to join in the clapping.

Reverend Gladstone bounded onstage to soak himself in the girls' glory and remind everyone to drop their extra contributions into cans conveniently held by hulking Panther types stationed at each exit. "We can't stay enriched without riches, folks!" he shouted over continuing applause. "Open your hearts and your wallets to these children!"

I followed Wade out but didn't add a dollar to his contribution. One of the bereted bruisers shook his can at me as I brushed by. I shrugged at his scowl—Jesus, I'd already paid precious bucks to see the damn thing. "Somehow," I told Wade, "I really doubt that all this money is going for the girls' dance class. And I'm not sure West Oakland needs a red tractor, so what do you think it's for?"

"Man, I think you're a terrible cynic."

"They're using little girls to raise money for their commie empire, and *I'm* a cynic?"

"Is it so hard to believe that Gladstone is really a benefactor, Guy? With no hidden motives? A holy man in the true sense of the word? Man, can't you see what he's done for this neighborhood?"

I sighed. The housing authority had condemned and demolished a whole block of infested slum dwellings two blocks away. CJ Properties was damn lucky no one had inspected their apartment house recently.

I was afraid Wade would become disgusted with my so-called cynicism. I sure didn't want to fake him out, though, declaring beliefs I didn't hold. It was like I had to be true to my faith in nothing. But I sure as hell didn't want to lose the guy I was crazy about because he thought I was a moral zero.

We crossed to the Beast across the dirt lot just as a boy trapped an alley cat under a shopping basket. As Wade scolded the little squirt and stooped to free the caterwauling beast, I felt even worse. People going to their cars stared at us, tsk-tsking, as if we were the cat abusers.

This is what I wanted, right, spending time with Wade? I just happened to attend tractor ballets on dates because I was involved with a guy who was good at heart, while mine pumped nothing but bile and confusion and defiance.

Wade held the cat and soothed it with kindly murmurings. I kicked the damn wire basket.

IMMEDIATELY AFTER the tractor ballet, we had coffee and cake with Penni and Lester. When I foolishly told Penni I'd be in Oakland on Saturday night, she'd insisted, intent on meeting Wade. She promised "something tasty," as if I hadn't learned a single thing in seventeen years.

In fact, she served us a nonwheat, sugar-free cake in her Rockridge kitchen. Flavor was as scarce as Lester. "I thought you said he'd be here, Mom."

"Lester has an afternoon thing with his son and daughter I'd forgotten about. But he'll be here shortly. How's the cake, Wade?"

"Interesting, ma'am." Wade smiled and shoveled another bite. "I reckon."

I laughed at Wade's cowboy manners around adults. I'd already set my inedible wedge aside, claiming that we'd had refreshments at the church dance recital, a heaven-sent white lie.

"So... Mrs., uh, Dimchek?"

"Penni, please, Wade." Penni smiled, batting her eyes. She rested her chin on her fist to stare at my adorable, jug-eared boyfriend.

"You're following a macrobiotic diet?" Wade managed to try a third bite, though the sample he forked was hardly more than a few crumbs.

"Sort of," Penni began. "Actually, I'm moving into combining macrobiotic with a high-protein, high-energy regimen. I'm working out now, following the advice of my physical consultant, and starting to jog a few times a week. That's why this cake uses soy flour. But carob is the secret."

The secret entrance to The Third Circle of Dessert Hell, where the cakes make sinners beg for lima beans and brussels sprouts?

Despite her regimen, Penni didn't look so hot tonight. When she wasn't blushing over one of Wade's compliments, her complexion went pasty. As her ponytail unraveled, her hair hung in clumps around her ears. Though I'd expected her to get dolled up for Wade—like she did for the postman and meter reader—she wore this burgundy outfit she called a "running suit," zippered chintz that made her look like a throw pillow on starvation rations. I wondered if Penni's new kick was some crackpot diet that had her jogging while starving.

"This *physical consultant*," I asked, "does she have some special theory on fitness?"

"*He*'s into vegetarian proteins and holistic, cardiovascular exercise. Really, Guy, he's changed my life. I needed drastic intervention. You may not realize it, Wade, but I was prematurely withering into a little old lady."

"For Pete's sake, Mom," I cried, adding another white lie. "You look great, like always."

"Every day I praise God there are parts of my body that people never see."

God earned my praise when Penni changed the subject. She pumped Wade with questions about his family and involvement in the Brethren Community Church, which, though she'd never attended, she claimed to "value as a positive force for West Oakland."

When there was a rap at the front door, Penni sent me to answer so she could extract more choice revelations from Wade. There, under the porch light, stood Lester, hands scrunched in coat pockets, looking cold and sheepish.

"Forgot my keys," he admitted, shaking my hand. "Sorry I had to miss this."

"You didn't, Lester." Calling back to the kitchen, I announced his arrival. "Hey, there's still plenty of cake."

"I'm sure there is." He smiled, but it was brief and sad.

"So is everything okay, with your kids and all?"

Lester nodded. For some reason, we kept standing there, near the doorway in the dark living room. Lester touched my arm, speaking just above a whisper. "It wasn't easy, though, Guy. I had to tell my kids I'm leaving town for a while. Well, I didn't *have* to tell them. I *chose* to."

This was SELF talking, that instant revision of verbs—meant to "take responsibility for one's own actions through mindful language"—but the hesitance and sadness in Lester's tone couldn't have been more real.

"So," I asked, "are you doing a visiting professor thing next semester?"

"No. Actually, I'm resigning from the college next term. That's what I chose to discuss with my kids. I'm headed for LA to become a certified trainer for SELF."

"Wow. Wow," I stalled, struck dumb, thinking of Penni's dishevelment. I realized, despite her motto-muttering, she'd been drifting away from SELF while Lester just kept getting more deeply involved. "How's Mom taking it?"

"Not well. I'm sorry to say that, because you know how much I care about her. But shared communication has not been our strong point lately. Who knows, maybe the time apart will do us some good."

"So you're really moving to LA? You're not going to teach fine arts anymore?"

"No. SELF insists, rightly, that trainers give up their ties to old careers. 'Past life, past. New life, newborn in the now.'"

Now, there was a saying for the ages. Poor old Lester! I remembered that he was wearing a Mao T-shirt the first time I saw him last winter and realized that my aversion to Mao & Friends went back before I ever saw a tractor folk opera. But I'd always liked Lester anyway, because I sensed his resistance to his own bullshit. I knew this decision had probably been among the hardest of his life. It was going to banish him from his career, his children, and his sweetheart to exile in Southern California for who knew how long, with who knew what result. Maybe when SELF spat him out, "certified," he'd just be another slick, babbling automaton. Why would a mellow art teacher want to become that?

Before I could think of anything intelligent or sympathetic to say, Lester pulled me into a gentle hug. For just a second he cried, his face buried in my shoulder. Then he took a big breath, clasped my shoulders with his hands, and headed into the bright kitchen.

While I listened to the introductions and Lester's attempt to force a hearty, welcoming tone for Wade's sake, my gaze caught the spread of East Bay lights out Penni's plate glass view to the west. A grid of boulevards dazzled toward the Oakland docks. I stood alone for a moment as the three—a Christian communist, a failed food faddist, and a self-improvement cultist—chatted in the kitchen. Before I joined them, I watched a yellow flare waver in the far distance over the waterfront. Watching it doused in the dark water, I imagined that some other misfit like me, barely afloat, had held up a beacon. He wasn't trying to declare some new faith or life-changing regimen. Before he went under, he just wanted to signal doubt, and second thoughts, and plain old wonder.

I THOUGHT Penni's cake and Lester's tears would pretty much mark the end of our big Saturday night, but I thought wrong. Way wrong. In fact, that night would mutate into a sleep-deprived, homeless odyssey that was just beginning.

To begin with, when I dropped Wade off on Camino Gordo, he practically begged me to come inside with him. His parents were throwing a small party for a missionary couple returning from Asia. I told Wade I'd be out of place, not to mention a potential embarrassment, given his mother's bluntness.

"You? Embarrass me? Guy, it's not like that. All anyone needs to know is that you're my friend. Which you are."

"I know, but your mom's suspicious. She's always insinuating that we're 'inseparable.'"

"Man, she can insinuate all she wants. You know, I was hoping to hold off coming out to my folks until I graduated. But being open with your mom, just now, that was so cool."

I'd parked the Beast a ways down the lane, beyond the station wagons and sedans lined up for the party. But even from this distance, we could see the square of light cast on the Harts' long front lawn, the shadowy flickers of guests passing back and forth in the bright living room window. I took Wade's hand and squeezed it. "I'll do whatever you want. I don't mind keeping quiet about our wild sex life."

"Yeah. It's funny, isn't it? We don't really have anything to hide."

"Other than the way I feel about you?"

Even though we were light in the loafers clear down to our soles, we were still two ordinary males, and this kind of talk was not easy. Saying the very words "I feel" paired with "about you" scared the hell out of me. I felt myself freezing up.

Now Wade squeezed my hand. "We can talk about it some other time, Guy. It's cool."

"I've just felt even more mixed-up than usual tonight. There's just so much crazy stuff going on with my family that's totally outside my influence. And meanwhile I've felt so intense. Inside me, when it comes to you. And it gets all mixed up with sex. Because I'm so attracted to you, and I like you so much, and…. Jesus. I'm babbling."

"Well, don't stop there. I like what you're babbling about."

"This is totally new." Virgin territory, I thought, except for messing around a little with Randy, which didn't really count. "I mean, between dreaming about having a boyfriend and actually having one, I have to cross a high wire."

"But you're really good at being a boyfriend, Guy. Like tonight. I knew that dance recital was the last place you wanted to be. And I'm pretty sure I know why you came to church with me in the first place. You just felt bad because nobody else signed up at orientation."

"No. It was more because of your eyes. And your ears. And your butt."

"Yeah, whatever. I'm just glad you've been willing to go through it. With me."

Now I felt ashamed of my irritation during the kids' tractor ballet. "Listen, I'll go inside with you."

"Great. I hate my parents' parties, but I've got to say hello to the guests of honor. They're my godparents. Anyway, if they're all loaded enough, we can score a beer or two."

I knew from Wade's laments that his parents' social life had taken an odd right turn from the Harts' Berkeley days as do-gooder missionaries. The couple they were welcoming back were the last of their old friends still involved with those Christian-socialist projects overseas. The din of the party spilled through open windows as we walked through the side yard on our way to the kitchen door.

The kitchen was packed with people, all seeming to talk at once in loud voices. Out of the pandemonium, the returning missionaries rushed to Wade to embrace their godson and gush over how much he'd grown in the last two years.

Meanwhile, Felicia Hart pulled me aside, pouring a punch. "It's virgin, don't worry, Guy. Far be it from me to corrupt my boy's best friend." She poured another one, this time adding a splash of vodka, for a passing guest, then gestured me farther toward an unoccupied corner. "Anyway, I've been meaning to thank you for being such a good friend to Wade. I always wonder about him, you know."

"Wonder what?"

"He's been such a loner. I mean, for such a smart, good-looking guy. Don't you think he's good-looking?"

Wade's mom, fueled by her lethal punch, was even more aggressive than usual. She'd cornered me too. I gestured to Wade, who was still chatting with his godparents, in hopes he'd hurry to my rescue. "Wade's an all-around good guy, Mrs. Hart."

"But this infatuation...."

"What infatuation?"

"With the Brethren Church, for God's sake! His father and I rue the day we ever took our kids there when they were little. We thought we were so progressive. So hip, you know, in those days. And now Gladstone's gone off the deep end. Guy, he's a goddamn Maoist!"

"A Maoist? Who?" Laughing, Wade's godmother appeared beside us, her arm in his.

"Betty, things have changed while you were gone," Felicia Hart said. "Gladstone's turned Commie Commissar, and Wade's been sneaking to his services. Every Sunday now."

"Sneaking?" Wade asked, arching a brow.

"I just said that for dramatic effect, dear. But be aware I'm not sending you there with my blessing."

"You're not sending me at all, Mom. I'm going of my own free will."

"And you're complaining, Felicia, because your son's going to Sunday services?" Betty laughed, topping off her punch with a shot of vodka.

"I'm going to need a goddamn deprogrammer, Betty, full-time. And maybe for poor Guy, here, who's been joining Wade for Gladstone's easy-listening totalitarianism." Felicia nudged me. "Have you met Wade's new friend? He and Wade have become very, very close in a very, very short time."

Betty smiled but seemed nonplussed by Felicia's innuendo. She was a thin, pleasant woman with long, kinky graying hair. Her prominent gold crucifix seemed incongruous with her dressy-hippie shawl and peasant dress, but then the Harts' whole scene mystified me. It was hard to imagine what would have fit with this household, and I was getting more and more jumpy about Felicia's suspicion about Wade and me. So I tried to change the subject. "You don't need to worry about getting a deprogrammer for me, Mrs. Hart. As Wade will tell you, I'm a strict nonbeliever."

"Good for you, Guy!" Felicia cried, clinking her punch cup to mine. "I'm so glad Wade hasn't corrupted your cynicism."

"Mom, come on," Wade said.

"No, I mean it. It takes guts to face this world without Marx or Jesus these days. It's just that when I look at you two boys, I have to wonder, Guy, who's corrupting whom."

Before I could absorb this attack, Wade's father and godfather carried their talk into our corner.

"It's getting real ugly over there," Wade's godfather was saying. "What's happening in Cambodia makes Mao's China look like a Baptist picnic. This bastard Pol Pot is ready to massacre the country's entire educated class. He's saying it loud and clear, but nobody gives a flying fuck. Pardon my French."

"In any language," Betty added, "if we stand by with our eyes closed, Cambodia's going to be the next Holocaust."

"See, Felicia?" Wade's father said. "Betty and Tom are still engaged with the world. Remember when we were like that?"

"Before you started sneaking Bloody Marys for breakfast?"

"I've got to get my fun somewhere, darling," Mr. Hart said.

Wade practically yanked me from my entrapment between his mother and his godparents. "Excuse us, folks," he said, hustling me back through the kitchen door.

"I'm sorry, Guy." We paced a distance under the full moon, crunching fallen oak leaves. The moonlight was so intense that each crumpled leaf cast a distinct shadow. "I guess my mom's plenty loaded."

"Listen, it doesn't look like anyone will miss either of us. Why don't you come to Circe Circle with me? I think Steve Martin's hosting *Saturday Night Live*, and there's that little TV in my room."

We started walking toward my car. "Thanks, Guy, but I better go back. Eventually they're going to notice I'm gone. Maybe I can lure Betty and Tom away from my folks. I'd like to hear more about their mission."

I realized he actually had a believer's investment in his godparents' work. Fresh from Felicia's firestorm of negation, I respected Wade's faith more. "Okay," I said, leaning against the Beast. "See you for church tomorrow morning?"

"Aw," Wade said, his gorgeous smile—I swear—reflecting the blazing moon. "First thing. You got a date, bud."

I pulled him into a kiss.

He responded, as always, with an ardent counter pucker that sucked me into ecstatic tongue wrestling. But this time he aborted it, pulling back.

"Before we went in," he whispered, "in the car, remember? You started to tell me how you feel."

"Yeah. Your mom's right. I want to corrupt you."

"Get serious, man. I feel a certain way about you too. Maybe you feel the same way?"

"Uh-huh. Pretty much." I reached for the back of his neck, trying to continue the kiss.

But he only bussed me quickly and paced back. "I'm just kinda reeling from this, Guy. This is big. Maybe we can figure out how to talk about it, after church or something?"

"Ain't no holy mystery!" I blurted, keeping my voice low. "It's *love*, Wade."

He paced farther away, laughing. "I know, I know!" He did one 360 twirl, a moon dance, showing off his tiny cowboy waist and perfect rear end, then headed back to the house. "Good night."

Life would probably not have many flawless moments, so I leaned back against the Beast, dizzy in the tug of Wade's presence. I shut my eyes to memorize his moonlit swirl, an image I wanted to store in my inner eye forever.

That's when I heard a distinct mechanical whirl, oddly emanating from the bushes across the narrow lane. Then an even more distinct "Fucking little fag" followed by "Sh!"

I knew exactly who it was. I was more pissed off that it had wrecked my flawless moment than for any violation of my privacy. I snuck across the lane, kicking back a waist-high hedge.

Two big guys leaped back, hurtling into a neighbor's wide lawn. I sprinted after the heavier, slower one with the camera and easily overtook him, grabbing it. For a second, I exulted, imagining the fun of developing the confiscated film and the heroic tale I'd relate to Dad and Adrian.

But heroics were knocked out of me in the first blow. With a hard metal smack across my upper back, the camera sailed out of my hands. From another direction, rough hands shoved me face-first to the ground. My face thumped against damp grass. My tongue licked a bloody, warm, iron slick. From both directions, boots kicked each hip. "This is what happens to queers in the real world, kid."

Last thing I saw, two pairs of boots stomped across the lawn. A clumsy, heavy-breathing ballet nobody would pay three cents to see.

My hip bones ached so bad when I tried to pull myself up, I almost howled. Everything went black. How'd these thugs from CREWP shut off the moon?

I CAME to after a couple minutes. I expected retreating taillights at the far end of Camino Gordo, but there was nothing but an empty lane in the moonlight. Though raised voices and laughter floated over from the Harts' party, nothing stirred around me. It seemed like the temperature had dropped. My hips killed me when I hobbled up. My upper back, just below my shoulders, hurt like hell along a straight welt of pain. What had that been, a tire iron?

I drove home practically comatose, not as much from the body blows and hard face-plant as from numb bewilderment. God, were my dad's opponents really that mean and desperate?

I was scared too. I admit it. I could understand the sneaky photography, as much as it disgusted me, and the sly blackmail they had planned. But no matter what the stakes were statewide, I never expected CREWP—in a suburban assembly campaign!—to stoop to assault. Fag bashing. Did my attackers attend some right-wingers' thug school, Smear the Queer Academy, where they'd learned how to focus a telephoto lens, then slam a crowbar whack to the back and kicks to the hips? Perfect, since the wounds wouldn't be obvious. They wouldn't even break the skin. It'd just deliver a stars-and-bars spangle of bloodless, blinding pain. As I winced and blinked my watery eyes, Burrito Boulevard's new Save Our Schools billboard blurred by, doubled up, gloating.

I negotiated Casket Curve, knowing I was in the doghouse for attending the ballet at Gladstone's church. Though I considered using the attack as a ploy for forgiveness and sympathy, when I pulled up to the house and saw Adrian's Jag in the driveway, I decided to save the story for later. My brain was as sore as my back. I'd grab a few aspirin and sink to my bed. Maybe Steve Martin would cheer me up. *Well, excuuuse me!*

I slipped through the garage door into the kitchen, where Dad kept an emergency bottle of aspirin for his hangovers, whether from too much scotch or politics or too much of both together. Since Dad, Liz, and Adrian looked so intent, hunched around a coffee table in the family room, I hoped I could get away with a wave and a good-night.

It looked as if they'd been talking for hours. Still in his bathing suit for the poolside commercial, Dad wore a green campaign sweatshirt, CHECK DIMCHEK. He filled a shot glass with Johnnie Walker. Liz wore the same jeans and shirt and had a tiny circular Band-Aid on her forehead. To the mountain of teabags on a saucer, she dropped another. Adrian, though, was in a dress shirt, slacks, and tie, sipping on a beer. He'd been busy with legal damage control somewhere.

I slugged back the aspirin while I stared at Conrad Binder's painting, propped against a corner chair, of that young soldier collapsing forward into a Soviet snow bank. I called good night across the kitchen counter island.

But all three stopped talking to stare at me. "What's going on with you, Guy?" Adrian asked. "You look like hell."

"I hope you haven't been drinking," Liz said, not accusatory so much as hopeful.

"Just coffee at Mom's and punch at Wade's parents'." I started for my room.

"You've got huge grass stains running up your jeans," Dad said. "Are you all right?"

"Wade and I were… horsing around. Wrestling on the lawn. Well, see you in the morning."

"Just a minute, Guy," Dad said. "Grab a soda and come over here. What we're talking about involves you. Big time."

"Oh, Paul," Liz said. "Do you have to be so dramatic? Guy looks like he needs to get to bed, anyway."

"No, Liz, Paul's right," Adrian said. "We've talked about this from every angle we know. But Guy's really at the heart of this, and we need his perspective."

"But that is my whole point!" Liz seethed, instantly vexed, as always, whenever any ordinary mortal dared to veto her ideas. "It is for Guy's sake that we cannot personalize this. We should be protecting him from these monsters. Monsters who will attack the minute we approach the gay issue as a family matter."

"That's precisely why Guy should give his input," Adrian said evenly, "because it is a family matter."

"Yes, Adrian," Liz said, crossing her arms. "And unlike you and everyone else who has been overreacting to Will Peters and his ridiculous pledge, Guy is actually a member of our family."

Once again, as with the TV interview at the Oakland Army Depot, I marveled at how Liz embraced me as "family" when it suited her argument. So I changed my mind. I wasn't gonna miss this for anything.

"Don't forget, Liz, that Adrian's my godfather." I eased myself carefully onto a footstool, cringing so I wouldn't yowl in pain and, agonizing, positioned my back into its usual slouch. "Adrian was always part of the original Dimchek so-called family," I said, trying to imitate my normal, cheerful sarcasm. "He claims to have wiped strained peas off my chin."

"I wiped the other end off too," Adrian said. "That's gotta count for more than blood."

Liz just stared ahead, arms still crossed, her tea steaming. "A charming walk down memory street, but—"

"Memory lane," Dad said flatly. "Guy, we've been hashing over what I should do about signing Will Peters's Moral Pledge. Liz thinks it's harmless, but Adrian—"

"We can't mimic the enemy," Adrian jumped in, "and hope to win. I know I asked you to stay quiet on the gay front for the campaign's sake, Guy. And for the sake of your minor status if nothing else, I'd still advise that. But we're the adults, and we can't put our principles in the closet."

"It's no different for me," I said. "Should I put my principles in the closet just because I'm seventeen?"

"Okay." Adrian smiled. "I figure we're not going to win a single vote in this district if we just offer a milder version of Will Peters and CREWP and his statewide machine. The people who are going to vote for us would want Paul Dimchek to be proud of his son and stand up for everyone's rights."

"I like this line of reasoning," Dad said. "But I'm not very proud of my son tonight." He glanced at me, contempt crinkled in his brow. "Considering he completely blew me off."

"I'm sorry, Dad. I regretted it, okay? The whole program was kind of a waste of time."

"Not to the campaign news editors," Liz said.

I was going to say that no one snapped any shots of us at the tractor ballet but stopped myself. How did I know that? After all, those goons had probably been following Wade and me all evening.

"Their pictures—their blackmail—they're not going to matter," Adrian said. "Not if there aren't any secrets to keep. That's why I think we preempt Peters's Moral Pledge schoolyard press conference Monday in a big way. So here's what I'm proposing, Guy. A while back, Harvey Milk invited Paul to a fundraiser for his antidiscrimination initiative."

"Which we ignored," Liz said, "because Harvey Milk is mixing politics with a Halloween theme party for transvestites and sadomasochists and street people from the Castro District."

"Sounds like fun," I said. "I met him when Dad was precinct captain for Ashbury Heights, remember? Harvey Milk is a great guy."

"Anyway, it's tomorrow night," Adrian said, "and I think Paul should go in support of Harvey's proposal. If we finesse a little, I'm sure Harvey will give Paul some podium time. That's when Paul exposes Peters's pledge for what it really is. He announces that as a matter of principle, as a matter of civil rights and respect for California's educators, he's not going to sign. Even if he's the only candidate in the state to refuse."

"This gay business is going to sink us," Liz said.

"But that's the beauty of it, Liz," Adrian said. I could tell he was straining to remain calm. "The only gay thing about this is the venue. Paul completely skips over the connection to Guy and makes this an issue about human rights and education."

"Are you serious, Adrian?" Liz leaned forward, pointing at the TV set's cold green eye. "If Paul crosses Harvey Milk's threshold, the local news stations will lead with the image of our Olympic hero, our Claimjumper champion, our Finish Line man, in the arms of the gay supervisor. Along with his drag queens and sex fiends. We do not need that distraction when we have much bigger battles to fight. Instead, we keep concentrating on real family issues like better schools. And especially the ecology. It is right there on your sweatshirt, Paul, 'For a Greener California.' Remember how that was Bart Morgan's legacy, Adrian? The environment got Paul into this candidacy in the first place."

So Liz, whose idea of a nature outing was to park her Porsche in the shade of a pruned sycamore on her way to the Emporium, suddenly talked like a green crusader. I would've laughed if it weren't for my cracking back.

But Adrian wasn't so amused. "We've already got the environmental vote, Liz. We can't let Peters have the votes on everything else."

"No," Liz insisted flatly. "We quietly surrender on Save Our Schools. Let him have that victory."

Adrian rose with his emptied beer. I could tell he was both flabbergasted and mad as hell, and for a second I wondered if he was going to clobber my pregnant stepmother with a bottle of Heineken. Instead, he carried it toward the kitchen and leaned against the counter. He sighed.

"Liz. You can't have it both ways. You can't advocate the high ground, then stoop to Peters's tactics."

"You can have things five ways in politics, Adrian, if you refuse to be naive. If we get this silly pledge and even Save Our Schools out of the news, the voters will forget about it when they go to the polls. We will probably be able to kill it in the courts, anyway. So we play his game, a little. We cut a deal with Peters."

"Where does this kind of thinking stop?" Adrian dropped the bottle in the trash with a sharp thud. "At what point would we *not* cut a deal with fascists?"

"Adrian!" Liz rose to her feet. "You take that back!"

"I just asked a question, Liz." He started for the foyer, then, on the steps, turned back. "And I've got another. At what point did you become the self-appointed queen of this campaign?" Adrian reached the front door. Before he slammed it behind him, he called to Dad, "I'll call you tomorrow about the Harvey Milk thing."

Liz seethed, and if Dad hadn't caressed her arm, then pressed it, I think she would have hurled her teacup at Adrian's departure. "That settles it, Paul," she said, constrained in his grip. "That makes the last of my dealings with Adrian. I was just waiting for him to play the Nazi card. How cruel of him, Paul! After the media just dragged my father through Nazi accusations."

"Come on, Liz," Dad said. "He just said *fascist*."

Liz wriggled from Dad's arm, carrying her teacup to the kitchen. "It will be political suicide to attend Harvey Milk's party," she called from the sink in a milder tone. "We have other campaign events to choose from tomorrow, especially the teachers' union banquet. And that's on this side of the Bay, Paul, where we belong. So, you can take Adrian's advice, or take mine."

"Adrian was still way out of bounds with that fascist crack," Dad said, "but I know him. He'll mull it over and apologize. Liz, nobody has any fixed roles in this campaign. We've valued everyone's talents all along. We've done our best. Let's just keep it that way."

"Fine." Liz dried her hands. "You are always so open to so many talents and ideas. Except for mine. Adrian will be happy leading you into some homosexual orgy in the Castro. That does it, Paul." She tossed the dish towel with a flourish and headed for the stairs. "You can attend as Adrian's whipping boy. Won't that make a nice impression on the thousands of voters who find homosexual acts disgusting?"

Dad moved in the direction of the stairs but didn't follow her up. "I never said I would go to Milk's damn rally, did I? I know it would be suicide...," he called up, then found his glass and belted the last of his scotch back. "I planned on going to the teachers' union all along."

"What do you think, Dad?" When I stood, pain stabbed me so hard I had to shut my eyes. "So, you gonna sign the Moral Pledge?"

Sinking back to the couch, Dad poured himself a fresh whiskey. No ice, just the pure poison. "I'm just listening to both sides."

"Yeah, I noticed you didn't have much to say."

He sipped, staring at me, then pinched the space between his eyebrows, the sure sign of an oncoming headache. He didn't say anything, and I was sure he was waiting for me to go to my room and get out of his hair. With everyone around him so passionate, so crusading, it must have been hard to maintain his bland center.

He really was a handsome guy, sitting there, giving the impression—so slick and vivid in commercials—that something interesting was going on underneath that Olympian brow. I'd spoken my role through several takes of his predigested commercial script that very afternoon, though it seemed like a different century ago.

A sensation started up my spine, igniting the ache across my back, then burning toward my misfiring brain. Disgust alloyed with anger. Didn't he have a damn thing to say after all that? Was he so used to my giving in that he took it for granted? "You're going to have to decide some response to your gay son dilemma," I said, still standing above him, trying to ignore pulses of shooting pain. "'Cause they got some juicy pictures tonight. Me kissing Wade, I guess."

"At that damn church?"

"No. Wade's house. I was kissing him good night. When I tried to confiscate the camera, they really whacked me. They got away with the film."

"Once again, thanks a lot for obeying my wishes."

"Thanks a lot for giving a rat's ass about me, Dad! I wasn't making a spectacle of myself, was I? On a quiet lane in the dark?"

He stood up, as if it were just sinking in. "How hard did they hit you?" He put his hands on my shoulders. "How bad are you hurt? Who the hell were they?"

"Damn it, Dad! Like you really care!" I shoved my way out of his grip without realizing how hard, because he toppled back, falling on his butt. Still down for the count, he scrambled to recover his drink, a spectacle that sickened me even more. "You really ought to let Liz run the whole damn campaign from here on out. You're completely out of your depth, Dad. You could sign Peters's pledge *at* the teachers' union. That'd be another high-jumping photo opportunity for you, huh? You get to sail high in the sky. Looking pretty and grabbing the gold to squelch the queers."

I stopped for a breath. I stared at him there, still on the floor, steadying his tumbler of scotch, and tried to stop myself. But I didn't, I just couldn't, and went on, "This time the big jump required that you have some principles. And you don't know what the hell to do, do you?"

He'd staggered to his feet, the emptied tumbler in his hand, the stench of scotch soaked into his clothes and the carpet. He looked so pathetic. When he tried to approach me, I stepped back, holding him off. "No, don't. I swear I'll knock you back to the goddamn floor."

"Jesus, Guy. Cut the macho crap. Let me look at your injuries."

"I mean it, Dad. I'm disgusted with you. Don't you have one single idea of your own? One lousy conviction? I look at you and see a middle-aged drunk. For the first time, I can understand why Mom left you." I eased myself toward the front door, afraid he'd follow, but he stayed where he was. "Don't wait up for me, okay? I'll be at Mom's."

I slipped out the door, calling back, "There's nothing to you, Dad. Nothing at all."

Chapter 12

DREAMS I knew were dreams kept replacing each other, rapid-fire, like outtakes from different bad movies. Like releasing Dad's hand just as he yelled for me to clasp it, then watching him plunge through a chrome-lined portal into deep space.

Or a figure off in the dark, keeping time with a snare drum, while two guys took turns whacking my back with a metal stick.

"It's okay, Guy, really," Wade whispered from the Beast's passenger seat. "Everything's going to turn out just fine." This dream clip featured realistic Smell-o-Rama, the toxic scent of old red vinyl and prehistoric Cheetos powder warming in the sun. I reached to take Wade's hand, but my fingers caught tufts of seat-cushion foam from a crack in the empty passenger seat.

"You shouldn't be leanin' on that crappy old car," a girl's voice warned nearby. "There's some bum sleeping in there!"

Fingers drumming on the passenger door halted. Laughing, the guy shoved himself off.

Lurching forward to grab the steering wheel as if I'd fallen asleep while driving, I realized I was awake in my parked car, the sun just up over the Oakland hills. I studied the guy and his girlfriend, relieved to see they weren't CREWP creeps but kids, about my age. Maybe they'd stayed out all night too.

Nothing menacing in the rearview either, just the rusty grille of a dinky Renault. No one stirred on the narrow Oakland side street, around this Rockridge corner from Penni's, and I finally felt free to exhale. It felt like I'd been holding my breath all night since I left Dad soaking in his own scotch on Mount Olympus. My back and hip bones were still sore as hell.

The night before, when I'd reached Burrito Boulevard after my fight with Dad, it had hit me that the same CREWP thugs who'd tracked me to Wade's might be behind me now. Although I hoped they'd gotten what they craved, a moonlit snapshot of two teenagers kissing good night, their crowbar's blow hinted they weren't through with me yet.

After deciding to take Penni up on her standing offer of the extra bedroom to crash in, I'd headed to Oakland by a lunatic route, snaking up the moon-luminous Berkeley Hills on Fish Ranch Road. I had the whole switchbacking, uninhabited route to myself. If they were following me, they had to be doing it with their headlights off.

On the Berkeley side, I'd slipped along quiet streets south through hill-hugging neighborhoods, navigating constant dead ends, cul-de-sacs, and T-intersections until I arrived at Penni's well past midnight. But except for the porch light she left on all night, her little rooftop perch was completely dark. Through the opened half of the front bedroom window, I could hear steady, contented snoring. Damn! I raised my hand to knock on the front door, then hesitated. After my theatrics with Dad, I figured I didn't need to alarm Penni and Lester in the middle of the night with more drama.

I had thought for a second of heading back through the tunnel to Wade's, rapping on his window and tumbling into his arms and his warm bed. Then I realized CREWP might still have its gestapo stationed along Camino Gordo.

For a split second, I'd even entertained sneaking back home to my own warm bed. But even cowards draw a line between comfort and pride. I decided not to cross it, still furious about the big blowup with Dad and tired of thinking about it.

Later, I wouldn't be able to think about anything else.

What the hell. I was due to work with Randy for CJ Properties at the apartments on Madrone Street that afternoon, so I might as well stay put in Oakland. Still, heading down Penni's steps and back to the street seemed to shrink my guts. By the time I landed on the sidewalk, I'd felt like I was about six years old, lonely, scared, and longing for my mommy. Every little noise jolted: my soles creaking with every footfall, the Grateful Dead refrain in a car passing by, a broken streetlamp's buzz. The Beast's door croaked open extra loud, and I sank into the wobbly bucket seat, the welts on my back aching against the cracked vinyl. How did my big declaration of love to Wade lead to the sorest, loneliest night of my life?

Now, waking up behind the Beast's steering wheel, grateful for the sun on my bare arms and for Wade's soothing words in that last dream clip—Holy Jesus!—I realized that in a short while, he was expecting me to pick him up for church.

WHEN I called from a pay phone and told Wade about the CREWP guys snapping our kiss, I decided to spare him the news of the assault until we were face to face.

"Maybe you shouldn't show your face at church today, Guy."

"I don't see what difference it makes now. I'll meet you there."

"Okay, but I don't want you to feel obliged."

"Wade, there is nowhere on this planet I'd rather be than sitting in that church with you."

I knew Penni and Lester would still be snoozing, sleeping in like every Sunday morning, so I decided to head west and take advantage of the Marxist Matrix's free breakfast. After washing in the Matrix's public lavatories, I realized it was so early that, in the bungalow kitchen across from the church, coffee was still brewing.

A tall, thin girl emerged from the kitchen dressed in the plain gray shift and scarf of Gladstone's Panther-Commie-Christian-Soldier nuns, a Pilgrim Sister. "What are you waiting for, white boy?"

When I recognized her as the former Catholic schoolgirl, her transformation irritated me instantly. "Black girl," I said, with a slight bow, "I was waiting for breakfast."

She stared now, her brow knotted, her expression grim. "Oh. It's you. Man, you've been haunting this block lately, haven't you? Doesn't your daddy own my building? Isn't he a big shot with male perfume or something?"

"Or something. I'm hungry, Sister."

"Don't sister me! If you're hungry, Son of Slumlord, then give me a hand."

So, after a fix of weak coffee, I found myself stirring a huge vat of pancake batter. I learned from my fellow lapsed mackerel snapper, Sister Diana, that she'd been planning to jump into Sister Pilgrimhood as soon as she finished up her senior year at the Catholic high school. Like me, she was graduating early, in January, and decided to practice her new devotion on weekends until she went under the scarf full-time.

I asked her how her own sister was doing now, and for the first time, Diana softened her bristling attitude. "She's just gone downhill so fast. First, my momma and I thought the wheelchair would just be a help, you know. But then my sister needed to use it all the time, even for the shortest distance. Then her throat kind of seized up, so she can hardly speak now. Fact is, she's got to stay confined at home most of the time, under poor Momma's constant care. It's not looking good at all. Boy, you've got to stir the batter harder, till it's smooth. Yeah, like that."

Diana filled me in on some backstage gossip. A schism had divided the Marxist Matrix and Gladstone's religious loyalists. As the reverend's Sunday morning shows became more popular, drawing white suburbanites and local celebrities hungering for Gladstone's seal of approval, lots of the radicals had become more and more critical about the whole shebang becoming too white. "Some even want it to return to its days as an all-black church."

"What are you going to do with the whites?"

"I don't worry about white folk," Diana said, mixing a huge batch of orange powdered drink. "I suppose we can always put 'em to work in the kitchen." She couldn't hide her big smile.

I was just about to try the batter on the griddle when Wade appeared, crossing Madrone with a searching look. He wore those jeans that showed off his cowboy waistline. The wind had blown his brown forelocks back, off his forehead. He looked so compelling that while I stared, dazzled, I drizzled pancake batter on my own jeans. "I figured you'd be here," Wade laughed, coming in. "In your never-ending quest for nourishment."

While I cooked up a pancake for each of us, Wade and Diana became acquainted. When she found out he'd grown up in the neighborhood just north, they started reminiscing about the playground where they both played: "Maybe that's why you look so familiar," Diana announced. "We probably pushed each other off that rusty old jungle gym."

"Did you hear they're gonna replace it with this new plastic equipment?" Wade asked, and they were off, tearing into urban renewal plans. Nothing bonded city kids like memories of their junky playgrounds, I thought. I flipped my pancakes, proud of their gold, wheaten inner rings.

"I hope those taste as good as they look" came a booming voice through the open door. The Reverend Gladstone breezed in, wearing a dark suit, holding the door for an entourage—an older Sister Pilgrim who led a middle-aged white man, tall, dark, and broad-faced, in a good suit and open-collar dress shirt. He never took off his mirrored sunglasses and glanced around, tight-lipped. Gladstone thanked me and Diana for our efforts, then reached for paper plates. I reluctantly surrendered this first perfect batch, meant for us, the kitchen crew, and understood the true nature of Great-Man Communism. The great man always gets fed first.

While I slid the pancakes onto the visitors' plates, I eavesdropped as I started a new griddle full. Wade listened too. Gladstone seemed to be rehearsing a brief presentation for the morning's service, in which he'd introduce Mirrored Sunglasses and his good works. At first I wondered if he might be some hotshot journalist, a Hunter S. Thompson type who would undercover another fear-and-loathing political exposé:

DIMCHEK SON CONSPIRES
WITH SOCIALIST "PANCAKE CULT"

But Gladstone referred to him as Reverend Brother.

"During the service, I'll say the piece about equalitarian community building," Gladstone said, "and draw the parallels between your good efforts in the wilds of South America and ours here on the wild streets of West Oakland."

"Excellent," said Mirror Sunglasses, his lips barely parting.

"Then I'll explain how the People's Temple has branched out into good works in the city, how Mayor Moscone appointed you to the housing commission."

Leaning in beside me at the griddle, Diana nudged my arm and whispered, "Now Reverend Jones is the ultimate white slumlord."

"With your model people's faith community in the third world," Gladstone continued, "I'll stress our solidarity with the global poor. Point out that even as we speak, your next pilgrims are massing at Oakland Airport to join the joyful mission in Guyana. Then I'll turn the microphone over to you, Reverend Brother."

"Excellent," said Mirror Sunglasses, washing down his pancake with orange Kool-Aid.

A SERIES of letters spilled across the apartment's linoleum from a children's charity providing skin grafts for burn victims. Though they must have been pitched on the tenants' moving day, the letters fanned out neatly like a deck of cards. Dated over months, they told a short, aborted story, from "Thanks for your inquiry" to "We regret that we must discontinue your child's course of treatments." Cleaning up around the rest of the abandoned little bedroom in CJ Properties' Madrone Street slum, I found a Service to Discontinue notice from the power company, five Past Due notices from a diaper service, and a flyer, A Circle of Nourishment, A Circle of Love. In interlocking circles around the smiling face of Reverend Gladstone, it advertised an emergency food bank.

Randy cried out, "What pigs!" from the tiny bathroom.

"What now?"

"Kotex! A whole bloody paper bag full of bloody goddamn Kotex. Stuffed under the drainpipe. Like that's how you dispose of 'em, right? Geez, these people were freakin' animals."

"Yeah," I called, "but it sure looks like their problems were piling up."

"My heart bleeds, Guy. We've both probably seen more disgusting renters' messes than anybody else in history, but these swine win the prize, okay?" Randy appeared in the doorway, snapping his rubber gloves. "Can you imagine filling an entire closet with shitty baby diapers and just leaving them behind? No wonder the neighbors were complaining about the stink. Jesus H. Jimmy Carter Christ!"

Randy reached for the offending sack of Kotex and tossed it into a larger plastic bag, the one we hoped would be our last to fill for the afternoon. Following the soap opera of Saturday night, and despite the stabbing pain every time I bent my hips, I was actually glad for this mindless, familiar work and Randy's rambunctious company.

I wasn't sure where I'd end up the rest of the day. I knew I had to contact my dad eventually and just face up to my hostile exit, but I figured for tonight I'd stay at Penni's. I could head from there to school on Monday—I had the big Hamlet True Son vs. Spoiled Brat presentation to give for Pullman's class—and stop by the CJ office afterward. If I talked to Dad in his office, in the sober light of Monday afternoon, with Leon there to mediate, we might be able to talk it out calmly.

Randy started to scrub the bathroom, and I gathered up the letters, stacking them neatly as if there were any reason to save them. What the hell was going to become of that burn-scarred little kid now?

So far I hadn't told Randy about the attack or the fight with Dad, no matter how I was tempted to dramatize the tale and make myself the hero. I still felt dazed, nagged by the edge of a feeling that, far from victim-hero, I'd somehow been responsible. Not for the crowbar whacks but for being reckless, for putting so much in jeopardy for Wade and for Dad so I could go my merry gay way in the world.

I hadn't told Wade about my injuries either, mostly because I hadn't had a chance. After church, he had to hustle to his new weekend job as a hotel clerk. I just wanted so bad to go back to last night and stop the clock at that moment when I'd said "It's called love."

Instead, here I was with Randy in another Madrone Street slum. He laughed at my neat stack of letters. "Let's just toss 'em, Guy," he said, sweeping them up in his gloved hand and sliding them into the trash bag. Then with deliberate slippery-rubber audio effects, *pppft*, he dropped his gloves in the trash too. "Well, I'm pretty much done. I gotta get moving. Janine's fixing Sunday dinner early so we can both study tonight."

"Okay, I'll do the windows," I said, turning to them.

Randy shocked me by hugging me from behind, his chest slamming against the welt under my shoulder blades. I flinched, wincing. I froze up when I felt his groin pressing against my sore hipbones. "Come on, Guy," Randy laughed, "don't go frigid on me like a little virgin."

"Guess what? I'm not so little anymore. But I am still a virgin."

"Wow. You mean, you and Wade haven't...?"

I shook my head.

"Well, I was just hugging you good-bye. You seemed so down today. You okay?"

When I turned around, Randy moved his hands to my shoulders, as if I needed to be steadied. "I'm okay. Just preoccupied." I told him the short version of my night and morning, then my plans to stay at Penni and Lester's for a while. "I'll just drop a sleeping bag down among their art supplies."

"Listen," Randy said, heading out, "if it doesn't work out, you can always crash on our couch."

The sun slipped behind the vacant building across the way, so I hustled with the squeegee. As I wiped down the sill, I noticed Diana, still in her gray Sister Pilgrim habit, pushing the wheelchair out from the apartment entry and onto the sidewalk. At first I thought she must be using it to transport a large wrapped bundle until I realized the bundle was her sister, now scrunched up into a painful ball, her twisted feet dangling from the shawl that covered her.

Easing down Madrone, turning onto Manzanita, a slick Porsche coupe appeared, headlights scanning the wheelchair, casting a glint in the metal spokes. I noticed that one of the coupe's side panel lights was out and strained to follow Liz's progress to the corner. She stopped briefly beside an empty lot, just where those front steps led straight into nothing. The Porsche zoomed away as fast as it came, its taillights visible, strobe-like in the gaps between demolished homes.

AT THE base of Penni's steps, a jumble of packed boxes puzzled me. A few paces down the sidewalk, a young guy in sweat pants and a tight T-shirt stood over a rowing machine. He watched me sidestep my way through the boxes and start up the stairs. "Hey, kid," he said, "you going up to Penni's?"

Kid? He didn't look much older than me. When I nodded, he asked me if I would help him carry the rowing contraption up. "That Lester guy was going to help me, but he's kept me waiting for like, ten minutes."

That Lester guy was actually on his way down the steps. "Guy!" he called. "Are you all right?"

Grunting under the downhill end of the rowing machine, I managed to yell up, "Yeah! Except for the three hernias I'm gonna have."

"Man," Tight T-Shirt said between heaving breaths, "these stairs alone are a great cardiovascular workout."

He was right, especially because we had to negotiate Penni's hanging garden of potted geraniums. This was so stupid. Even while I panted under the full weight of the machine, I knew this was going to screw up my healing time. Lester lent his help from the halfway point, relieving the extra pain on my hips, thank God, and from there we had it up, across the deck, and into the art studio/guest bedroom.

Tight T-Shirt directed us to set the rowing machine facing the window so, "Penni can meditate on her garden when she's doing cardio."

The effort of hauling the damn thing must have herniated my brain. When had the art room become so spacious? Penni's big sketching desk and easel had been shoved against a far corner, her art supplies stashed in stacked boxes. Where dashed-off watercolors had always been taped on the wall to dry, she'd taped up a poster of stretching exercises. Where Lester's drawing table had stood, a red foam pad waited for sit-ups. In the room's old art-making chaos, I had never noticed its polished hardwood floors. Now the room looked like a spare little chapel to worship the Body Beautiful.

I also couldn't figure out why Tight T-Shirt, the home fitness delivery guy, was working on Sunday evening or knew so much about my mother's habits. He kept standing there, contemplating the alignment of the rowing machine in Penni's temple.

Lester pulled me aside, clutching my arm. "Guy," he said, "we've been concerned about you. Your mother's been frantic."

"Oh! You're Penni's son? The kid who's been AWOL?" asked Tight T-Shirt. "Man, you're a lot older than I expected."

Irked, I turned to Lester. "I'm fine. I worked all afternoon on Madrone Street. What's up with Mom?"

"Must be fun," Tight T-Shirt speculated, "having such a young mother."

"Fun as a barrel of baboons," I told him. "But when I need it, home cookin' and wise guidance too."

The muscular boy nodded. "She's a great lady."

The great lady appeared, bizarre in a leopard-skin sweatshirt over a black leotard. Though she was carefully made up and scented by expensive chemicals, her red eyes looked swollen and her face splotchy, as if she'd been dabbing at the goop on her face.

"Guy...," she sighed. She threw herself against me and held on tight. "I was so relieved when I heard your voice."

"You okay, Mom?" I pulled back, but she wouldn't let go.

"I've been worried all day. Your dad called this morning expecting you to be here. To have stayed here, I mean. Last night."

"I meant to, but I swear, I got here so late you and Lester were already asleep. I heard snoring through the bedroom window."

Lester coughed and looked at the floor. Tight T-Shirt lowered his eyes to the same fascinating spot. What the hell was going on? When Mom finally managed to extricate herself from my precious being, I could see that her tears had started up again.

"I'm just so glad you're all right, Guy. When Paul called, I even thought of calling the police."

Her overreaction irritated the hell out of me. Since when did Penni have a stake in worrying about my whereabouts? Where were her tears when I was a junior science geek fending off the leering clones on Castro and living off takeout burritos? And if she was so fragile about my single night of homelessness, what could I do to prepare her for the bigger shocks to come? Like pix of her son in compromising positions and our good name screaming across the *Tribune*?

"I'm glad you decided to keep the police out of it, Mom," I said finally. At least missing person wouldn't be added to my mounting rap sheet. "I'll call Dad and let him know I'm okay."

"You'd better hurry, because he's off to some campaign event later tonight."

"Yeah, the teachers' union. So, he's not exactly paralyzed by panic over my disappearance?"

"Only because he called Randy, and Janine told him you both were working in West Oakland today."

"See? There was nothing to be upset about. Not only did I punch the clock for CJ Properties, I even helped deliver your new toy."

Penni glanced at the rowing machine and tried to form an appreciative expression. Then, smearing her eyes with a well-used tissue, she introduced me to Tight T-Shirt, who was not just the delivery boy but her *physical consultant*.

"Cary has been a godsend, Guy. Especially with the extra stress I've had, taking on so much of Liz's work. He's earning his certification as a professional trainer."

Cary nodded, crouching to the rowing machine to make an adjustment. "I'm also studying at the East/West Center on eclectic massage work."

"Wonderful, amazing work," Penni put in, "harmonizing the body and spirit."

I cringed, trying not to imagine Cary harmonizing my mother's naked back. It bugged me how they kept using the word "work" in that weird way, maybe because they were ashamed it was just play.

Lester's eyes met mine. He was too much of a gentleman to roll them, but he sighed and slipped out of the room, explaining he had to keep an eye on the boxes in the street below.

Okay, I was slow on the uptake, but I finally got it. While Penni insisted on making tea and Cary got to work attaching pulleys, I followed Lester out to the deck. "So, you're moving out now? Already?"

"Yeah. I should've told you yesterday, but I just didn't have the heart."

"Oh God. Oh God. How old is the trainer boy, Lester?"

"Nineteen, maybe twenty."

We both inhaled deeply, leaning side by side on the deck rail. The day's summerlike heat had ripened into a rare, warm East Bay fall evening. The night was so clear I could spot a huge vessel slipping from Treasure Island, its lights ablaze across the dark bay.

Lester told me he still loved my mom but couldn't overcome their tensions over SELF.

"It's provided insight after insight for me," Lester explained, "forcing me to demand more of myself and my capabilities. You know, 'Any doubt you have is yours by choice.' Penni's obviously moving into a different place, less introspective, more physical."

I didn't want to dwell on Penni's physical quest just then. "What's going on with your guys' art careers, though, Lester? Are you really going to give it up?"

"Your mom is trying to juggle some commercial art projects with managing Aspirations Unlimited again. She has a contract with a plumbing company to do a series for the Sunday *Tribune*. As for me, like we say at SELF, 'Any remnants of the lives we discard only go into safe storage.'"

I went down the steps with Lester, who'd already packed the many boxes of art supplies, the portfolios of sketches and watercolors, the frame of his sketch table. With it all jammed tight in his pickup's bed, it gave me the willies, like SELF had just packed good ol' Lester's old life into "safe storage" for some night journey into the unknown.

Penni appeared on the steps above. "Guy, your tea's ready. Lester, would you like some? It's black Tibetan Tantric, very potent and hearty!"

Lester begged off but followed me up the steps to say good-bye to my mom. Even in the dark, despite her cheery hospitality, I could see the tears dashing her cheeks.

I couldn't turn around to see it, but I heard Lester and Penni fall into a sighing, sobbing embrace.

Cary stood in the kitchen doorway, holding a cup of tea. I could barely bring myself to cross the dark living room. His physique, one of those perfect, compact V-shapes from his bulked-up shoulders to his narrow waist, got exaggerated in the bright outline of the doorframe. It felt so freaky. I wanted like hell to punch him smack in his flat abdomen, knock the tantric teacup to nirvana, then bloody his smug, boyish face.

"Here you go, Guy," Cary said, extending the teacup to me.

"Thanks," I said. My hands shook so bad I immediately set the cup on Penni's big, messy coffee table next to her knockoff Giacometti stone statuette. I didn't have Cary's muscle, I knew, but he only came up to my shoulders. I was so much taller, I probably outweighed the little gym rat by twenty or thirty pounds.

While Cary went into the kitchen to prepare a cup for Penni and himself, the craving to commit violence coursed through my evil blood. I sat on the sofa, forcing my hands to clutch my knees. Then pulses of self-rebuke collided in my brain.

One, I was a sexist hypocrite, since I'd never reacted to my dad's young female sex partners like this.

Two, I was a fraud if I didn't attack, since I was supposed to protect my mom from adolescent sex predators like Cary.

Three, I was a total freak, a fairy boy with a random psycho-macho streak.

My urges were Greek-lit clichés. I could just hear Pullman satirizing my oedipal jealousy and rage. Still, no matter what, that Giacometti statue would crush Cary's empty cranium in a single slam.

When Cary sat with his tea in the armchair nearby, he asked me about my college plans. I managed small talk about my plan to major in aquatic biology, but all the while I tightened my grip on my own knees and stared at the statuette with blood-struck longing. When Penni wandered through the front door, dabbing her eyes with that same damn crumpled tissue, I excused myself and tried to head out.

"Guy!" Penni about-faced and followed me out to the deck. "Where are you going?"

"I've got this huge project due tomorrow, Mom. In my English class." I tried to shove off down the stairs. "I'm, like, the whole period's main event. I gotta go."

Penni grabbed my arm. "So you're going back to Mount Olympus?"

"Yeah," I lied, smirking at our subdivision's cheesy name. "Sure. Right back to good ol' Circe Circle."

"If you need to stay here, Guy, you know you can have the extra room. We'll just leave you alone so you can study." Now she tightened her grip on my arm. "We'll move the futon in there. Next to the rowing machine."

"Thanks. But all my notes are at home. You know."

"I do, but the scare today just made me wonder if *you know*, Guy. If I've ever given you the impression this isn't your home just as much as your father's house, I just haven't been clear enough. I don't care who's sleeping or snoring, you just let yourself in."

"Okay, Mom."

"Good. You wouldn't believe how much you occupy my best thoughts. For the record, I love you, okay?"

"You like 'em young, huh?"

Penni gasped, sinking to steady herself on the railing as if from a body blow. Catching a last glimpse of Cary in my mother's armchair, his mouth agape, I plunged toward the warm, dark street.

PULLMAN, WHO commuted against the commute to teach at Diablo View, lived in the Oakland hills just across the 24 Freeway from Penni's. Once, when I had to miss class due to a campaign chore, I'd dropped off an essay in her home mail slot to meet her strict deadline. She acted like she'd done me a huge favor.

"Understand that I'm not offering clemency because I'm a Democrat, Mr. Dimchek. I would extend the same mercy to the child of a Peace and Freedom candidate, say, or a Socialist Worker."

Now, parking the Beast on her street, I realized I really did need Pullman's mercy. I hated to bother a teacher on Sunday night—probably a capital crime in some states—but there was no way, as this evening's endless fourth act got bloodier, that I'd ever be ready for my *Hamlet* presentation.

No way was I going back to Circe Circle. I was sure Dad was still totally stressed, especially because of whatever Penni was bound to report by telephone, and probably furious. I figured my only option would be to take Randy up on that offer to crash on their couch in the city.

Laughter from somebody's yard party spilled over the block's high stucco walls. Sweet, powerful scents massed from the gardens all around, too-ripe fruits and herbs, wafting on the evening's tropical breeze. At Pullman's front gate, encouraged by the blazing porch light, I indulged a fantasy that she'd actually invite me in. I imagined she and her husband would just be sitting down to Sunday dinner. A pot roast, maybe. She'd insist I stay, then torture me at the table with references to Prince Hamlet, lateness, and lame excuses.

When she came to the door all dolled up, I realized Pullman already had company. In fact, after crying my name, she shut the door to the loud talk and laughter inside and pulled me aside on her entryway.

"Don't tell me. Did my youngest niece decide to surprise me by inviting you? Does she know you from somewhere?"

"No, no... ma'am. I'm sorry...," I fumbled.

Now she narrowed her gaze, leaning back to scrutinize me, then touched my shoulder. "Are you all right, Guy?"

Pullman looked so small now, out of the classroom, the top of her gray head barely reaching my collarbone. She acted so kindly that I felt abashed. I explained I'd fallen behind on my project, due to an "unexpected family thing." I apologized for messing up her Monday plans.

"That's really why you came all this way?" Pullman asked, now wide-eyed.

As far as the assignment, she almost laughed it off.

"I've been teaching for almost thirty years. I think I can dream up something on Hamlet for fifty minutes." But she kept staring at me all concerned and sympathetic, as if she expected me to have a nervous breakdown right there on her porch.

I realized I looked like hell and probably smelled worse, scruffy from the day's chores and way too many hours from my last shower. Pullman had never seen Prince Dimchek befouled by his role as a weekend slave for CJ Properties. She was probably freaked that, in my real life, I was such a bum. I apologized again for interrupting her party and thanked her, then started back to the street.

"Oh, Guy, for God's sake." She grabbed my arm, tugging me toward the front door. "Now, my nieces are throwing a party for my anniversary, and I want to introduce you to some nice folks."

She wouldn't take no, leading me past a heaping buffet table groaning under salads, veggies, scalloped potatoes, and I swear, a big roast, carved into thick pink slices, still steaming from the oven. All kinds of people swarmed around the kitchen, sampling the feast and pouring drinks. As she led me across the living room, I met the nieces, other relatives, even Pullman's tiny white-headed parents, who beamed identical smiles.

Still, my English teacher guided me with determination toward the back deck. Her bungalow perched on a steep downslope, and her deck overlooked a brick patio below, lit up for the party with tiki lights and strung bulbs. Down there, like a convention of amazons, laughing women of all ages clustered among a few children and an occasional solitary guy trying to hold his own. Pullman called to one of the amazons, a tall, stocky blonde about Penni's age. "Deb," she cried, "look who's here. It's Guy Dimchek."

Deb smiled and waved up to me. "Wow! Your favorite student, right, Lillian?"

"I thought I was your favorite student," a much younger woman beside Deb shouted. "Now that I'm in college, you drop me, Lil?"

"I never drop my favorites," Pullman cried. "Fact is, I'm in love with all the little buggers, God help me. But this guy…." Pullman hesitated, as the clusters below coalesced into one mass, all of them quiet, turning their faces up to her. Suddenly she'd morphed from "Lil" back into the formidable Ms. Pullman, asking everyone for their attention. "Listen, people! A very special guest just showed up to help celebrate Deb's and my anniversary. This is Guy Dimchek. He's Paul Dimchek's son!"

The sudden whoops and applause shocked the devil out of me. All these women, in their party clothes, earrings, jewels, and fussed-over hair, screamed out the loudest, rowdiest group cheer for my dad. Then, in unison, they all raised glasses in a toast to my father. "Tell him how grateful we are, Guy!" a middle-aged woman cried. "He's the only candidate with any guts or integrity in this whole damn state."

A younger woman beside her stepped forward, her free hand sweeping grandly from the kiss she blew toward me. "That's for your dad, straight from me. No pun intended."

"SO MANY Christians have deluded themselves," Gas 'n' Jesus thundered on the radio, "with their comforting lie of a merciful, forgiving God." Even more than usual, the Beast shimmied in its off-kilter progress across the Bay Bridge. Harold Pruedhoe's Sunday talk show, "From the Right Side," had suddenly preempted the space on the car's AM-only dial of my favorite, an all-Motown program. "God shows mercy and forgiveness only to the deserving. Only to those who have already surrendered their souls to him. The rest are cast irretrievably into sin. They have condemned their souls to an eternity in Hell."

As if to follow hell-bent on the sermon's finale, a program note welcomed a new sponsor, the Committee to Re-elect Will Peters. The studio audience applauded wildly when they heard Will Peters himself was tonight's special guest. Along with an even more special guest, joining by phone from a sister station in Miami, a spokeswoman for Florida Orange Growers.

"Will, keep fightin' the good fight out there in the Golden State. I understand your victory's almost assured."

"We'll only feel like winners when we've accomplished half of what you've done," Will Peters crooned, "to save the children of the Sunshine State."

"I'm praying for you all," Anita Bryant said.

"*Pray for me*, Orange Juice Lady," I whispered, snapping off the radio. I longed for the Temptations or Aretha. After Will Peters installed his regime up in Sacramento, would he silence all the spots on California's dial for soul music and quirky love?

Defying my mood, the city shimmered in the balmy night, the TransAmerica Pyramid and Coit Tower beacon-like against the far hilltops, where city lights melted into the stars over Twin Peaks. From the upper deck of the bridge, San Francisco never appeared to be a peninsular point but an island, a self-contained utopia, too gorgeous even to touch the mainland.

Then, after my exit, the city showed its usual skid-road, wilted-produce, peeling-paint true face as I headed through South of Market's skanky streets, meaning to follow Market Street's diagonal across the city, then over Twin Peaks to Randy and Janine's.

I'd slipped out of Pullman's house when the crowd on the back patio turned back to wine and conversation. Kind of numb from the shock and despite all the warmth and hospitality, I felt too out of place. I'd congratulated Pullman and Deb on their anniversary and whispered my farewell, citing my "family thing" excuses. I would have been better off hanging out at Pullman's, probably, because multiple shocks still crouched, waiting to pounce in the dark like more thugs with crowbars.

Market Street was jammed up around a movie palace for a special screening of *Invasion of the Body Snatchers*, highlighting the local actors who'd appeared in the new version. Past the light beams and movie mobs, when I reached Castro and Seventeenth, a guy in jeans and a Harvey Milk T-shirt handed me a flyer. But when the green light flashed to cross to Upper Market, as if my Beast were on fixed tracks, it took me on a hard right, up the steep incline of Seventeenth to Ashbury, an involuntary detour to Montes Terrace.

Maybe something about the prospect of spending the night at Randy and Janine's daunted me. Their student-housing place was tiny, and Randy said they'd be trying to study. Then, at the top of the hill, the Beast itself seemed to decide that I had to keep heading north on Masonic, cross the Panhandle, and follow its homing instinct back to the Pescatore house on Hayes Street. Rob might change his mind about me now. Maybe I was too stinky and homeless to turn away. It was a long shot but worth a try, and I'd crashed at the Pescatore house so many times since first grade that maybe I still had my permanent squatter's rights.

Just as I guided the Beast around the corner onto Rob's street, his house lights flickered off, and a motorcycle bolted away from the garage driveway underneath. So I drove back up the hill to Montes Terrace, thinking of how I'd memorized every inch of this route since I was seven or eight, either walking or riding with Rob and his mom in this very Beast, then shiny and clean of Cheetos microbes.

So maybe I'd sleep in my car again. If I could find a parking place on any of the streets around Montes Terrace, it'd be quiet, safe, and familiar. I was in luck. A fat Peugeot was just pulling out as I eased up the narrow, curving lanes above Ashbury. Uncontrolled parking under a spreading tree, paradise for teenaged vagrants. Right across the street, beside the basketball court for the parish junior high, was a pay phone.

Since Dad was attending the teachers' union banquet by now, I shot a quick lie to CJ's answering service: "Tell him I'm fine. That I'm on my way to Randy Blanding's to spend the night over here. That I'll see him after school tomorrow when I check in at CJ." Cool as I tried to sound, my heart did belly flops when I finished the message and hung up. I wondered if lives of crime started with simple acts like plotting murder with Giacometti sculptures, then lying to phone services, recording a trail of deceit for prosecuting attorneys.

Four boys improvised a half-court game, shooting hoops under the streetlights, taking me back to that happy, scary freedom I felt here on October nights like this last year, when my dad was busy prowling for female company. I leaned against the mesh fence, watching one kid shoot right over another's upraised hands, a perfect arc into the basket.

Just down from me, two nuns occupied a bench where the Parish Schools office overlooked the playing court.

"I'm worried about this new confirmation class," the plump sister was saying. "Tomorrow I'm teaching a session on original sin, and I'm expecting a passel of challenges and questions."

"This whole generation struggles to accept the very concept of sin," the thin, quieter nun said. "It's as if the flower children inoculated them with 'God Is Love' when they were still in kindergarten, and they've never matured beyond that."

"*Matured* is the word, Frederika. I don't know how to convince them of the reality of sinfulness. They think they were born perfect in the palm of their hippie God."

The other sister laughed. So this was Sister Fred! I kind of laughed too, though it was the last thing I wanted to do. But I saw myself in their complaint, in the easy way I'd said adios to my own absent God. I'd dumped two millennia of Catholic theology and never looked back.

"Excuse me, young man?" the plump sister asked, standing up. "We've reserved these courts for the younger pupils in the evenings now. We're asking the high schoolers to use the courts at their own campus."

"We've had some problems with bullying and loitering," Sister Fred explained gently, still seated.

I shoved off from the fence. There was that damn word, *loitering*. "Okay. I used to play here, though. I went to Precious Suffering...."

"That's nice, dear," the plump one said, still standing.

"Don't you recognize me?" Starting down the walk, I moved closer to the bench, toward Sister Fred.

The plump sister crossed her arms and planted her feet wider apart, as if to protect her smaller colleague. "Please, son, we've asked you nicely. Don't make us contact the authorities. Just move along, now."

Maybe the darkness freaked her out. Anyway, it was crazy to think Sister Fred would recognize me in the flickering streetlight, from years ago when I was such a squirt. Suddenly I saw Fred in a whole different light. She wasn't a nun who existed only to annoy me, but a devoted teacher, protective of the little kids. She was one of those adults who gave a damn and aimed her whole life toward her conception of the truth. Meanwhile, in her eyes, I'd evolved into a tall, threatening stranger lurking like a pervert where children played.

I couldn't very well cross the street now and take a snooze in my car, or the sisters really would call the cops. Anyway, I wasn't sleepy anymore. I kept walking toward Montes and Ashbury, hoping to tire myself into a stupor. Maybe the nuns would be gone when I circled back.

It was like the reverse of those height bars they have to prohibit too-little kids from carnival rides. Suddenly I'd outgrown some measuring stick and lost the right to hang out in my old neighborhood without attracting a criminal investigation. Zombified, I kept walking. The truth is, I felt creepy and way too alone and despised the brim of tears welling up because I didn't want to feel anything. I blinked my eyes dry.

Approaching Lola Montes Terrace, I thought the sight of our old house might cheer me up. I didn't plan to *loiter*, okay? Just stroll by and say hi to the old dump.

Yet when I got near, my way was blocked. Our old stove just sat there, at the base of the front steps, out in the sidewalk. Two big guys in jeans and T-shirts even scruffier than mine leaned against a dumpster, one smoking a cigarette, the other sipping a beer.

"Hey, kid," one of the men called to me. "You the guy Lennie sent up? We gotta get that old piece of crap out of our way before morning."

I stood there, shaking my head, staring down at the stove in the light of a work lamp clamped on the dumpster. Oh God, oh God what wouldn't I give for another round of Penni's pheasant bladders in curry or salamander livers in brine? Now egg yolk and some brown goop were mired in the burner grates, like the poor old range had been exiled to death row while cooking its own last meal.

Behind it, swooping over the sidewalk, a chute ran into the dumpster. I looked up. My bedroom windows had been completely knocked out. The long chute had been fastened to the base of the smashed-out casings. The lath and plaster knocked from the walls of my old room stuck there, dangling at the chute's lip like some drunk's vomit. More to myself than the men, I said, "I used to live here."

The smoking guy laughed. "Yeah, right."

"You never lived here, kid," the beer guy said. "Last guy owned this place was a bachelor."

"That Finish Line guy. He didn't have any kids."

"Had a Playboy Mansion thing going on here."

"Chicks in and out at all hours." The smoking guy laughed, humping the air with his thrusting waist. He tossed his cigarette into Penni's ice plant. "So, kid, maybe you wanna keep moving, huh?"

So I kept moving. I felt stupid for even thinking I had a claim to Montes Terrace anymore. I'd run out of ideas. Suddenly I didn't feel like sleeping in my car by myself and decided to drive to Randy and Janine's after all and make my lie true.

When I got back to the Parish Schools building, the kids' game was over. The nuns had vanished too. I crossed to the Beast and put the key in the ignition, but instead of turning it over, I just sank my forehead to the wheel.

Maybe because I was out of the public eye, parked under the tree's canopy and out of streetlight range, my tired old psyche didn't have the oomph to maintain my zombie trance. I started crying in a crazy, quiet way. Not like I'd bawled as a kid, no blubbering. Just this steady stream of tears. I couldn't quite catch my breath either. It was like half of me was watching the other half, astonished that a human male could cry for so long without stopping.

Throughout the marathon of tears, the main thing I felt was shame. Pullman's entire party had cheered for my dad. Cary and Lester had moved their lives and equipment up and down and in and out in adoration of Penni. But when my turn came to uphold my parents, I just inflicted smartass venom.

Head pressed against the steering wheel, going nowhere, I'd reached the real end of my road. Maybe Gas 'n' Jesus was right, and the plump nun too. I'd been living so deep in a state of sin that I hadn't even recognized it. For all I knew, God promised no mercy to the sinner and issued tire irons to CREWP to enforce his punishment.

Like our house on Montes Terrace, I had to be gutted. I'd probably helped cause the divorce that led to our house being abandoned in the first place. Maybe I'd created a wedge between Penni and Paul, never having become the kind of son they'd expected. Maybe their slow disappointment with me fed the distance between them. I'd never been the popular, physically talented type they'd both been as kids. Here they'd gone and done the shotgun wedding routine as teenagers themselves, and what had issued from that misfire? A smart-mouthed little dork with no special qualities at all.

Come to think of it, they'd been downright graceful and uncomplaining, considering what a letdown I must've been. To top it off, I'd turned out to be playing on the wrong team, letting them down again, no matter how accepting they'd been on the surface. What a joke. After all their efforts not to admit how crushed they were by the dork in their midst, the dork turned out to be a fag. A dorky fag. Their grand prize. What could they think, let alone say, to console each other in private?

And now, in the space of a day, I'd gone and attacked each of them where it hurt the most. I could apologize for centuries, continents might shift into brainless new shapes, but it would never blot my cruel words from the geologic record. That's why I slammed my head down. That's why I couldn't raise it and go forward. Like a rough hand, self-hatred mashed my face against the steering wheel.

"WELL, IF you can't talk to Harold Pruedhoe, I'd sure love to," Janine was telling Randy in their squeezed little student-housing apartment just across from the San Francisco State campus. "Let's invite Harold and your mom for dinner. I'd love to serve him a piece of my mind about his Sunday talk show. If this idiotic Save Our Schools thing passes, at least three of my favorite teachers from Walt Whitman are going to be fired."

"Baby, that wouldn't persuade Harold," Randy called. "He only goes by strict Biblical arguments, okay?"

"Then I'll turn the Bible against him, sweetie. I'll sit here with Ivan in my arms and ask Reverend Harold if masturbators should be fired too. After all, the Bible is just as unforgiving about the sin of Onan. If everyone who ever jacked off can't teach either, we won't have a single classroom open in the state." Leaning into the table, she removed her glasses and rested her head on the massive Advanced Aquatic Biology text in front of her.

When I'd arrived, Janine confessed that she'd listened to the entire Gas 'n' Jesus interview with Will Peters and the Florida Orange Juice Queen and now faced an insurmountable mountain of reading. Now she murmured, muffled by the text, "Maybe we should invite you to this dinner with Harold, Guy. You could be the poster child for gay rights. Smart and sweet."

"And square," Randy put in, getting drinks for each of us. "A preppy Boy Scout."

"So what do you think, Guy? Are you up for meeting Gas 'n' Jesus and charming the bile out of him?"

"I already met him," I said, accepting a beer from Randy. "Last spring, out in the Delta at Randy's mom's place."

"That's right," Randy said, sitting beside me and sliding a glass of warm milk to Janine, then popping open his beer. "Before he and Mom were even engaged."

"Yeah," I said. "They were just fornicating then."

Janine laughed. "If only our side had the cojones to play as dirty as the right-wingers! Imagine how we could skewer Will Peters's closest ally in the media. A countercharge of sexual immorality. With Randy's mom, no less."

"The only problem is," I said, "we'd be agreeing that sex is immoral."

"You're right," Janine said. "Damn. But anyway, I still think Harold should face an honest-to-God homosexual."

"Well, he didn't seem too impressed with me the first time. Besides, I'm not such a Boy Scout type anymore. I'm as evil and depraved as the next honest-to-God homosexual." Despite Randy and Janine's company, my mood continued to be as sour as my own workday stench. The cold-pepperoni-and-cardboard smell of the pizza they'd demolished before I arrived mixed with invading smells of other couples' cooking—Velveeta nachos, overcooked broccoli.

Janine shoved off from the table. "'Scuse me boys, I'm taking my biology text to bed." Even tired as she was, she looked so healthy and robust, her cheeks pink, her inquisitive eyes heavy-lidded and soft. "Well, evil one, you're way too tall for this sofa. I hope you'll be able to sleep." When she leaned over to buss me on the cheek, her long, wild brown hair grazing my neck, I swore her baby belly had swollen even more from our picnic, just last Saturday. It already seemed like an ancient memory.

I told Janine I'd be fine and got up to catch the blanket and pillow she tossed from the hallway cabinet before she bid us good night.

It wasn't even ten o'clock, but I had the strongest urge to collapse on their couch and press my head into a long, deep sleep. As we soaked up the beers, Randy had other ideas for me. He launched into a litany of his own college reading labors and midterm crises, then, pressing my leg under the table, implored me to help him study for a quiz he had in the morning.

"Make up a bunch of questions from the text and see how I do off the top of my head, okay?"

He was as eager and fresh as I was sunken into my own bitter, foul-smelling juices. I agreed to help only after I had a shower and borrowed some clean clothes.

I was just done shampooing when Randy knocked on the bathroom door. Through the shower door, I could see him setting a pile of clothes on the hamper lid. Then he slid the shower door open a crack and said, voice lowered, "Janine's exhausted. Nodded off right in the middle of her chapter. She's fast asleep already."

Before he slid the door shut, I thanked him for the clothes and ducked my soapy hair under the water. Each clean hair follicle felt so good I started to apply a second gob to lather when, with my eyes tight shut, I felt Randy slip behind me. Naked, of course, pressing against me in that cramped little shower stall.

He rinsed my hair and soaped down my back, my butt, and the backs of my legs. Using the detachable showerhead, he sent a surge of water down from my shoulders, massaging my back, then reached for the soap to slide across my chest, my stomach, and downward. His hands flinched when he reached my hips. "What's with these big bruises? You okay?"

I didn't answer, which he must've taken for consent to proceed. Pressing himself hard against my back, he slipped his chin against my neck and then proceeded to stroke me in his strong, soapy grip.

"Remember when we used to talk about free love? Just like old times."

"We never went this far, Randy." I tried to pry his hand off my dick.

"Not like we didn't want to, babe," he whispered, still gripping me tight. "Don't act like you don't want it."

"I don't, Randy, honest. And I really am sore as hell all over down there."

He kissed my ear, licking it and sighing while his hard-on slipped up and down against my ass. I could feel him soaping his dick with his other hand, then pressing it right into me. "Let me inside! I've wanted this so bad for so long," he muttered, his lips still sampling the flesh of my ears. "You want this as much as I do." He thrust farther in, a blinding jab.

In a split second, I pulled myself off him and turned around. He took this as a signal to slide his tongue into my mouth until I shoved him back against the tiles. "Randy!" I cried, too loud, then whispered. "Janine's in the next room, damn it. Remember, your pregnant wife?"

Undaunted, Randy grabbed my hand. "Come on. Geez, it's different now. Janine's tired all the time."

"Don't blame it on Janine. What's different is that you're married now."

"What's wrong with a little playing around among friends? It's been torture, okay? Watching you wag that little butt around when we work together—"

"Then maybe we shouldn't work together—"

"—especially since you told me you and Wade aren't getting it on." Slow, unwilling, he stopped gripping my hand. "Damn."

I blundered out of the shower stall. "I love him, okay? I want Wade to be the first one."

Limp, leaning back against the shower tiles, Randy murmured, "What the hell do you know, little boy, about love?"

I hustled from the apartment, back in the same filthy clothes.

I PATROLLED every side street in the Castro District in search of a parking space. Leaving Randy's, I'd spied the Harvey Milk flyer I'd tossed on the passenger seat. It advertised that rally Dad, Liz, and Adrian had been arguing about, promising a party that would "Rock on Past Midnight." I decided I had nothing to lose by trying to get in the door. Maybe I could snag some snack food. The whole thing would occupy my churning brain until I got tired enough, again, to sleep away the long night in my car.

So I hoped to park on another quiet back street off noisy Castro as my refuge for the night. It briefly crossed my mind to head home to Circe Circle and apologize to Dad, but I didn't want to have to explain why I'd changed my mind about staying at Randy's and tell my four millionth lie of the day. I'd be okay. I'd go to CJ after school Monday just like I planned, and humble myself before my dad. Then I'd force down tantric tea with Penni and do the same. I'd apologize for being such an ass.

The night stayed warm past eleven, inspiring throngs to cruise the Castro's commercial blocks. As I crisscrossed the throbbing street scenes in search of a space, jaywalkers thumped my car or cried obscenities through my open windows. Halloween was a month-long orgy around here. All the usual costume types—cowboys or sailors or motorcycle cops or bearded nuns—spilled in and out of the bars, mingled with the usual drag queens in sequins and Dolly Parton falsies and the usual clones in the standard tight, frayed jeans and T-shirts. I finally found a spot up on Dubose, then hiked down into the gay canyons spoking from Castro and Market. Shoved and shoving forward, I couldn't imagine feeling more disconnected, like a mourner at a wedding party.

I don't know what the hell I was grieving. I tried to concentrate on following the flyer's directions downhill to an old Eureka Valley Knights of Columbus Hall. Right at my old bus stop, this poor kid waited for the 33 bus, clutching his backpack, alone and dead still. He had his red windbreaker zipped up to his throat in the breezeless, sultry air, trying to cover every inch of his schoolboy skin as flimsy protection against the packs of predators in Levi's. I felt so sorry for this little shrimp of about fifteen. I was sure he had pond scum samples in that pack and was muttering Hail Marys under his breath for that heaven-sent Muni bus to pluck him up to Ashbury Heights. I wanted to stand there with him until it arrived.

Two guys in black leather vests over naked chests waited at the light beside me, turning their necks in unison to leer at the kid. "I want my candy fix," the bearded one said. "Daddy likes the red pieces best."

Somehow the kid in the red windbreaker managed to stand even stiffer, slipping his hands deeper into his pockets. I sidled over beside him and asked if he was okay.

He looked at me with Bambi-in-the-headlights eyes, then quickly turned away, hunching his shoulders.

"Mister, please, just leave me alone?"

The Walk sign flashed, and I was swept across Castro with the crowd, jostled back beside the leather-vested men. The bearded one glanced across at me. "Hey!" he cried, then wolf-whistled. He slipped his paw into my back pocket and squeezed. "You got a sweet ass, big boy."

I slipped out of his grip and pressed forward through the crowd, past the Castro Café and Without Reservations to stumble in front of a bar. Its garage-door facade opened to expose the packed, dark interior to the street. As I passed, one guy sitting on a beer box nudged me with the bottle in his hand. "New in town, sailor?"

Mister, please, just leave me alone. Another time, with gay men and women from around the whole country converging on these few blocks, it all would have been a blast. The foursome of guys dressed as the Village People. The beautiful black guy, a dead ringer for Grace Jones in a skintight iridescent sheath. Four gorgeous, shirtless guys in an open Cadillac convertible, plastic pink flamingoes crowning each head. The Little Sisters of the Martyred Torso on roller skates, their habits slit to reveal their shaved, lacquered chests.

As I slipped ever deeper into this life, would these giggling man-sisters be my spiritual guides? Could I make a Cadillac confession to a boy bombshell with hard nipples and a pink plastic bird bobbing on a headband? After all, I had so much to confess. It wasn't like Randy was some evil molester. I probably had been wagging my butt in his direction, since God knows I'd never stopped lusting after him in my dreams and fantasies. Even as self-righteous as I acted in the shower, I could have taken him up inside me just as easily as I refused it. That was the truth, and no matter how I protested my loyalty to Wade, Randy had a point. What did I know about love?

Nothing. Just one more homo horndogging around the city. No wonder that schoolboy begged me to let him alone. No matter how I felt sometimes, I wasn't a schoolboy anymore.

Around the next corner, a crowd loitered in front of the Knights of Columbus Hall while people milled up and down the old wooden steps. Tables on the sidewalk covered with election flyers were manned by gauzy princesses, Marine MPs with nightsticks, and a grinning Jimmy-Carter-masked guy dressed as a peanut. Real

SFPD cops stationed themselves in watchful positions around the doorway and curbside.

I started up the steps beside a couple emerging from a limo. A perfumed woman in an evening dress and her dashing tuxedoed escort chatted about the opera. The guy taking checks at a cheap folding table and the bodyguard behind him were so bowled over by this celebrity, fawning over him with "Mr. Moscone!" this and "Mr. Mayor" that, and even "Your Honor," that I easily slipped past and into the rowdy, smoky hall.

Inside, most people weren't in costume, and despite the prevalence of the Castro clone look, most folks were ordinary, young and middle-aged guys outnumbering a fair number of actual, natural-born females. As I expected, the TV media attended in force with their thickets of lights and cameras, but now they were turned on the crowd, parting as Mayor Moscone strolled to the stage. The place was so packed, and I was shoved so hopelessly far back on the fringes, any CREWP operatives posing as reporters just couldn't find me.

I joined in the raucous applause and hooting when the drag queen MC, Joan Bra-Ford, kissed the mayor, leaving a Hollywood-red lipstick smack on his cheek. In a dress with massive shoulder pads, a huge exterior brassiere tied around the bustline, and a shellacked, complicated forties 'do, Joan Bra-Ford then anointed Mayor Moscone, tapping his head and each shoulder with the touch of a padded coat hanger.

The mayor spoke generalities about the city's diverse population being its greatest strength. At length he praised Supervisor Milk for forming a "partnership between the city government and its gay community," which earned another round of applause and hoots.

"And thank God Joan didn't use her wire hanger," Harvey Milk joked, leaning into the microphone as he and Moscone posed arm in arm for flashing cameras.

"Listen, buster," Joan Bra-Ford warned Supervisor Milk, shoving him aside, "you'll see the business end of my wire hanger if you don't stop upstaging me." She led the mayor offstage with wounded grandeur, leaving Harvey Milk to face the crowd alone.

Harvey took the chance to read messages of support from other supervisors and candidates, and from a network of politicians nationwide. With his everyday looks and casual manners, Harvey Milk mirrored the majority of his supporters. He had big, dark eyes, a shock of unruly dark hair across his forehead, and an almost goofy smile.

The whole time Harvey attempted to read those messages, a huge Styrofoam orange strutted behind him on stage in high-heeled Army boots. Under a massive brunette bouffant and hairy exposed shoulders, the enormous human orange wore a sash reading "Miss Fresh-Squeezed Florida Orange Juice." The foam-fruit Anita Bryant angled for the microphone, then wrested it from Harvey to vamp beauty-queen poses and gushings while the crowd booed.

"Wait, wait, let me tell you what we think of Harvey down in Flor-i-da!" she shouted, smiling, oblivious to the return of Joan Bra-Ford, who appeared behind her armed with a wire coat hanger.

"I like my orange juice with lots of pulp, Anita!" Joan screamed, hacking at the Styrofoam savagely. Joan hustled the orange offstage.

Watching the antics, Harvey laughed, then turned to face the audience. "I know you're all ready for the politics to end and the dancing to start," he began as a glitter ball descended from the ceiling on cue, bathing the darkened room in little diamonds of floating light. Cheers erupted all around, but Harvey, now spotlit from an overhead klieg, signaled for everyone to quiet. "And we will. We'll dance the rest of Sunday night away—you can all call in sick in the morning— but not until I introduce one more of our friends from across the Bay. This gentleman is the only statewide candidate who accepted my invitation to grace our stage tonight. You'll all recognize him as—"

From somewhere near the stage, the candidate jumped beside Harvey and into the spot of light, ducking to the mike to finish the introduction himself.

"...as one more Democratic Assembly candidate from the suburban wilds beyond the Berkeley Hills."

"Paul Dimchek, ladies and gentlemen," Harvey shouted to uproarious applause. "Paul has committed to be the only candidate to refuse to sign Will Peters's so-called Moral Pledge. Which you all know is nothing more than a witch hunt to scare teachers and candidates." Harvey peered off in the dark toward the media thicket. "Did you catch that, Channel 5? Channel 7? Darling newshounds, are you taking notes? This man isn't scared of Will Peters and his stooges, but his colleagues in other races are bloodless cowards, and you can quote me on that!"

After more wild applause, hoots, and unison cheers, Dad, laughing, lowered his hands and begged everyone to let him squeeze in a word. "I just decided I couldn't face my family, let alone myself, if I didn't fight Peters on this one. My boy is still in high school, and he's benefited from so many great teachers. We can't stand aside and betray a single one of these dedicated public servants. Anyway, I wanted to thank Harvey for inviting me. Let's encourage every supervisor to vote for Harvey's gay rights initiative."

But before Dad could shake Harvey's hand and disappear into the crowd, Joan Bra-Ford reappeared on stage, bearing the Anita Bryant wig like a gladiator with a severed head. She minced her forward steps, then grabbed my dad by the arm before he could exit. "Just a minute, Mr. Finish Line man, not so fast!" When she had him in her clutches, the dark wig dangling, she looked him up and down—and down and down—to much giggling and laughter. "He's even more adorable in person, boys, and—" She sniffed him. "—he smells just as dreamy as you might expect. Listen, darlings, get out there and buy all the Finish Line products you can. Walgreens is open twenty-four hours. Get some on the way home tonight! Then send a few bucks to that little assembly district east of those Berkeley Hills! And if it's any help, I'll organize every drag queen in San Francisco to canvass your district door to door. Now, can we start dancing, or is there anyone out there who wants to... oh, I don't know, endorse another suburban assembly candidate?"

It was a huge risk, daring to delay the start of the disco in a roomful of homosexuals, but I was so elated I'd lost all my hesitation. I raised my hand.

Joan looked toward me with a hand cupped over her squinting eyes. "Who? Who?"

A technician dropped a spot in my direction.

"Oh, you there? Oh, my, darling, you're very, very young, aren't you? Did you wander in, hoping you'd find your dad attending the Knights of Columbus?"

"Not exactly," I shouted. "He was the last person I thought I'd find here." Then I told the drag queen whose son I was.

DAD INSISTED on walking me up to my car on Dubose Street, and that's when I had my chance to apologize. He was easy about it and pointed out that, in our seventeen years together, those had been our only angry moments.

"If we keep our cool, we might go for seventeen more without resorting to fisticuffs."

He was actually angrier that I'd slept in my car "exposed to every East Bay thug," and a lot more concerned about my Camino Gordo attackers the night before. He mentioned that an investigation was underway and asked if I could identify the CREWP guys well enough to press charges.

"For all I know, Dad, they might have been large, extremely mean women. Besides, it'd be one more time I dragged Wade into this whole mess with CREWP. Those guys have photographs of him and me making out. If they actually got caught, the pictures might end up in the police report. And the media, right?"

Dad nodded, grim-faced. "It's so asinine that this is anybody's business at all. That anyone could try to use this as scandal fodder in 1978!"

"Yeah, good ol' 1978. When California is ready to fire state employees just because they're gay."

"Yep, I guess we still have a long way to go."

"Dad." I leaned against the Beast, mentally searching my thin thesaurus in vain for "gratitude." So I blurted, "That was a hell of a thing you just did. You're gonna lose, but I'm not going to forget this."

"Good. You know, Guy, now that it's hopeless, the campaign's going to speak a lot straighter." He laughed. "And gayer. Lots of gaiety, merriment, and even more pizza."

I smiled, but for some reason I flashed back to that crazy glimpse of Liz, darting down Manzanita Street at nightfall. I asked Dad how Liz felt about his appearance at Harvey Milk's rally.

He fell silent for a while. "She didn't approve and refused to come with me," he finally admitted, shrugging. "We had words. She's been upset all evening. In fact, I better get home and face the music. And I would deeply appreciate your best behavior."

"You got it. I'll see you at Circe Circle."

"Yes, Guy, that's where you live. And sleep. It is your domicile, understand?"

"Right." But I told him I had to make one last stop on the way to Mount Olympus.

THE LATE-NIGHT clerk at the El Diablo Inn told me Wade was almost through for the night. "He's learning how to close on his paperwork. Then he's done." The guy pointed me down a hallway behind the front desk.

If I managed the place, I'd have to fire the guy for letting an uncouth scum like me in, still in my slum-clearance work clothes. Through an open office door, I heard a female voice.

"Then just total your petty cash, Wade."

I paced forward, just shy of the doorway, aware of my thudding heart. After the whirr and clatter of an electric adding machine, I heard Wade curse, apologize, then cheer, "Yeah!"

They joked about a persnickety manager, then called numbers back and forth for a while. Once the whirring resumed, the female asked, "So, what were you saying about your love life, Wade?"

"I wasn't saying anything about it."

"I know. Why are you being so mysterious?"

Wade sighed. I halted, pressing myself against the wall just outside the office doorway.

"I'm not really ready to talk about it," he told her. "It's all happened real fast, and it's just gotten kind of serious."

"Oh, so you've fallen in love?"

"Well, I've been in love since we met. But it wasn't until last night that I found out the feeling was mutual."

I waited a decent interval, then knocked on the open door and ducked in. The inquisitive blonde who'd been training him was barely older than Wade and I. She batted her brown eyes at me.

But she wasn't nearly as pretty as Wade, spiffy in his blue blazer and striped tie. His hair was actually combed, swept back off his high forehead. I grinned at him.

"I just wanted to see how you survived your first day on the job, bro."

"Oh!" The blonde rose from her desk and shook my hand. "You didn't tell me you had a brother…."

"Big brother," I said, laughing.

"Like hell!" Wade said, pushing me back out the door. "I'm older and bigger and stronger than you, little Guy."

We jostled each other out to the parking lot. We'd each had such a vast, endless twenty-four hours to tell each other about. Wade had relost his godparents back to Asia and started a new job. I had realienated my mother, survived a physical assault by CREWP goons and the goon named Randy, and regained my father. Because I was sure the shocks of the day were over, and it was past midnight on a school night, I knew we would have to catch each other up another time. Though I planned never to tell him about my near-miss tryst in the shower with Randy. On a technicality, I still considered myself a virgin, and I wanted Wade to be the one who cured me of that condition.

As we leaned side by side against his Datsun, though, I knew I had to tell him about the assault in Camino Gordo. "I'm sorry," I said, finishing the roundup of bad news, "that you've been implicated in my family's messes. Jesus, be careful."

"But we can't live like we're under surveillance," Wade said. "Even if we are. And if I see any sign of the scum who hit you, I'm not going to exercise any Christian restraint. Man, I'm going to show them what a crowbar feels like."

"No, no, Wade. Like a wise man once told me, this is not the time to be macho. We've got two weeks till Dad loses this election. Then this idiocy becomes a footnote in some political almanac."

"Then I'll just have to deal with being your boyfriend."

The moon dropped behind a screen of palm trees between us and the golf course. "I told my dad I'd meet him at the house, and I'm running way late."

Wade shoved off from the car and positioned himself in front of me. Hands on my waist, he pulled me close. "This'll make a nice picture."

"Very nice. But I'm sure these clothes don't smell so nice."

"I have the solution for that." He slipped my T-shirt upward.

Oh God. Just the touch of Wade's fingers on my bare chest counted for more than a thousand of Randy's sneaky probes. "I overheard what you told your supervisor," I confessed, speaking low. "And I wanted you to know that you're right. The feeling is mutual."

We kissed, quick. But just to confirm this "I love you" moment, I leaned in for more, surprised at the warmth of his lips, the slow, delicious slide of his tongue. For once, no one seemed to be watching but the sinking moon.

IN THE Beast, heading home, I finally had to switch from the AM talk-show channel when some woman declared, "Marriage is sacred because its only purpose is procreation." I dialed over to one of the Bay Area's abominable AM music stations playing the hit "Just the Way You Are" as an ambulance screamed between the oncoming lanes of Burrito Boulevard. In a schlocky, lovestruck mood, I sang along with Billy Joel as I pulled back into traffic. Voice raised to the chorus, out of habit, I raised my middle finger to Will Peters's illuminated billboard for Save Our Schools.

In the afternoon tomorrow, as almost three thousand suburban students commuted home from Diablo View High, Peters himself would nail the final coffin in my dad's campaign with his publicity stunt across from the school. He would promise to defend us vulnerable children from our most terrifying scourge, consenting-adult, same-sex-smooching teachers. Every state candidate but one would meet his challenge by signing his Moral Pledge. Then, as Dad took to saying lately, we would have two more years to "get our act together for real and send Peters packing in 1980." Of course we would, I figured, since by then Will Peters would be headed to victory as governor of his new, morally cleansed California.

Then a commercial. "Tape the future on Betamax! Clear, crisp, lasting, Beta is your best bet in videotape!" As I turned onto the winding lane up to Mount Olympus, I wondered why the hell somebody had strung blinking lights on the roof of the collapsing pioneer farm building just ahead.

But the lights were blinking well beyond that, up on Casket Curve. Then the red strobes across the cab of a tow truck flashed ever closer, forcing me onto the narrow shoulder as it approached. It carried an unrecognizable, flattened vehicle.

When I reached the wide spot on the switchbacks, near the pioneer graveyard, the late-night guard slowed me down with a waving flashlight. Ahead, three police cars and an ambulance parked at angles, pulsing white and red against the grassy bluffs. Amid the glitter of broken glass, the scattered metal debris, officers interviewed passengers of two halted cars parked beside Dad's dark, motionless Volvo station wagon.

The guard seemed to be expecting me. He took off his cap and leaned into my open window, his hand on my arm. "Son, I've got some terrible news."

February, 1979

A BELLY dancer's bikini top flaps from our window on Madrone Street like the silk flag of a newly independent nation. To dry it in the February sun, my de facto roommate, Amy, fastened it to the window sash. But the sun has sunk behind the Oakland shipyards, and I've got to tussle with the silk top to close the window against the cold.

I'm pretty sure I've seen Amy, a belly dancer from South Dakota, before she moved in with Adrian and me. Since I've never been to the Greek restaurant in Berkeley where she gyrates, she must be the belly dancer I spotted coming out of my dad's bedroom on Montes Terrace more than a year ago, during his sex-fiend phase between Penni and Liz.

Adrian claims he met Amy at a bar mitzvah in Piedmont, where she, the entertainment, and he, the family's legal advisor, simultaneously stuck their forks into the fondue. Since then, they've been dipping into each other's fondue for almost a month. Right now Amy's moving more of her wardrobe from her apartment in the city to cram into the closet she shares with Adrian.

"I never thought I'd wind up in West Oakland," she said the other day, when she dropped off her good toothbrush, contact lens boiler, and vast collection of occupational clickers, clackers, transparent tops, and ankle bracelets. "Life sure isn't slow pitch when it comes to changes," she'd mused, "just fastball after fastball."

Though I would've expected comparisons to shimmies, bumps, and grinds, it's not her baseball analogies that have got me jumpy. It's that my dad is on his way over too, along with the rest of the family. I don't want to see him get all embarrassed when Amy wanders through dinner carrying a box of her unmentionables.

And I'm jumpy enough, just hosting this birthday-dinner deal. My own fault too. My original idea was just to show off how I'm living semi-on-my-own, attending college, buying my own groceries. A lot of trouble to prove what a big man I am, especially now. With fastball velocity, it's all evolved into an event. Since Dad's been staying at

Granny's in Sacramento, Granny's driving down with him to attend the birthday feast. Then I invited old friends, new friends, and my boyfriend. Penni invited hers.

I'm following the "easy" spaghetti recipe Granny dictated to me over the phone. Now she and Dad are cruising down here, after a quick detour to Circe Circle, to sit at the meal I've promised them. So I'm on my own, simmering the tomatoes Granny canned from her garden down to what I hope is going to be an edible sauce.

Dashing through on his way to a fundraiser for a legal assistance center, Adrian inspects the simmering pot. He shoves a few garlic cloves my way. "Here, dice these up. Can I borrow the Beast, Guy?"

"Sure," I tell him. Adrian's Jaguar got sabotaged by CREWP (we think). Foam rubber in the carburetor during the last days of the campaign. It hasn't been the same since, spending more time hiccupping to the mechanic's than on the road. "But I'm warning ya, the Beast won't make the right impression on the donors."

"Doesn't matter. At least the foam rubber's where it belongs, poking out of the front seats. Not infecting the engine's lifeblood." Adrian checks his tie, reflected in the saltwater aquarium that divides the kitchen from the living room. In its murky depths lives a crab suffering from a lingering terminal illness. The tank's a gift from one of Adrian's cash-strapped clients. Others decorate the living room: a stolen parking meter, a stuffed raven, a carousel horsey with a flat saddle that doubles as a coffee table. "Give my best to everybody," Adrian says. "I may make it back here in time for dessert."

"Yeah, Mom's bringing something. Tofu-bulgur cupcakes."

"Then I'll just have coffee, thanks."

"But Granny's bringing the birthday cake."

"Ah. Perfect with coffee." He snags my keys. "I'll be back."

Adrian's gliding off on the manic breeze gusting his sails since the end of Dad's campaign. As if to make up for the free time left after all those months of banquets, press conferences, back room dealings, and second-guessings, Adrian's thrown himself into this legal assistance center. It's a drop-in storefront on San Pablo Avenue not far from here.

At the end of this past, evil November, after the twinned assassinations at San Francisco city hall and in the throes of a breakup with another girlfriend, Adrian decided to put his townhouse on the market.

When a top-floor apartment at Madrone Street became vacant, a larger three bedroom, Adrian dispatched Randy and me to cleanse it of the usual mortal stains and death-defying stench. Just as I never imagined I'd go on being friends with Randy (we made up before Christmas, establishing a no-bodily-contact policy, because I missed Janine and the baby), I never dreamed Adrian would actually move into this ghetto himself.

Or that I'd move in with him. Before I started at Berkeley in January, Adrian told me, "You know, the Cal campus is a straight shot up Telegraph Avenue from my slum." I knew it was really a conspiracy between him and Dad, keeping one slightly underage college boy tethered to their orbit. They even offered me "a break on the rent" to keep me in indentured servitude to CJ Properties.

The extra bedroom between Adrian's and mine helps muffle the full volume of his all-night contortions with Amy the belly dancer. It's now a home office devoted to Adrian's other preoccupation. He's using his legal savvy and contacts to document CREWP's dirty tricks during the campaign. No matter how after the fact it might seem, Adrian's planning to press criminal charges. He managed to publicize the attack on me days before the election, so at least Will Peters had to distance himself from "violent elements acting without authorization."

The worst part for Dad and Adrian, though, followed from their brief, just restarted bond with Harvey Milk. After Dad's appearance at the gay rights rally, the three took up their old acquaintance. They even combined campaign efforts across the Bay. Harvey really did have Joan Bra-Ford dispatch a team of drag queens to Dad's district, where they pretended to celebrate Will Peters's final rallies along Burrito Boulevard. They carried signs of support, cheered his every word on family morality, and sprinkled glitter on buttoned-up Republicans under the banner WILL'S GOT OUR KIND OF PETER! To a campaign with nothing left to lose, Joan's drag queens brought laughs and unbelievable, bitchy exuberance.

A big contrast to the murderous phase to come.

After Harvey Milk and Mayor Moscone got shot to death in their city hall offices on November 27, Adrian began to question how deep CREWP's roots might reach. Supervisor Dan White, the assassin, a religious conservative so unhappy with a gay rights initiative that he quit his elected office, believed that murdering the mayor and the supervisor was the Christian thing to do. Since Gas 'n' Jesus organized the Dan White Defense Fund, Adrian wondered if a right-wing plot actually stretched back to Bart Morgan's strange demise in June, whether that cliff-top photo shoot was staged to conceal a political murder. Paranoid maybe, but no one's been able to locate the "photographer" enlisted "to fill in" for the campaign that day. I can't help but wonder if it was the big guy with the camera who was hiding at Wade's when I got crowbar bashed. Anyway, Adrian's new answering machine keeps collecting obscene and bloody "Christian" curses and threats. His desk gets piled under more evidence whose stink leads back to CREWP.

"Wonderful! Guy! I can smell it from out here!" It's Penni, who's let herself in after meeting Adrian on his way out. She sets the birthday package, protected in butcher-paper wrapping, beside the doorway. I help her out of her black coat, then finger the collar's fur fringe. "How many baby seals got bashed for this, Mom?"

"Come on, Guy." Penni crosses her arms and leans against the counter. In the aquarium, the doomed crab listlessly raises a claw in her direction. "It's synthetic. I'm not wearing the ecology around my neck, so spare me the interrogation. It was my Christmas present from Cary."

Draping the coat over the parking meter, I can't hold back a chance to comment on her twenty-year-old *physical consultant.* "Are you sure it wasn't really financed by his parents' lunch money allowance?"

"Cary always speaks well of you, Guy."

In sweater and slacks, Penni actually does look fit, and I hold back my next snide question: teenaged lover or rowing machine? Since I can vouch for the invigorating effects of having a handsome young boyfriend, I know I've got to get over my resentment of hers. "So where is he?"

"On his way from a late class. Spiritual Foundations of Personal Physical Training."

"Great." I nod to the package. "So, how'd our present turn out?"

"Surprisingly well."

Sister Diana leans in the door, a paperback in hand, wide smile. She's traveled all the way across the hall, so I signal her in for introductions. After sharing demure nods with Penni, Diana turns to me in exasperation. "Well, I am all done with your reading suggestions, neighbor," she tells me, shoving *The Stranger* my way.

"I have no idea what's wrong with your Berkeley professors, assigning such a pointless novel."

"That's the point, isn't it? Pointlessness?"

"What's the point of pointlessness? The whole story's spiritually dead." As if that alerts her to my cooking, Diana turns toward the steaming pot. "Guy! You've got to mince this garlic more, then sauté it, then let it simmer into the marinara. Here...."

"Yes!" cries Penni, whose authority as a chef is legendary. As the two of them bustle around the stove, dicing, stirring, exhorting me to add the ground sausage, the buzzer sounds, and I have to hustle three flights down to the foyer. Naturally, with our slumlord being CJ Properties, our security release is broken again, and anyone, friend, foe, or mass murderer, can just sashay inside.

But Cary's waiting politely on the front step beside Wade, underage gents who each bear wine borrowed—I'm guessing—from parental stashes. Cary shakes my hand as he finishes a comment to Wade.

"Yeah, you should definitely go out for track. You have the endomorphic physique for it. Just let me know and I'll get you started on the right training program." Cary seems to be running in place as he speaks, all brilliant blue in his running suit and sneakers, and just keeps on truckin' by as he dashes up the stairs. "Penni up there yet, Guy?"

"Yeah, and she could use your help with the spaghetti sauce," I call after him, then bar Wade's attempt to follow with my arm across the doorway. "Let's stay right here for a second," I tell him. "It's been a while."

"Yeah, since Sunday," Wade says. We've lowered our voices to the hush level we kept in the good ol' days of our ten-minute make-out sessions in the abandoned vending nook at Diablo View High.

"It's weird that now I'm an emancipated college man, I see my boyfriend less—and less of my boyfriend—than when I was a little schoolboy."

"Maybe that's because your boyfriend is still a schoolboy. And, man, you mock your mother for rocking the cradle."

I smile because Wade is slightly taller and slightly older than I am. I lean in for a quick kiss. It's almost full dark already, and of course the porch lights are out, one broken, one shot out by a Saturday night reveler. "We always seem to be face to face in dismal hideaways."

"That's why we're so chaste."

"Must be a conspiracy. Your dad sets you up in a job that keeps you occupied every weekend night, and I've been conned into living with my godfather. A stealth chaperone."

"A sleazy chaperone," Wade says. "How come Adrian gets to sleep with a belly dancer while we suffer like monks?"

I study the barren lot across the street, thinking that the pointless universe must have a great sense of humor. Oakland's urban renewal bulldozers have just knocked down the slum across the street, exposing an old Foul Line billboard to full view atop a warehouse. Though most of the ads featuring Dad got eliminated during his brief life as a political candidate, this one got overlooked. Funny how the bogus California lifestyle of the billboard image—pools and palm trees and surfer chicks—unravels in tatters over the real California of tattered, unraveling San Pablo Avenue, with its hustlers and hustlerees, strugglers and sad sacks. So Dad smiles down on me now, from the usual Olympian heights, all-powerful and all-seeing even as I come and go from my own front steps.

"Dad rules from afar," I tell Wade. "But Adrian's the moral guardian of my life. He gets to flirt with money, invest in women, cavort with criminals, and then redeem himself with good causes. Meanwhile, I'm tied to this ascetic's rack."

"I'd like to rack your ascetic, myself," Wade says, pulling me close. I slip my bare arms under his big overcoat.

"Less than a week…," I mutter, meaning our plan to snag champagne and an empty room at the inn after his Saturday shift, which happens to follow Valentine's Day. We're going to see "what evolves." No pressure, of course. But one thing that's for sure? We're going to celebrate the end of the ugly season that began with the crowbar attack and Liz's accident.

In the November interval following Election Day and the Jonestown massacre, Wade and I wandered half-catatonic. The Bay Area seemed unrecognizable, body-snatched, surrendered to violence. When we attended the city's mass candlelight vigil after the assassinations of Harvey Milk and Mayor Moscone, I strained to find one positive thing. I could only locate one, at the end of my fingers: Wade's hand, squeezing mine like bloody murder.

After that, Wade stopped attending Sunday services at Brethren Community Church. No matter how much Gladstone backpedaled, blamed, and denied, Wade couldn't overcome the Marxist Matrix's connection to the Reverend Jim Jones and his support for the doomed Guyana colony. No million-strong army of little ballerinas with bayonets could force Wade back.

So, starting in December, I've tried to fill Wade's Sunday mornings with outings to my places of worship. After breakfast with his parents, we've been hiking the wilds around the Bay, Muir Woods, Mount Tamalpais, and Point Reyes. Along the way, if we followed a stream, I could indulge my mania for fresh water ecologies and try to tempt Wade toward my passion. But the more I tell him about really keen streambed microbes, the more he claims to be interested in studying social sciences. Meanwhile, the more I learn about people and the way they operate, the more intrigued I am by water and the bugs that wiggle in it.

As soon as I've led Wade upstairs and uncorked the wine, I lose him to the trio in the tiny kitchen. As I stand in the open doorway, watching Diana, Penni, and Cary raid our meager supply of spices for the pasta sauce, I hear quick steps groaning the hallway boards behind me. The tall guy almost looks unreal, both futuristic and macho, in a thick, tufted motorcycle jacket. He carries his helmet and yet another bottle of wine lifted, for sure, from his parents' supply.

"Smells good, Guy. I caught a whiff of the garlic from the bottom of the stairs and just followed it up. What a cool old building, man!"

The Pest had mellowed out, finally, just before Christmas vacation, when his mom invited me for a family dinner to celebrate my early graduation. Celeste Pescatore kind of orchestrated things, not even letting Rob know I was coming over. Since it was cold, windy, and raining like hell, he couldn't really escape on his motorcycle. Rob grudgingly sat down with me just for irresistible chicken cacciatore, then, just as grudgingly, joined in our conversation about the good old days of the Beast. Celeste reminded us how they bought it new the same year Rob and I were born, and we all got wistful about other Beastly rites of passage in our lives, like when I joined the Pescatores on a drive up to Lake Tahoe and Rob got to drive, for his first time, on the interstate. Pretty soon the Pest and I were breaking bread again, grudge free, over our love of that big, wobbly boat of a car, and all our schemes—sanitized in front of Celeste—we'd had when we first tooled around the city at sixteen.

Rob hasn't even taken off his motorcycle jacket before he's joining the great spaghetti sauce debate that's still rattling the kitchen rafters.

"My mom's big on oregano," Cary says, elbowing his way between Penni and Wade to sprinkle it athletically over the roiling red mass.

"My mom's secret is a bay leaf," Wade says, searching the cabinets beside Diana.

"My mom's is a pinch of cayenne pepper," Rob insists, "and I'm a full-blooded Italian, guys, so just be glad I'm letting you in on the real secret."

Diana shouts, "Ah-hah!" and produces a tin of cayenne from the shelf, which Rob takes from her hands after a lingering stare—at Diana, not the cayenne. It really is beginning to smell like something edible might be born in that pot.

Meanwhile, Dad has arrived with his entourage, and between hugs and uncoatings and present-stackings, I'm distracted by Granny. After she sets down the birthday cake and pours us each a half glass of Chianti, she pulls me into the living room beside the stuffed raven to gush over how proud I should be of her Pee Dee.

"It's a shame we didn't know his legislation was going to rotate into session today, Guy. It's a shame Liz wasn't around to see it too. It would've been wonderful if you could have heard what your father had to say."

Before I can glean the true extent of Pee Dee's wonderfulness, Amy's entrance distracts everyone. She's concealed behind an enormous box of unmentionables, and after she adjusts it to wave at everyone, she apologizes for her big rush. "I'm running late for my evening shift in Berkeley. Wish I could join you! Guy, the sauce smells heavenly." She retrieves the box and hustles into Adrian's room to change.

Dad, who's been on the wagon since Liz's accident, has helped himself to a glass of Amy's organic apple juice, on the rocks, and raises it in her wake as he approaches Granny and me. He truly doesn't seem to have made the connection or glimpsed enough of Amy to spur the recollection—if he even remembers.

"What's it like, Guy," he asks, "living with a belly dancer?"

"Strangely familiar," I say, "given the crowd I've been living with all my life."

Granny laughs. "She certainly has the figure for it," she says, then turns back to me. "Anyway, your father had his chance to introduce the legislation today. On his very first day addressing the entire assembly. And he was just brilliant!"

Dad smiles sheepishly, basking in his mother's adoration. Then his grin widens. "Yep, I have to admit, it went pretty well. I didn't think our bill would come up today, so I really had to wing it. Made a little speech. Hope I didn't sound too asinine."

"Asinine!" Granny's hand goes to her collar in mock horror. "It was just the opposite, Pee Dee. You were as eloquent as you've ever been. 'If you hope, as I hope, that one more of our heroes hasn't been slain....'" She trails off, dreamy with a mom's pride.

"'Slain, gunned down in vain,'" Dad recites, picking it up, "'we can end one last form of legal discrimination. To advance full citizenship for every Californian, I urge you to vote with me on the Harvey Milk Human Rights Amendment.' Or words to that effect."

"Dad," I say, overcome myself with a son's pride, "those are the most nonasinine words I've ever heard a politician say."

We toast each other just as Amy rushes from the bedroom in her dance slippers and silken trousers, bubbling with apology again, face covered in her gauzy veil. With crossed arms, she clutches shut her spangled vest.

"Guy! I think my top is still hanging out the window. Sorry, 'scuse me everyone," she says, urging me to unlatch the living room window. "Oh thank God!" she cries when I pass her the tiny silk bra. "It's cold but dry!" After a detour to fasten it on in the bathroom, she grabs her jacket and purse, waves good night to everyone, and heads off for work.

Dad's followed her every move. "Now, what were we saying?"

"Oh nothing, Dad. Just another civil rights speech by some freshman assemblyman."

"Yep, our state bill is modeled almost word for word on Harvey's San Francisco ordinance. Best memorial we could think of."

For some reason, this reminds me of the surprise gift, still exposed beside the doorway, the large rectangle obvious in its paper wrap. I'm having second thoughts about it now. The recipient can be so unsentimental and unpredictable. I figure we better not make a big deal out of it, putting her on the spot in front of everyone. After all, she's going to have to endure cake-candles-make-a-wish after dinner.

I share my plan with Mom, who gives me the nod before she pours more wine for herself and Granny. Over the cauldron of sauce, the kitchen group is testing Diana's encyclopedic knowledge of every known Rocky and Bullwinkle story line, while the last three of the arriving guests join in. Randy, still in his jacket, lobs Diana an easy question about Bullwinkle's birth in Frostbite Falls, Minnesota. Dad gazes into his apple juice wistfully, as if it might alchemize into scotch if he stares long enough. I pick up the package and, before slipping with it into my room, knock on my bedroom door.

"It is all right, Guy. You can come in." It's dark, with only enough light flooding through the door to see that Liz has propped herself on my pillows. She'd hustled into my bedroom with her bundle as soon as she arrived with Granny and Dad. Now, his head poking from under a tiny blanket spread across Liz's shoulders, my baby brother suckles. "See? I was not being unsociable," she whispers. "Just as I wished I could have been with Paul in Sacramento for today's session. But I have to live by Conrad's demands, now."

It was Dad's idea to name him after Liz's father ("Plus, it's a cool name," he'd decided). Liz went along without obvious enthusiasm. Considering the little guy's already a survivor, he has a better chance of living a longer life than his namesake.

Maybe the whole namesake deal inspired the gift in the first place. I sit on a chair beside the bed, propping the package against the wall in Liz's range of sight, and tell her about how it came to be. "We used the slide of this painting, that portrait your father did of you," I said. "I hope you don't mind our sneaking around. We wanted to surprise you on your birthday."

Liz raises her eyebrows, staring at the package. "To be honest, I have forgotten about it. We have had so much more to think about than my father's art."

Okay. I take a breath. "So, I had the slide blown up to the size of the original. And I took it to my mom's so she could frame it with her matte cutter. But Mom got all excited about the idea of repainting it. Since she's been fooling around with this whole photorealist style in her commercial art, I guess Mom wanted a challenge." I realize I'm babbling and probably boring Liz. But she's remained attentive. I don't tell her that as part of Penni's "commission" for her labor I'll spend the entire spring weeding her hillside garden. "So anyway,

Mom's all jazzed with how well it turned out." I touch the paper wrapper. "You ready?"

"Yes." Liz adjusts herself, then nudges Conrad upward, higher on the pillows. With her free hand, she switches on the lamp as I unwrap the portrait.

Penni's photographic-paint method overlays a modern touch on Conrad's blurrier, more wavering sense of time. But somehow the weird mix bridges the thirty-five years between painting and repainting.

Lisabeth is poised on a wooden bench in a sun-flooded kitchen. Her back is erect. Her arms fold across her stomach, one hand's fingers pinching her red jumper, the other dangling a little bouquet of wildflowers. Her legs dangle too, her bare feet crossing in midair.

Yet every line leads back to her face, more sharply focused than the rest. Her father has turned her face slightly aside, and Lisabeth has offered the slightest hint of a smile at the corners of her mouth. Lisabeth's eyes glance from the angle, straight into the viewer's.

I can't guess what Liz is thinking as she regards her three-year-old self interpreted by her father and reinterpreted by her husband's ex-wife. But I'm thinking this is the opposite of any damn Foul Line commercial or any number of Penni's sketches for real estate throwaways, the opposite of hard-sell fantasies where love is easy and family life is an effortless cartwheel of laughs among poolside lounge chairs. Where somehow our bayonets, suburban apartheid, and infested slums never make it into the picture. Even reinterpreted, Liz's father painted the truth, even if subconscious, even if against his will. Though he exaggerates the shade of Prussian blue Liz's eyes really have, he can't lie. Even then the eyes seem to chill all the portrait's points of warmth. He does nothing to disguise their hard blankness. There's no exchange to them, absorbing, patient, unlaughing, giving nothing back.

I kind of dread Liz's reaction. She stares and stares. She shuffles Conrad, who's fussing now, studying the picture with her head at a different angle and a slight smile. "Thank you," she says at last.

I finally breathe. "I'm glad you like it."

"Now that I have a child of my own, I think I have a glimmer of how difficult it must have been. He had to have me sit still for this painting, study me, then hold me close. Then to have to return to the battlefields in Russia, alone."

Abrupt, she holds Conrad out to me. "Here, Guy, please. Just for a while." When I take the baby, she buttons her blouse and combs her short hair back with her fingers. The scars on her neck and jaw look red and raw even in the faint lamplight but so much better since she started treatments.

Sometimes, gazing down Manzanita Street from my bedroom window as night falls, I'm still unhinged by that glimpse of Liz in the dinged-up Porsche, cruising these streets the night of her crash. Sometimes I wonder if I really saw it, if it really was Liz. Was she saying good-bye to her old life, to Good-Time Charlie and the ghost children her body never could deliver?

Or did she want to ask me something, tell me something? Without close friends or confidants, would her gay stepson have to do for whatever she couldn't discuss with Dad? But she'd chickened out and sped back into the long night that would end in a one-car smashup on Casket Curve.

Her desperation scared the hell out of me. I'd never asked Liz about my sight of her that evening. For sure, I never mentioned it to the investigators and insurance people who interviewed me while Liz was still recovering. I've tried to make sense of that sequence of little "accidents." Those dings on the Porsche, aborted attempts that finally led to her near-fatal crash the night Dad attended Harvey Milk's gay rights rally against her wishes. How wrecked she must have felt, after losing the big fight with Dad. I'm sure, like the rest of us, she expected Dad to lose the election and was sure she would have another miscarriage. What did she mean to annihilate?

After Liz swerved off Casket Curve, she rolled out the open door into tall grass just before the rotating Porsche completely caved in on itself. Now, stretching her shoulders, massaging her upper arms, she stands by the window. Headlights flicker through the braces of the double-decker Cypress Freeway and the far shapes of warehouses, lighted cranes on piers, dark outlines of seagoing freighters, the red dabs of light on their smokestacks.

"I'll tell you the truth, Guy. In the hospital, I continued to wonder how much I really wanted a child." She turns from the window to face me. "Maybe I always was afraid I wasn't fit to be a mother. But the doctors kept saying I had such resolve, such a will to live. They said the same thing about Conrad. No one expected either of us to come through this so well."

Part of me wants to spout some autopilot baloney from my religious indoctrination, like "Yes, it's a miracle," but I kick my inner Catholic in his shins. *Miracle?* It was Liz's perseverance, combined with the emergency ward's skills, along with support from us, her stepfamily. Plus that "will to live." Let me tell you, it stood for a hell of a lot more in my book than to sucker yourself to hoaxes, or surrender the field to hype, or worship a Great Man's charismatic Kool-Aid.

Even the other "miracle," Dad's unthinkable victory, vaulted from Liz's and my dark nights of the soul back in October. With Liz in the hospital, her life and the baby's suspended by a flimsy thread right up until Election Day, voters' compassion probably pushed Dad ahead. When Dad joined Harvey Milk on the eleven o'clock news to detail CREWP's blackmail attempts, tire irons and full-moon photo peep shows, everybody got creeped out. After Adrian made sure voters heard about CREWP's violence, they sympathized, even if I was a boy-kissin' degenerate. Funny that after a campaign that pitted "family values" against us, one new commentator pointed out the truth about our family: "Immigrant in origin, divorced, stepped, mobile, and scattered. Just like the rest of us, folks, still hanging together." What's weird is how, after all our disconnecting, we keep re-rebounding.

After a tap on the door, Janine pokes her head through, her eyes meeting mine. "Okay if I come in? Your dad said your room is the perfect baby feeding spot...." She smiles at Liz, who's still gazing out to Madrone Street, then crinkles her nose for Conrad's sake, who's fidgeting a little in my arms, bundled in his blankie. "I checked out that poor crab in the aquarium, Guy," she says, gently rocking her own baby, "and I think we can help it. It needs a viable marine ecosystem."

"In other words, we need to clean the damn fish tank."

"Exactly." Her baby's cradled, squirming against Janine, so she and I stand like it's a baby-to-baby fussing contest until Janine sits on my bed and starts to nurse Ivan.

I can't exactly do the same for Conrad, and Liz isn't making any move away from the window, so I move nearer to her, kind of bouncing my brother the way I've seen Dad do it. Believe me, I've calculated Conrad's conception in the privacy of my own head. With normal human gestation, he must've been conceived around my April birthday.

On a cold but sunny Sunday afternoon a few weeks before Christmas, Janine and Randy surprised me at an Ocean Beach picnic, the first time I'd ventured over to their student apartment to see Baby Ivan. During a little ceremony at the water's edge, in which they had me anoint Ivan's head with a dribble of seawater, I was pronounced his godfather.

"I'm a fraud, you know, a nonbeliever," I told the proud parents. "I never know what god to pray to. But I'm open to suggestions."

"Neptune will do just fine," Janine had said, laughing as she propped Ivan to face the swelling breakers.

If godless Adrian could godfather me, I supposed, I would do my best for Ivan.

Pressed against my chest, my brother looks up at me, sighs, and kind of coos. He closes his eyes, sealing them with his downy lashes. Conrad's whole hand splays out to seize my forefinger. You know, no matter what, Liz will be my brother's mother for as long as we all shall live, and I want to live well. So finally I start to coax Liz back to reality with, "It's amazing how well we've all—"

"We're all starving, Guy." Granny cuts me off, whispering for the babies' sake in the bedroom doorway, leaving it open to the apartment's laughter. "Your sauce is ready, but what about the pasta?"

"Here, Gran." I pass Conrad to her waiting arms as we prepare to join the kitchen's many cooks. Holding up *The Stranger*, Rob is trying to form some long-shot analogy to impress Diana.

"I've got to write an essay on it for Senior English. Maybe I can work in Bullwinkle, with your help." Diana laughs, and Wade shoots me a goofy smile as he suspends the spaghetti over boiling water.

"Yes, yes!" Granny cries to Wade. "Get the spaghetti boiling so we can celebrate Liz's birthday sometime before midnight." Patting Conrad, she calls to me. "And Guy, put out the salad! Your friends are hungry. We all are. You've got a family to feed."

LEE PATTON enjoyed a free-range childhood on northern California's Mendocino Coast, attended college in Sacramento and the Bay Area, including ed-school at San Francisco State. He fled to Colorado to teach high school writing and literature, climb the easiest 14'ers, raft the most placid whitewater, and bike the wimpiest singletrack. After earning his MA in the University of Denver's Writing Program, he developed an accidental career as a mystery novelist. He woke from a ten-year spell as an accidental playwright to concentrate on fiction and poetry. In nonfiction, he's focused on political satire, travel and environmental reportage.

Patton has a knack for finding himself at the wrong place at the wrong time—he left Rio the day before Carnival and arrived in New Orleans the day after Mardi Gras. He crossed the Iron Curtain just after the Chernobyl meltdown in Ukraine, visited Vietnam during avian flu, and India right after the Mumbai terror attacks. Unreliable sources insist that he may even be responsible for the breakup of Yugoslavia, which he visited shortly before it descended into ethnic strife and civil war.

E-mail: lee_patton@hotmail.com
Facebook: www.facebook.com/lee.patton.370
Website: leepatton.net

Dirk Hunter

AFTER SCHOOL ACTIVITIES

www.dreamspinnerpress.com

Louise Lyons

BEAUTIFUL THUNDER

www.dreamspinnerpress.com

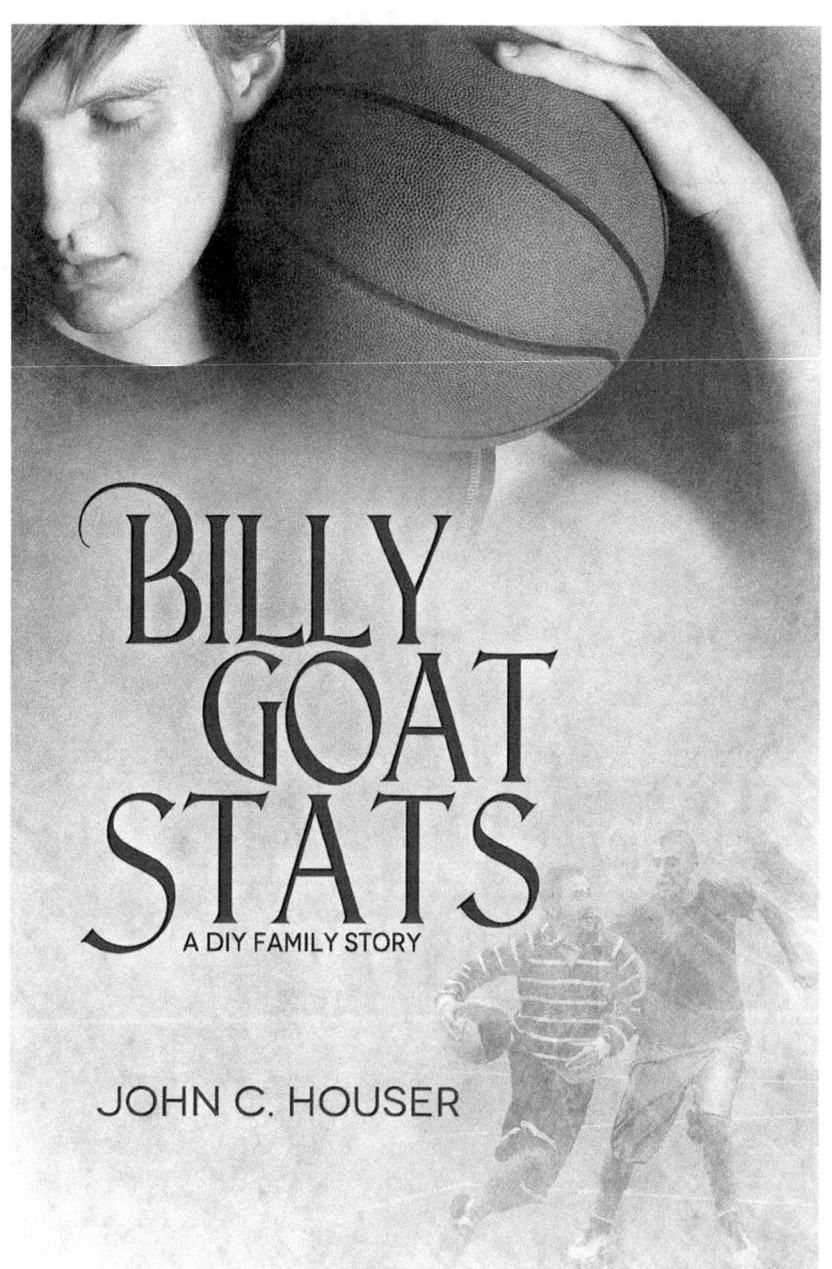

BILLY GOAT STATS

A DIY FAMILY STORY

JOHN C. HOUSER

www.dreamspinnerpress.com

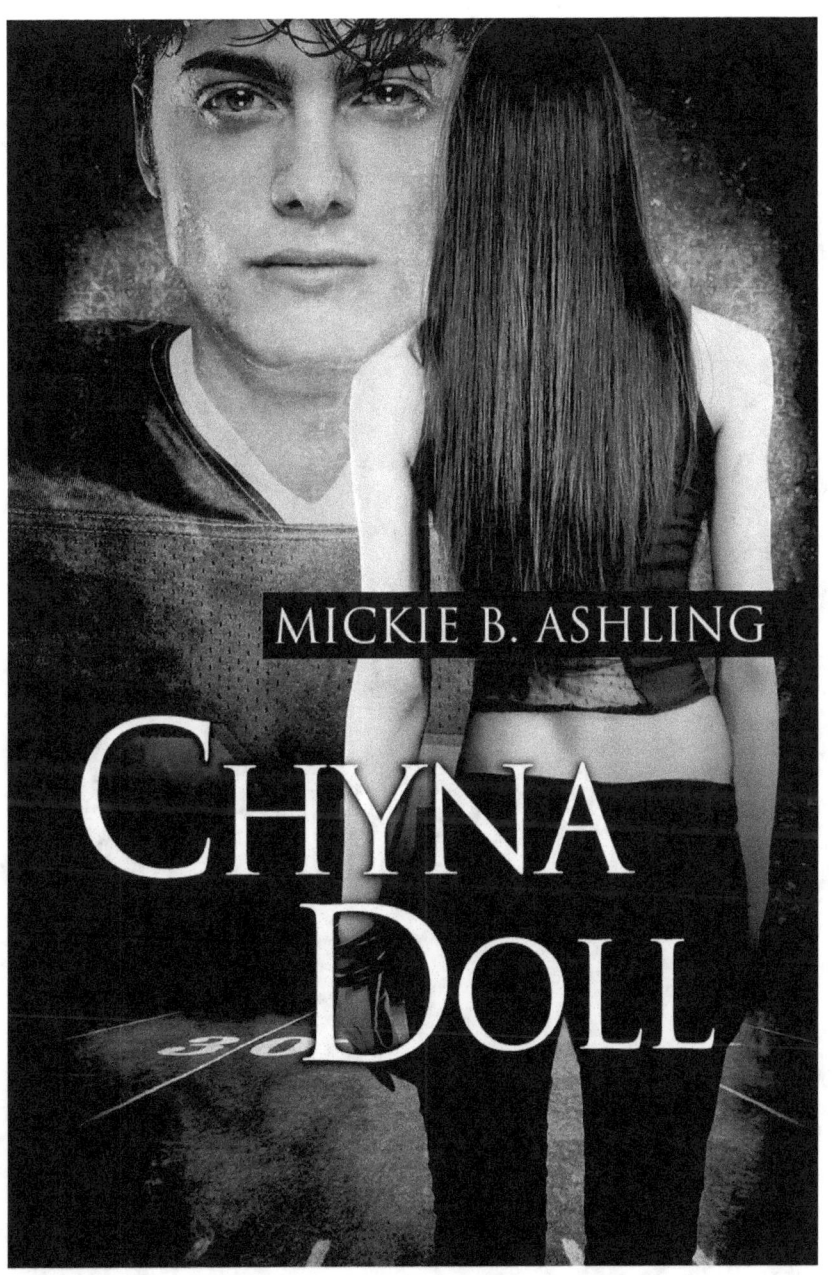

MICKIE B. ASHLING

Chyna
Doll

www.dreamspinnerpress.com

Where love is on the menu

DINNER
at FIORELLO'S

RICK R. REED

www.dreamspinnerpress.com

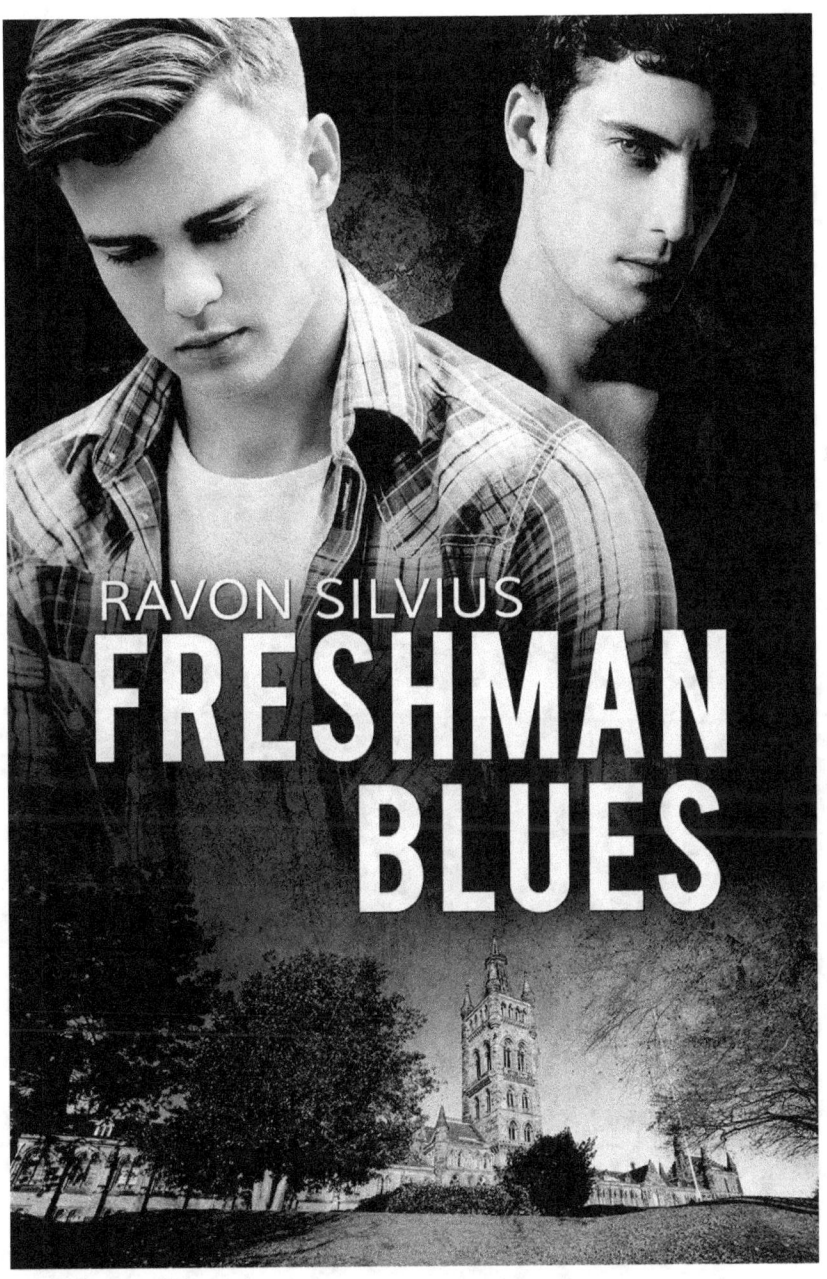

RAVON SILVIUS

FRESHMAN
BLUES

www.dreamspinnerpress.com

ONE VOICE
BOOK TWO

HERE
WITHOUT
YOU

Mia Kerick

www.dreamspinnerpress.com

Signs

ANNA MARTIN

www.dreamspinnerpress.com

www.ingramcontent.com/pod-product-compliance
Lightning Source LLC
Chambersburg PA
CBHW070108260626
47160CB00004B/1367